Chi Warrior

The Protectors Book 1
Vijaya Schartz

Print ISBNs
Amazon print 9780228637622
Ingram Spark 9780228637646
Barnes & Noble 9780228637639
BWL Print 9780228637653

Copyright 2025 by Vijaya Schartz
Editor Victoria Chatham
Cover artist Michelle Lee

Dedication

*To all my Tai-Chi students, who reward me
with their constant progress.
You inspired me to write this book.*

Acknowledgements

I am forever grateful to my teacher, Charles Gill, head of South West Taiji, for introducing me to the art and technique of this unique Martial Art, and to the ancient philosophy and wisdom of the Dao. Thank you, Charlie, for your generosity and your teachings. They matter more than you'll ever know, changing lives for the better.

Table of Contents

Prologue

Temple of the Celestial Gate

The entire Temple complex shook with a powerful vibration. Wang steadied himself and closed the trunk he'd been filling with ancient scrolls to keep them safe. "What now?"

As he rushed out on the Temple terrace, the Celestial Gate whined and the ground shook, but he kept his balance. He shaded his eyes against the fierce sandstorm churning the desert around Temple Rock. Then he descended the steps to the main courtyard, fighting the gusts that whipped his long white hair and twisted his flowing robes around his legs. He could taste fine sand on his lips, nesting in his beard, and filling the gaps between his toes through the open sandals.

Lightning flashed above the two giant square pillars framing the empty space, through which travelers from other parts of the universe manifested from time to time. The ancient script covering the entire surface of the pillars now glowed and undulated with the vibrations, rewriting the story... the visitors' point of origin.

Wang did not recognize the planet. Who in their right mind would want to visit at such a perilous time?

Who was it? He had better things to do than play host to uninvited guests, especially at a time like this. The spoiled and the privileged had no regard for the struggles of the local people.

A large protective bubble formed around the Celestial gate, shimmering with energy. Inside it, a silvery frigate in the shape of an egg emerged between the two square pillars, impervious to the surrounding weather. The smooth vessel hovered, steady over the cobblestones of the vast courtyard.

Wang recognized the ship and it worsened his mood. Fighting his way against sand and wind, he crossed into the shimmering sphere of calm surrounding the gate. Once inside the bubble, he sighed and willed himself to relax. Losing his cool would only make things worse... instead, he should appreciate the short respite from the sandstorm.

As the frigate hovered a foot above the ground, its belly ramp unfolded. When it touched the cobblestones, six tall beings in pastel robes of shimmering silk glided solemnly toward Wang. They all sported smooth faces, and immaculate black hair tied with gold ornaments. Holding their backs straight, they proudly displayed the bejeweled seal of their galactic dynasty on their puffed chests. The green water dragon. Immortals...

Suddenly self-conscious about his unrefined appearance, Wang shook the sand from his hair and rough robes. Immortals could be so critical.

His celestial brothers and sisters glanced at his disheveled state with concern in their narrowed blue eyes, but also judgement. They disapproved of his decision to stay.

His number one brother brushed an invisible speck off his lavender sleeve then bowed slightly. A sweet scent of heavenly musk filled the air. "Are you well, brother? You look old."

Wang saluted, right fist in the left palm. "I assure you I am fine, older brother."

"Are you certain you want to remain on this savage world?" The Immortal's gaze scanned the growing sandstorm raging over the dunes below the cliffs. "The village and the fields surrounding this rocky promontory will not survive. The planetary alignment has barely begun to ravage this planet. The worst is yet to come."

"I know." Wang couldn't expect his siblings to understand.

"There is space for you on the frigate if you wish to return home with us." His number one brother paused, perfect brow rising in silent question.

Wang shook his head. "Not unless you agree to take with us the four hundred souls who live in this monastery and the farmers residing in the village below."

"What you ask is against the rules and you know it, Wang." His number one brother's eyebrows met in a scowl, then his face relaxed and he sighed. "But, please, reconsider... this is too hard a life for any of our kind... and quite unnecessary."

Wang pinched his lips together to stifle a sharp comment about his brother's lack of compassion. Instead, he exhaled slowly. "I have dedicated my life to teaching these people. What kind of example would I set if I abandoned them in their time of need?"

"Indeed." His brother's shoulders dropped and he shook his head. "But since you decided to ignore our advice and stay, as we anticipated... we have brought you a gift."

"A gift?" Wang couldn't hide his surprise. Generosity wasn't one of his brother's traits. His siblings had never contributed anything to his altruistic projects.

Out of the frigate, a rectangular coffer, covered with a black veil, floated toward them, then hovered between Wang and his oldest brother.

Wang stared at the coffer. "What is it?"

"A few necessities..." His brother paused and checked his impeccable fingernails. "And a Celestial Gem."

"A Celestial Gem?" Wang could barely breathe.

His brother flashed a disdainful smile. "You must promise to hide and protect this rare treasure with your life... until it is needed."

Wang placed both hands on his fast-beating heart and took a knee. "I solemnly promise to protect the Celestial Gem, Honorable Brother."

"Good. After the cataclysm passes, as the prophecy foretold, a new ruler of Immortal blood will rise for whoever survived." Number one brother straightened his frame, looking even taller. "This new leader will rid this planet of any tyrants who would oppress it then claim the Celestial Gem."

Wang rose to his feet and gazed into his brother's dark blue eyes. "Thank you, Honorable Brother, for bringing us hope for a brighter future."

"Do not thank me yet, brother. The prophecy also says that if the wrong ruler controls the gem, this planet will be plundered by unscrupulous galactic species, depleted of its natural resources, and forever condemned to slavery, poverty, and famine."

Wang nodded. He had seen it happen on faraway worlds. "I guess I may never see you again, brother. At least, not for a very long time."

"I'm afraid so." No regret in his brother's voice. "Time flows differently in our spheres. But we trust you to guard and keep the Celestial Gate in good working order until our return."

"I will." Wang bowed to his number one brother, and to the five other siblings standing behind him.

None of them returned his bow. Instead, his brothers and sisters turned around and walked up the ramp of the frigate, in a slow, deliberate stride, not one hair, or one single fold of their shimmering robes out of place. Immortals... they had no respect for him, or anyone else.

Although he was one of them by birth, Wang realized his pampered siblings could never understand the plight of the human population on this humble planet. With no technology to fight the forces of nature, and no way to escape off world, they would be helpless when the elements unleashed their wrath.

As the frigate's hatch closed and sealed with a metallic clunk, the familiar whine of the Celestial Gate humming to life prompted Wang to hurry. He grabbed one side handle of the floating coffer and hurried out of the protective bubble surrounding the pillars.

Fighting the fierce wind, he climbed the Temple steps two by two with the floating coffer in tow. At the top of the steps, he glanced back to see the frigate and its bubble vanish through the Celestial Gate. Now, the gate stood still and empty, like a stone relic from a faraway past, blasted by sand and wind. "Farewell, my siblings."

Safe inside the stone Temple, Wang led the floating coffer across the main hall, then hurried down narrow stone stairs and along torchlit tunnels. At the end of a passage, he entered a small chamber and deposited the coffer in a corner.

A village woman rushed in, holding a white cat in her arms. "Master Wang, everyone we could find is gathered in the cellars with the provisions to weather the storm."

"Good. What of the animals?" They would be needed later if the people survived.

"Burden beasts, steeds, dairy cows, and flocks are stabled with the hay, in the caves by the underground river as you suggested, Master Wang. We stored the carts, tools, and gears in the caves as well.

"Good." Wang sighed. "The upheaval will last for many days, but we are prepared."

Wang hoped they wouldn't be buried alive in those caves and would still have a livable planet after the alignment subsided... if they survived the cataclysm.

As they all gathered underground and sat, ready to wait out the wrath of nature, he wondered if he had made the right decision. What if he'd only led these people to a delayed but certain death? He shook his head to dispel the doubts. No fear. He must remain positive.

When he closed his eyes, Wang could focus his mind and see outside the Temple. Hurricane-force winds shifted the sand dunes, while lightning melted sand into glass and ignited the frond-roofs in the village and the dried-up fields. Even the trees, shriveled by the wind, were blazing like tinder.

As he expanded his mind awareness, Wang could see what happened in faraway lands as well. Everywhere his mind's eye looked, the ground shook. Among the cries of horrified populations, he saw cities engulfed in flames as the ground caved under them, and mountains of dirt folded over to bury them. New volcanoes erupted, spurting fire high in the sky, and blackening the snow below them. Tidal waves unfurled, destroying coastal towns in their path and flooding the lowlands with mud flow and debris. The coastline changed, so did the flow of the Great River. Then new lakes formed inland along the previous river bed.

Inside their stone refuge, the ground also shook. During times of respite, loud moans rose from the deep, like a monster's voice, scaring the children. The animals screamed in panic at every quake, every cracking of stone. Dust fell from the ceiling, and the cave floor seemed to move.

At night, mothers held their babies close, in a protective embrace. Young children held on to their fathers for reassurance. Men, young and old, glanced at each other with serious faces and fear in their eyes.

And Wang prayed the refugees would remain safe in the lower cellars, and in the caves where the underground river flowed.

Forty days and forty nights, nature raged, shaking the ground and the rocky caves. When the deep tremors ceased and the stormy wind and thunder abated outside, Wang knew the many planets of the system had moved out of alignment. The cataclysmic event wouldn't happen again for sixty millennia. Stability would gradually return to this planet, but was the surface still habitable?

He led the survivors up the steep stairs and secret passages, and they emerged outside, on the flat outcrop where the Temple complex still stood. Wang took a deep breath and smiled. At least the air was clean.

He was also glad the monastery he called home, erected with hefty stones many centuries ago, had survived the destruction... although not unscathed. Many broken tiles from the pagoda roofs were strewn on the ground. A few secondary buildings showed cracks, and one section of the kitchen wall had fallen into what used to be a pond... now just sand. But all that could be repaired.

Shading his eyes from the reddish sunlight, Wang could hardly recognize the courtyard, filled with sand, debris, and fallen trees. The square pillars of the Celestial Gate, once imposing landmarks visible from many miles away, now stood half-buried in sand and debris. Would the gate still function when cleared? Not that any space traveler would want to visit a wrecked world... not for a long time. Wang was now marooned on this planet.

But the Celestial Gem was safe, and there was hope for the future of this world.

The survivors climbed to the top of the great stone wall surrounding the compound built upon Temple Rock, then they gazed down the cliff and around. No village remained, no field, no stables, no barns, no trees, no structure of any kind. Only sand.

The villagers, huddled atop the great wall and glanced at each other with dismay, holding hands as they realized the depth of their loss.

A young student gazed up at Wang, eyes round in disbelief. "Master Wang, what are we going to do?"

Wang smiled. "Well, young one, we shall clean up this mess, clear the paths, salvage whatever we can find and rebuild. We shall plant the seeds we stored underground and dig new wells to irrigate the fields. We'll work hard. With a little faith and a positive attitude, we shall overcome the obstacles."

"We are going to need a lot of luck," a man holding a child's hand volunteered.

"We should be thankful. It could have been much worse. We must remain hopeful." Wang didn't believe in luck, but he must help these villagers manifest their own power. "Remember, our thoughts shape our reality and our destiny."

"Master Wang," a young girl asked in a weak voice. "Is everyone else dead?"

Wang shook his head. "No, young one. Just as we survived, many others must have survived as well. In time, we shall meet them and help each other rebuild a new civilization."

But it would take time...

Chapter 1

Temple of the Celestial Gate, two decades later

Anila struggled to breathe, as if trapped underwater. She sensed the darkness but must not yield to fear.

A horde of barbarians in dark furs and boots galloped down the mountains on black steeds. They unfurled across the grassy plains like demons, as if to engulf the entire continent. Fierce and determined, they rode, with black markings on their faces, and long black hair bound on the top of their heads. Red banners floated above their army like rivers of blood.

Flocks of falcons and golden eagles flew ahead of them on the wind, along with blood-curdling battle cries. The barbarians brandished spears and wide, curved swords, while archers shot long arrows from the saddle of their galloping steeds. Alongside the dark horde, like lowly servants begging for scraps, tall wolves ran in packs to share in the carnage.

And at their head, leading men and beasts, rode the fiercest of them all. A tall, muscular man with black symbols on his face and determination in his piercing green eyes. His warriors called him Bayor Khan!

Anila awoke in a cold sweat, her heart beating like a runaway drum. She sat up on her mat and shuddered. What was that? Just a horrible dream? Something she imagined? Or a vision of things to come?

Around her, the Acolytes slept, like soft bundles of sand-colored cloth left on the floor overnight. Anila rose to her bare feet, rolled her thin mat, quietly tiptoed around the sleeping forms, stored the mat on the wall rack, then headed toward the door.

The Temple gong hadn't tolled yet, but she needed fresh air and peace.

It was still dark and cool outside when she retrieved her sandals and stepped onto the blue tile of the main courtyard. There, familiar cats, black, white, or patched like the Yin-Yang, the Tai-Chi symbol, played, stretched, yawned, or groomed themselves. The chimes hanging from roofs and windows emitted soft, crystalline notes in the cool breeze.

Between two stone buildings, Anila caught a glimpse of shadowy figures with shaved heads, in black flowing pants and loose white shirts. They carried long spears. Double-edge swords and knives protruded from their low-hanging belts. The Protectors of the Celestial Gate... She hoped to become one of them someday.

The Protectors glided in total silence like weightless ghosts, in a single file, toward their private practice hall. Said to be lethal, they were a mysterious bunch who never spoke and never attended seasonal celebrations. They kept to themselves and didn't mingle with the other residents.

Birds trilled their ode to sunrise in the highest branches of the leafy banyan tree shading the stone benches. A few Acolytes sitting on individual mats meditated along the walls, eyes closed and legs crossed. Early bees buzzed around the yellow blossoms in the flower beds and the white and pink lotus flowers in the shallow ponds where frogs sang.

Along the kitchen wall, a dozen Tai-Chi kittens lapped milk and raw eggs. At the well, an Acolyte on kitchen duty raised a pail from the depths and carried it toward the back garden. On the cool breeze wafted the aroma of baking bread and strong tea being brewed.

"Sifu Anila!" An Acolyte at the kitchen door, one of her students, beckoned to her. "Come have some tea." He handed her a warm mug.

"Thank you." Anila smiled and accepted the aromatic brew.

Mug in hand, she climbed up the narrow steps along the great wall surrounding the compound and crossed the wide top to sit at the outside edge. Letting her legs dangle over the steep drop, she sipped the honeyed spiced tea, gazing toward the far horizon upon the vast expanse of sand that went on for several riding days. From this height in the predawn light, she could barely distinguish the sand road snaking around the dunes.

Straight down, at the foot of the cliffy promontory upon which the Temple complex was built long ago, lay the village getting its life force from the Temple, and its water from the underground stream. A rosy dawn bathed the smattering of small abodes, sheds, and stables made of fronds, mud bricks, and straw. Around the village, carefully manicured gardens alternated with small fields, meadows, and palm trees... an oasis of green with red and yellow blossoms, surrounded by a sea of sand.

In the small community below, life was also stirring. A rooster crowed, goats bleated, and cows mooed. A beast of burden pulling a cart full of manure brayed, causing a hound to bark in response.

Grabbing her pendant in her free hand, Anila found comfort in its smooth contact. She could feel energy in its warmth. Carved in red jasper, it represented the Great Ultimate, the Tai-Chi symbol. Some called it the Yin-Yang, light and darkness, the feminine and the masculine, the perfect balance of energy, harmony between all things and all people.

She cherished the stone as the last remnant of her family, killed like so many others in the great cataclysm, over two decades ago. She knew nothing about her dead parents, and sometimes, she wished she had known them. It must be nice to belong, to have a family, like an anchor of unconditional love, no matter what. Although the monastery was her home, sometimes, she felt like a lost ship on that sea of sand.

A familiar white cat nudged her elbow, and Anila set down her mug to oblige the feline with a scratch under the chin. "Good morning to you, too, Cottonball. And thank you for keeping the grounds free of vermin and the evil spirits at bay."

The cat purred under her ministrations, and all seemed right again in Anila's small world. Maybe, her nightmare was born of irrational dread... but she must not fear. Fearful thoughts created negative futures. Fear invited evil.

Then the red sun rose, setting ablaze the eastern horizon, highlighting the ancient markings etched upon the massive pillars of the Celestial Gate in a long-forgotten language. Ancient scrolls said the characters changed when the gate came to life. But to her knowledge, no one had ever seen it open.

Anila knew the perfect remedy to regain her serenity. She slipped off her sandals and rose atop the great wall, facing the direction of the rising sun. Emptying her mind, she straightened her frame, calmed her thoughts, lowered her shoulders, softened her knees, then sank into the Tai-Chi form.

The Chi was strong around Temple Rock. She relaxed into each slow movement, like meditation in motion, as she shaped energy through the air. Drawing Chi from the stone under her bare feet, she gathered it into a ball between her hands, molded it, then threw it to catch it again. Soon, she immersed herself in the form, and all her fears vanished as she became one with the forces of nature, one with the energy of the planet, one with the universal Chi.

The Temple gong resonated through the entire compound. Now serene and fully energized, Anila closed the form and saluted the sun. Time for her morning ablutions, meditation, then weapons training. During her morning break, she might consult Master Wang about the disturbing dream.

* * *

Wang enjoyed teaching the young children who sat in a semicircle under the banyan tree. How this new generation emerged after the cataclysm could be considered a miracle... but he knew better. The strong Chi emanating from the Temple was helping the people stay healthy, happy, and vigorous.

Legs crossed on the blue tile of the courtyard, the children petted the occasional cat begging for attention... three dozen pupils, all eyes on him, thirsty for knowledge. Their eagerness to learn gave him hope for the future of the oasis, the village, and the Temple.

When he saw Anila step into the courtyard, Wang detected a disturbance of red and orange in her turquoise aura. Tall and svelte in her tan practice outfit, her cropped black hair ruffled by the breeze, she looked like any other Acolyte. But she walked with the calm confidence of a fully trained warrior. He noticed her tan skin, shiny from intense practice... and something different in her wide amber eyes. She seemed troubled.

Wang motioned to the pupils. "Let's welcome Sifu Anila to our circle."

The seated children pivoted and saluted from the ground, right fist in the left palm. "Good morning, Sifu Anila."

"Good morning, children." Anila smiled and returned the salute. "Master Wang, I had a strange dream, and I would like a word with you... when you have the time."

"Time is an artificial concept, Anila. Now is always the right time for the truth." Wang wanted the children to understand that grownups, too, had problems to solve and fears to overcome. "Speak freely, Anila, and maybe together we shall find the answer you seek."

Anila hesitated. "It might be scary for the children."

"We have no fear of dreams." Wang waved away the thought. "Right, children? No fear."

"No fear," the children repeated then laughed.

"Go ahead, Anila. Tell us your dream." How could the children master their fears if they were kept in total ignorance?

Wang listened to Anila describing her nightmare in chilling details. The children seemed rivetted, eyes wide, suspended on every word.

When she was finished, Wang nodded. "This could be a true vision, Anila. I've been informed about wild tribes stirring in the north."

"Informed?" Anila's amber eyes widened. "How? when?"

Wang chuckled. "We are isolated, Anila, but I do get news from faraway places, once in a while."

"Sorry, Master." Anila nodded. "Could this be part of the prophecy?"

"Possibly." Wang couldn't reveal all he knew. The planet's inhabitants needed to draw their own conclusions, make their own decisions, evolve in their own way. "Prophecies are always vague, and prone to many interpretations, and I suspect that's on purpose."

A young pupil named Taran raised his hand. "Master Wang, what does the prophecy say?"

Wang took a slow breath. He wouldn't mention the dark side. "It says that after the planet recovers from the cataclysm, a new ruler will rise."

A child raised his hand. "He will claim the Celestial Gem to help him govern the planet in peace and harmony."

Wang smiled. He couldn't divulge what else he knew.

"Master Wang, when is this supposed to happen?" Taran again.

"Master Wang," another pupil interrupted. "Is Sifu Anila's pendant the Celestial Gem?"

"Slow down. Give me time to answer." Wang raised both hands to shore the flood of questions. "One question at a time."

Anila was staring at him.

Wang winked at her. "But no, Anila's pendant is not the Celestial Gem. The Celestial Gem is something extremely rare and precious. And no one knows exactly what the prophecy means, or when it will manifest." He turned to Anila. "I will meditate on your dream and get back to you, young lady. Let's talk again tomorrow."

"Thank you, Master Wang." Anila saluted, turned around on one heel then walked away with new assurance and serenity.

Wang watched her disappear around the corner of a building, wondering if Anila's dream confirmed the time of the prophecy had come. Was the world ready for it? Then he took a calming breath and switched his attention back to his young flock. "Next question."

A child in the front row raised his hand. "Master Wang? Why do we salute with the fist in the hand?"

"Good question." Wang had explained it several times, but it took many repetitions for them to remember. "The right fist symbolizes the martial aspect, the strong warrior side, while the open palm symbolizes friendship, peace, and togetherness." He did the gesture slowly. "We also tuck the left thumb between the first and second knuckles of the right fist, to symbolize humility."

All the children did the gesture, the youngest ones struggling with the fine points.

"Master Wang, what are wolves?" Taran's fresh face scrunched up in concentration.

Time to teach. "Wolves are wild beasts that look like hounds, but bigger than a man, and very aggressive. They have long fangs, are intelligent, and live in an organized society. Sometimes, they make alliances with other wolves, and even other species... and they use clever hunting tactics for the benefit of their entire pack."

"Could they eat us?" A timid girl whispered from the back row, holding a black kitten close to her chest.

"They would if they were very hungry." Wang smiled. "But they don't live in the desert, so we are safe from wolves." He didn't mention the poisonous snakes, the scorpions, or the panthers roaming the sand dunes. No need to frighten them.

The young pupils released a collective sigh of relief.

"Just like our Tai-Chi cats, who love the energy of this place, every living thing feeds on the Chi, the universal life force... from the smallest insects to the largest predators." Wang paused for emphasis. "Every life is precious. In the Chi, we are all brothers and sisters."

Taran frowned. "Even the wolves?"

"Yes, Taran." Wang chuckled. "Even the wolves."

* * *

Later that day, Anila stood in the practice yard as the sun lowered on the horizon, and the northern breeze tempered the heat. She taught a long pole class for a score of Acolytes, but her mind kept returning to the dream.

As she corrected the stance of a teenage boy in the front row, he straightened and faced her, holding his pole with both hands.

"Sifu? How can a wooden pole win against a sword?"

Anila shivered as she remembered the wicked blades the barbarians wielded in her dream. "For one thing, a long pole can be fitted with a blade for battle. But even without a blade, the length of the pole gives you the advantage of reach. You can strike enemies on their steeds and remain at a safe distance from their swords."

The boy frowned. "But won't the sharp sword edge slice the pole?"

"Not necessarily." Anila remembered struggling with the concept in her early training years. "When you strike, it's not the strength of wood or steel, or muscle that counts, but the speed, and the amount of energy expanded in the strike. It's the strength of your Chi. In training, we use the weapons to help us gather and focus the Chi."

"What do you mean, Sifu?" A student asked from the back row.

Anila couldn't help but smile as she walked toward the student. "How does a blade of straw bury itself into a wood pillar during a sand storm?"

"It shouldn't, Sifu." A girl on her left straightened. "The pillar is harder than the straw. The straw should bend or break."

"Exactly. Yet, during a deadly storm, the force of the wind expands so much energy that it strengthens the straw, allowing it to penetrate the harder wood." Anila scanned her students' eager faces. "The energy, or Chi, is stronger than matter."

The students stared at her, some in disbelief.

"So, the weapon is not as important as the Chi of its wielder." She searched her mind for an example they would remember. "With intense daily practice, a master can strike a death blow using the Chi alone, without making contact, without any weapon."

"Really?" The boy in the first row frowned. "Can you do it, Sifu?"

Anila chuckled. "I never tried, but no. I'm not a master. With intense practice, however, I feel my Chi getting stronger each day."

"Sifu? How long does it take to become a master?" The girl in the back stared at her teacher.

"It takes a lifetime." Anila enjoyed these questions. "Sometimes, several lifetimes."

"Sifu," another girl interrupted. "Raised in the Temple, you studied and practiced all your life... you are old enough. Why aren't you a Protector of the Celestial Gate?"

"It is my goal. I am a Protector in training. But I'm only a few cycles older than you are." Anila envied the innocence of the early years. Training with no strings attached. "But with deeper knowledge comes more responsibility." And both could be a burden. "In any case, I still have time before I take the vows of the Protectors."

"Celibacy, loyalty, humility, truth, courage," an Acolyte enunciated by rote.

"And the Protectors live like monks, they shave their heads and have a big Yin-Yang tattoo on the back of their skull," a boy volunteered.

Another Acolyte raised his hand. "And they only wear black and white, the colors of Tai-Chi."

"All true." Anila refrained from smiling to give weight to her words. "They also go on dangerous missions wherever the Temple sends them... and some never return."

The dinner gong resonated throughout the compound.

Anila realized she was hungry. She saluted her students, right fist in her left palm. "Class dismissed."

"Thank you, Sifu." The pupils saluted back then rushed toward the racks to store their long poles, before heading for the refectory.

* * *

After the evening meal, still haunted by the nightmare of the night before, Anila decided to go for a walk under the stars. It was Fall, and although the sun remained warm during the day, the nights would get cooler as the red sun laid its course toward the winter solstice.

The large moon and its small sister lit the stone pavers and the buildings.

Following a familiar path along the great wall, Anila found herself on a terrace with a stone balustrade at the edge of the cliff. She sat under a small tree, closed her eyes, and emptied her mind.

When something brought Anila out of her meditative state, she opened her eyes but did not move. The air was still and silent. Strange. Why did the night creatures stop making sounds?

A slim figure in a black cloak bent over the stone balustrade and glanced down the cliff. He had a beaked nose, and it seemed there was a very large bird behind him, flapping black wings. Then in the faint moonlight, in the play of light and shadow, the cloaked figure seemed to vanish, while the giant bird flapped its wide wings and flew over the balustrade. Moonlight flashed on something shiny, then the large bird circled high once and flew away into the night... North.

A homing bird? This was no pigeon. Master Wang mentioned he was receiving messages from afar. Was this how he remained informed? But why keep it a secret?

Who was the shadowy figure who vanished into the night without a sound? Probably a Protector. Anila wondered how they managed to be so stealthy. It seemed she still had a lot to learn to become one of them.

It was late. Anila needed her sleep. She wanted to be fully energized and alert for her classes and intense daily practice. Lack of focus could cause accidents. Other than blisters, bruises, and small cuts that healed in a day, she never had a training accident, and she wanted to keep that perfect record intact.

In the morning, maybe Master Wang would have an explanation for her dream.

Chapter 2

The next morning, as Anila stepped into the main courtyard, she was stunned by the stillness and the silence of the place. No bird songs. Had the birds fled for the winter? No breeze, no chimes, no bees, and a complete absence of cats. She'd never seen this before. Strange...

As she neared the kitchen, not even one kitten lapped the milk set by the wall. Why were they hiding? Cats could detect earthquakes and smell fire before anyone else. Did they sense something bad coming this way? Was the ground about to shake? She glanced at the clear sky. Was a big sandstorm coming?

Anila accepted a mug of hot tea from the girl serving at the kitchen window, then she headed for a stone bench, wondering about the eerie silence. Even the wildlife in the surrounding desert seemed to hold its breath. The students at the tables, or sitting on the low walls and stone benches, glanced around and at each other in wonder, forgetting to sip their tea.

The sound of a horn outside the wall broke the silence and bellowed in the air, followed by a cacophony of drums and trumpets. Loud music exploded, shattering the serenity.

"It's a caravan!" someone yelled from the top of the great wall. "A caravan is coming!"

A caravan? None had stopped by this oasis in many cycles. Anila was still a child then, but she remembered the excitement. Maybe what scared the animals was a good thing after all. She hoped so.

Everyone in the courtyard forgot their morning tea and rushed to the great wall, in a total lack of order, laughing and talking at the same time, racing each other up the steps, pushing and shoving, and wobbling out of breath at the top.

Anila followed sedately, noticing how easily young people forgot their training. She felt old compared to them, although they were close in age. She envied their excitement. Standing atop the wall, she shaded her eyes to gaze at the faint ribbon of road circling the dunes and saw the source of the ostentatious music.

Behind a group of riders in red armor, a full ensemble of musicians played while sitting in an open chariot pulled by oxen. It seemed the outside world was very different from the peaceful oasis. This riotous lifestyle seemed a far cry from the quiet serenity that reigned around the Temple of the Celestial Gate... until today.

A long convoy of camels, steeds, and covered chariots pulled by oxen followed the musicians, including another group of mounted soldiers in red armor, wearing swords and holding spears. Red and blue ribbons adorned their leather helmets. Closing the rear, several rows of archers on foot had crossbows strapped upon their backs.

Anila didn't know a caravan needed so much protection to traverse the desert... but protection from what? Wild predators? Thieves? To her knowledge, there was no war in the region. Or was there?

The image of the barbarian horde and their green-eyed leader from her nightmare made her shudder.

* * *

"Master Wang!" The teenage boy, an Acolyte, rushed into the Temple and bowed.

Wang looked up from the prophecy scroll he had been studying. Had the time really come? He straightened in his seat. "Speak."

"The caravan made camp outside the village, Master." The Acolyte paused and took a slow breath, as if to calm his frantic mind. "They are holding a market for the villagers to exchange goods."

"That's fine." But Wang didn't believe in coincidences. This visit must have a more important purpose. "Who is their leader?"

"His name is Prince Altan, Master, Ruler of the Southern Provinces."

"Ah! I know who he is." Could the visit be linked to Anila's dream? Or to the prophecy? "What about the soldiers and their general?"

"The soldiers staked their tents, and Prince Altan requested an audience for you to meet him and his noble retinue." The Acolyte stared down at his feet. "But they refuse to climb the steep path and the many steps to the monastery, Master."

Another bunch of privileged nobles... "They can take the rope elevator we use for heavy loads."

"No, Master. They deemed it smelly and unworthy of their rank." The boy took a deep breath. "Prince Altan is asking you to come meet them down in their camp instead."

"Really?" Wang guffawed. "They cross the desert to the Temple of the Celestial Gate, and they refuse to come up to see the said gate and our Temple?"

"Prince Altan says his noble ladies are delicate flowers, not fit to climb all those rocky trails and stairs." The boy giggled. "I've seen their fancy shoes, Master, and I believe it."

"Well, can they ride goat-mules?" That's how the villagers brought up their lighter loads.

"I guess they could, Master... but there are many women." The boy chuckled. "Prince Altan brought his entire harem."

"A harem?" How decadent. Wang refrained from rolling his eyes at such nonsense. "Send all the small mounts we have. The rest of the women can ride on the backs of sturdy farmers.”

“Yes, Master.” The boy saluted and ran out.

Wang smiled, imagining the awkward tableau on the steep incline, but he couldn’t let an outsider dictate his will upon the Temple. The Celestial Gate and its mighty Protectors should command respect, even from a feudal Prince traveling with a small armed force and a large harem.

According to a recent report from one of his undercover Protectors, Prince Altan was a lesser noble with great ambition. In this naïve new world, anyone could rise to power. Altan must have crossed the desert for an important reason… to claim the Celestial Gem? He would not turn around on account of a steep climb.

It had been a long time since Wang engaged in political intrigue, and today he would have a chance to practice this special skill. But he must prepare. Every detail should be perfect. Ambitious lords judged others on appearances.

He gestured to the Protector standing like an inconspicuous shadow at the Temple’s back door. The shaved warrior seemed to walk on air as she approached him, then took a knee. “Master?”

Wang whispered in her ear. “Full ceremonial protocol. Two hours from now, main courtyard.”

"Yes, Master." The Protector saluted, then rose, pivoted on one heel, revealing the large, round tattoo on the back of her shaved head, and vanished without a sound.

But Wang remembered his siblings' reaction to his humble garb. He couldn't impress an ambitious Prince while looking like a pauper. Time to open his Immortal bag of tricks… where did he store his shimmering robes, and his special flask of elixir?

* * *

Aware of his general awaiting an answer, Prince Altan, ruler of the Southern Provinces, paced his tent in front of his ancestral armor. Centuries old, made of ancient metal for a tall Immortal, the relic from glorious times was mounted on a frame. The finely crafted breastplate featured a silver dragon, containing a drop of blood from his ancestors —the symbol and proof of his Immortal bloodline, however diluted.

Altan fumed at the audacity of the Temple master. "By refusing to come to me, this Wang fellow insulted my noble birth and my authority!"

"True." General Torino, in his red armor made of boiled leather, glanced at the metalcraft wonder with obvious envy. "I heard the Temple master is quite old… could he be too feeble to comply, and too proud to admit it?"

"Possibly." The insult still stung. Why would Torino make excuses for the miscreant?

The general straightened his frame to look taller... in vain. "My Prince, if you are to defeat the barbarians and crown yourself king, you need the official support and the fighting power of the famous Protectors."

"I know." Altan sighed. "Let the messenger know we are on our way to meet his master."

"Yes, my Prince." The general paused. "Your courtly ladies aren't going to like this excursion, my Prince. May I suggest we climb without them?"

"Out of the question!" Was his general daft? "My harem is the only luxury I can flaunt in this inaccessible place. A mark of wealth and high status. Without it, I might as well be a simple tribal chief."

"My Prince, if I may..." General Torino bowed, as if to soften his borderline insolence. "Don't forget that you also command an impressive army."

"So does the uncouth Bayor Khan, who lives on his steed and sleeps with wolves." Altan resented having to explain, but he needed his general to understand. "Even a village leader can draft and train soldiers. It doesn't make him fit to be king."

"I understand, my Prince." Torino nodded. "Like this humble Temple and their communal village, producing the fiercest warriors in the land, but unfit to rule it."

"Exactly. I'm the only noble with enough Immortal blood to take the crown. The Protectors are formidable warriors, but poor. I can give them great status and fame." Altan picked up a red fruit from the bowl on the table and sat in the chair at the end... the high seat of the table. "By demonstrating our superiority through noble blood, wealth, education, and refined culture, we can rally the Temple to our cause and use its formidable Protectors to accomplish our goal."

Torino cleared his throat. "But, my Prince, what if the master refuses to give us his warriors?"

Altan bit into the sweet fruit and enjoyed its juicy pulp. "We'll just have to make certain he cannot refuse."

"By threatening the Temple?" The general shook his head. "My Prince, our small escort doesn't stand a chance against their Protectors. A few hundred of them, I heard."

"True." But Altan had foreseen that possibility. "General, there are more civilized ways to make alliances and ensure the loyalty of our vassals."

General Torino raised an interested brow. "Such as?"

Altan licked the juice from his fingers, leaned back in his chair, tucked both hands behind his head, and smiled. "General, did you ever wonder why I have so many ladies in my harem?"

Torino's dark eyes rounded in surprise. "It's not for me to judge, my Prince. You are rich, young, handsome, and I assume virile as well."

"All true... but that's not it, Torino. Think again..."

The light of understanding finally dawned in General Torino's eyes. "Ah... I see... The number of ladies in your harem shows how many vassal lords give you their support and their loyalty, by entrusting you with their daughters."

"Now, you understand, Torino." Time for Altan to wield his exceptional diplomatic gifts and make useful alliances.

* * *

Anila saw the master's messenger coming from the corner entrance of the practice yard toward her. When he reached her, she signaled her students to stop, then she listened to the young boy's whispered message. She didn't usually interrupt her class, but this was an unusual day.

"Thank you." She saluted the messenger, right fist in her left palm.

The boy returned the salute, then scampered away.

Anila turned to her students, all quiet and staring at her. "We have an official request from Master Wang. We are to dress in our best practice uniform and line up in the main courtyard to properly greet the visitors who came with the caravan.”

The Acolytes glanced at each other, excitement on their faces.

“We’ll go to the main courtyard as a group. We meet outside the dorm in fifteen. Class dismissed.” She saluted her students.

The Acolytes returned the salute then ran toward their dorms. Anila followed them at a more dignified pace to change into her newest practice clothes, the ones with no unraveling edges. Then she led her small group around buildings and gardens, toward the main courtyard.

Even before she reached the Temple yard, drums and music emanating from the flat terraces under the tiled pagoda roofs filled the air with palpable energy. The compound residents were lining up in perfect rows on each side of the gate, facing the Temple, leaving a wide central path from the gate pillars to the Temple terrace for the important guests.

The blue tile underfoot emitted a soft glow, and so did the red-painted columns of the Temple. Tai-Chi banners with the Yin-Yang symbol floated from high masts above the many pagoda roofs.

The two giant pillars framing the eastern gate seemed to hum to the vibrations of the soft bells, strings, and gongs. Anila could see the strange markings etched on the square pillars moving, as if they danced to the music. Did the alien characters shimmer?

No. Impossible. It must be her fertile imagination. To her knowledge, no one had ever seen the Celestial Gate come alive.

A whiff of incense floated in the air from inside the Temple, mixing with the sweet scent of the yellow bushes in the flower beds and the white lotus in the shallow ponds. Anila also detected the tantalizing aroma of baking goods wafting from the kitchen. There would be special treats.

On the terrace lining the Temple, atop the wide steps leading from the courtyard, the master's wooden chair stood like an empty throne, its green paint gleaming like jade in the morning sun. Then the music stopped.

In the following silence, a gong rang. From the Temple roof gallery came the loud booms of the huge Daiko drums, struck by young Acolytes with the power of the Chi in a frantic staccato, like a formidable roll of thunder from heaven. Then the drums came to an abrupt stop.

The Protectors glided out of the Temple in total silence, like black and white shadows, and lined up in four rows of twelve on both sides of the master's empty chair. They looked fierce, men and women alike, with shaved heads, sharp blades, long spears, and a ferocious expression on their faces. The tall ones stood in the back and the shorter ones in front.

Anila shivered at the intimidating sight. She also wondered where the rest of them were hiding. She knew there must be at least two hundred more in residence… not counting the many sent on special missions across the land.

Then, some heavenly notes from a flute floated on the breeze, and out of the Temple came a youthful man, also shaved under a black cap. Incredibly tall and elegant, he wore shimmering rainbow robes that changed colors as he walked. His smooth face glowed, and his gliding walk looked very familiar, despite the tall platform shoes.

Only when he sat in his chair did Anila recognize him. Master Wang? All shaved and dressed up, he looked young and heavenly, like the lofty Immortals portrayed on the ancient scrolls.

Never in her entire life had Anila seen such pomp and decorum. This must be a very important visitor.

A messenger in red regalia appeared at the eastern gate, between the two monumental pillars, then he took a deep breath and announced in a booming voice, "His Highness, Prince Altan, Ruler of the Southern Provinces, with General Torino, Commander of the great army, and the princely harem of noble ladies."

At the dry knock of two wooden bricks, everyone in the yard pivoted on one heel to face the central path. Anila held her breath. For whom did Master Wang go to such trouble?

Then a fanfare from beyond the gate confirmed the arrival. The messenger stepped aside and made way for the noble guest and his entourage. Two men walked into the courtyard.

The young one, tall and handsome, in blue and red silk, wore a silver dragon breastplate on his chest and carried a staff. Symbol of power? Or weapon? His short black hair contrasted with his blue eyes and fair skin.

The other man, darker, shorter, older, in red armor with a sword at his hip, had slightly bowed legs. Two steps behind his Prince, he walked onto the blue tile like marching into battle. An escort of six armed soldiers walked in step behind them.

Then appeared a strange flock of chatting ladies in full makeup and fancy hairdos, wearing brightly colored gowns, and fluffy dresses. These women teetered on unstable heels, lamenting in high-pitched voices about the unsightly climb. They fanned themselves frantically with gem-incrusted fans, despite the cool morning, and the fact that they certainly didn't expand any energy coming up the steep incline in these delicate shoes, or they would be in shreds.

Some boy behind Anila made hushed comments about the ladies and sneered. A girl giggled, remarking on Prince Altan's good looks. Anila silenced them both with a harsh stare. Any lack of respect would reflect badly on Master Wang.

Anila was more interested in the meaning of this unlikely display. Her gaze went to the guest of honor. Prince Altan. He walked head high, confident, sure of himself, and his fancy clothes, fitted to flatter his muscular physique, reeked of wealth and power. He obviously enjoyed the pomp and decorum... the mark of a big ego.

According to Anila's studies, his ancient breastplate design indicated he was descended from that particular dynasty of Immortals, the silver dragon emperor. But that was thousands of cycles ago. With each generation, the blood was diluted.

All nobles claimed Immortal blood, but most of them only had half a drop, if any. Prince Altan, however, must be an authentic blood prince, because she couldn't read him at all. She could always tell when someone was lying, or if a person was trustworthy or not... unless they had Immortal blood.

But she could not read Prince Altan... the same way she couldn't read Master Wang, who demonstrated today that he had more Immortal blood than she suspected. Curious... She might ask him about it.

As the prince reached the bottom of the Temple steps and faced Master Wang, Anila wished she could see his face... and hear the conversation.

Unfortunately, the gong signaled for the residents to return to their classes or assigned chores. So, she turned around and led her students back to the practice yard.

She hoped Master Wang would share the details of his encounter with Prince Altan later in the day. He did confide in Anila, sometimes, and this would be most interesting.

Chapter 3

Wang waited as the gongs and drums marked the orderly departure of the Temple residents from the courtyard. After all of them had left to resume their daily activities, only the four dozen Protectors behind him remained.

The effect of his little display of power on Prince Altan's classic face, straight nose and blue eyes made him chuckle inside. The smile of the would-be-king revealed perfect teeth, but he looked more nervous than jovial. He did not bow or salute, indicating he considered Wang his humble subject, but he seemed at a loss.

Good. Maybe this ceremonial display would bring his arrogance down a notch or two. Although Prince Altan was his official overlord and ruled the land where the monastery stood, Wang would never bow to him either. He could tell from Altan's dark, reddish aura, that he was greedy and quick to anger. But since Wang couldn't read his mind, Altan also had undeniable Immortal blood... at least some.

As for his military chief, General Torino, he stood with martial confidence, but repressed fear was making his small aura tremble. The six armored soldiers standing behind him seemed confused, casting quick glances at each other.

A wavy pool of a hundred or so ladies in gaudy attire with elaborate headdresses and makeup, teetered and limped on impossible heels. They looked flustered and tired. Some complained to each other in hushed tones, while others stared at the Protectors with open dread.

The strategy worked. The visitors expected a rough back-country welcome from a destitute monk they could dazzle, not a princely reception and a show of force.

"Master Wang." Prince Altan cleared his throat. "I now remember we met before, when I was but a child. You haven't aged at all... One might say you look even younger." His puzzled gaze searched Wang's face. "Also, I cannot read you. You must have an Immortal somewhere in your bloodline."

"Possibly." Wang refrained from laughing. "I detect a trace of Immortal blood in you, as well." Did Altan think he was the purest noble in the land? Was it how he planned to stake his claim to power?

"Pardon the ladies' frantic countenance." Prince Altan indicated his chattering harem in a state of disarray, panting and disheveled. "Brought up in the far provinces by lesser lords, they were not prepared for a harsh climb, nor for a reception fit for a king... or an emperor."

Emperor? Wang refrained from scoffing. Altan's aspirations were lofty indeed. Had he come to claim the Celestial Gem? Not on Wang's watch. But hospitality first.

Wang clapped his hands. "We should make these ladies more comfortable."

Out of an adjacent building, Acolytes carried long tables and benches and set them in the shade of the banyan tree. The ladies rushed to get off their feet, visibly happy to sit. Wang noticed their ridiculous shoes and remembered his messenger's giggles. Then, Acolytes on kitchen duty brought out trays of sweets, pastries, fruit, and other delicacies, as well as mugs for everyone, and jugs of sun tea with honey.

The Acolytes on kitchen duty had outdone themselves on such short notice. Wang would thank them in person later. As for the Protectors, they remained so still, they had become part of the scenery, almost invisible.

Prince Altan inclined his head. "Thank you, Master Wang, for being so considerate to my ladies. Be assured, they appreciate it."

Wang rose from his green chair and unfolded to his full height... including platform shoes that made him look even taller. "I believe it's time for you to tell me what brought you to this isolated oasis, so far from the path of the trading caravans." Wang indicated an open stone arch to the side, leading out of the courtyard. "Shall we walk the grounds? Just the two of us... Immortal to Immortal."

"Yes, of course." Prince Altan seemed baffled by the direct approach but nodded and motioned for his general and armed escort to remain behind.

Wang nodded to the Protectors. One blink confirmed they would observe from a distance. Their mere presence ensured the ladies and soldiers in the courtyard would remain respectful.

Wang smiled inside as they climbed down the temple stairs. Keeping Prince Altan guessing and off balance might trick him into revealing what he didn't intend to disclose. They left the courtyard through the arch, then walked in silence along the garden path.

Once out of earshot, Wang stopped, admiring a tall flower. "So, Prince Altan, why have you come?"

Altan straightened and took a deep breath. "The northern tribes have come down from their mountains, conquered the grasslands, and are about to cross the Great River to claim the Southern Provinces."

"I know." Wang waited for the request. "How is this our concern? This Temple has survived the cataclysm, and its great wall has never been breached. Besides, there is nothing here a barbarian would want."

"True. But we rely on each other for our subsistence." The prince's voice shook a little.

"No, we don't. This oasis is completely autonomous." Wang wondered why the long-winded runaround.

"We need your help, Master Wang. I fear the barbarians might overcome us." Prince Altan straightened his frame. "Having your Protectors fighting the black hordes at our side would tip the scales in our favor."

Wang couldn't believe such audacity. "The Protectors of the Celestial Gate are not soldiers... they are monks who respect life. They do not wear armor or go into battle to kill, neither do they take orders from military leaders."

"But, Master Wang, they are a formidable force. Why not use them? Together, we can push back the barbarians."

But Wang refused to take sides. "The Protectors' supreme duty is here, guarding the Celestial Gate."

"Surely the gate is safe enough." Prince Altan's brisk tone denoted impatience. "As you said, these walls have never been breached... and the Immortals who used that gate millennia ago may never return."

Wang did not correct him but realized the population at large must believe the Immortals had gone for good. Given their short lifespan, it must seem so to them. But they must believe in order for the prophecy to be realized. "All the same, the Protectors took vows that can never be broken."

"Then how about lending me a dozen of them to train my new recruits. They are peasants in need of serious training, and your Protectors are the best." Prince Altan paused, as if expecting an answer that did not come. "The Temple will be handsomely compensated, of course."

"We are monks, Prince Altan. Not mercenaries. We do not value material gifts."

"Then, what do you value?" The keen interest in Altan's blue eyes said much about his determination to succeed. How unsettling.

"We value truth, knowledge, loyalty, humility, purity of heart." Rare qualities among politicians.

Prince Altan rubbed his smooth chin. "I have a library full of ancient scrolls and rare manuscripts, collected by my ancestors over the centuries." He smiled. "If I lent you a hundred of them, while your Protectors are training my recruits, you could have them copied for the Temple's library, so our history and knowledge can be preserved and passed on to future generations."

"The spread of knowledge has always been the secondary function of this Temple." Wang couldn't help but admire Altan's sharp mind and quick thinking. "A dozen Protectors it is. But they will not fight your battles... only instruct your recruits."

"Of course. Thank you, Master Wang. We are in your debt." Prince Altan relaxed into a genuine smile. "I would love to see how you train your own recruits."

"Then let's take a tour of the training yards." Wang started back toward the compound, wondering if Altan also owned a prophecy scroll in his vast library.

The proud Prince walked with uncommon grace... with a spring in his step, like a trained warrior... or a cat. "Where do you find so many students, when the village is small and isolated?"

Wang welcomed the easy question. "They come to us from all over the land. We have a reputation for adopting orphans and offering refuge to those rejected by society. We welcome anyone seeking a higher purpose. I believe all who are led to this Temple are following the true path. And we do not discriminate on the basis of age, race or gender. We accept anyone with a true calling. The grueling training is enough to discourage the weak and the unworthy."

"You accept anyone? Even females? I didn't notice any among your students earlier. Of course, in that drab uniform and same cropped hair, who can tell what's underneath?" Prince Altan loosened his silk collar. "In my experience, girls are not as reliable as boys. I could not imagine any of my ladies having what it takes to be a warrior."

"Me neither." Wang cast Altan a stern look. "The women of your harem were victimized and conditioned since birth, told their only value is as chattel, to be traded by their fathers for political favors. You should be ashamed for perpetuating such unfair practices."

"These are some of our oldest traditions, Master Wang." Prince Altan's smile froze. Obviously, he didn't like to be challenged. "They served us well for many centuries."

"You mean they served the men who benefited from them. That doesn't make it right." Wang scoffed. "Given freedom and a favorable environment, women are every bit as reliable as men and make excellent warriors. We have many in training."

Prince Altan cast him a worried glance. "But they are not strong enough to ever become Protectors... right?"

"Wrong." Wang enjoyed playing with Altan's prejudices. "Half the Protectors you saw behind me in the courtyard earlier are women."

"Half?" The shocked expression on Altan's handsome face was priceless. "But they all look alike... and their heads are shaved... and tattooed!"

"Of course. All our monks shave their heads and get the Tai-Chi tattoo when they take the vows. It's our tradition, our way to ensure fairness and equality." Wang enjoyed the prince's discomfort, maybe more than he should.

A white cat crossed their path and hissed at the visitor, then bolted out of sight.

Prince Altan huffed. "I hate cats."

"It seems the feeling is mutual." Wang knew exactly how the cat felt.

They entered a training yard, where Anila was teaching a double-edged sword class. She demonstrated the movement first, then let the Acolytes practice in pairs in a constant hammering of metallic blades. Wang glanced up and gave a slow nod to the Protectors watching from the rooftops.

Prince Altan rolled his shoulders, as if aware he was being watched. He definitely had Immortal blood, with the extrasensory abilities that came with it.

Fortunately for Wang, even an Immortal could not read another Immortal. His secrets would remain safe. And he didn't need to read Prince Altan to guess his true motivations. The man reeked of ambition and thirst for power.

Prince Altan seemed fascinated by the sweaty Acolytes practicing with boundless energy. "Are the swords sharpened?"

"Not for practice." Wang locked his hands behind his back. "But they can still break bones or inflict severe bruises... and, wielded with enough force, a strike to a vital organ could kill, nevertheless."

Prince Altan squinted at Anila. "Is the instructor a young woman?"

"Yes. Her name is Anila. One of our best teachers... a Protector in training... by choice." Wang managed a detached tone.

"I sense Immortal blood in her. Who are her parents?" The intense interest in Prince Altan's blue stare was disturbing.

"Like many of our students, she came here as a baby, orphaned by the cataclysmic alignment over two decades ago." Wang averted his gaze to cover the lie. "We do not know who her parents were."

"Still, I would like her to become my bride." Prince Altan's matter-of-fact statement echoed in the air, over the clash of steel.

Wang stilled his mounting anger at such audacity. "You already have so many noble ladies to propagate your seed, my Prince."

"But none of my ladies have enough Immortal blood to carry the Silver Dragon line." Prince Altan relaxed with a confident smile. "I sense that this young lady's blood, however, is noble enough for this great honor."

Wang cleared his throat. "That wouldn't be wise, my Prince."

"Well, all the same, I would like to purchase her from the Temple." Prince Altan's sharp tone could cut stone.

"Purchase her?" Wang shook off the disgusted feeling invading him at the very thought. "We do not sell our people, my Prince. They are free and make their own decisions."

"Really? Even the women?" The surprise on Altan's perfect face didn't reach his eyes. "Freedom is such an illusion..."

"Not here." Wang scoffed. "Besides, Anila is a Protector in training. She chose that path a long time ago, and I doubt she will renounce it to further your bloodline."

"Then let me present the offer to her in person, right now." So much arrogance in the way Altan held his head high and squared his shoulders.

"Anila is strong-headed and outspoken, my Prince. She will refuse, causing you public humiliation." Maybe that would make Altan think twice.

Prince Altan rubbed his smooth chin, and his lips curled into a slow smile. "Then add her to the group of Protectors I will take home with me. Given a chance, and with a little time for her to know me, I'm certain I can persuade her."

Wang wanted to refuse, but he must not interfere. Still... "Prince Altan, she hasn't completed her training. She is not a Protector, yet. She is not ready."

"You do not understand, Master Wang." Prince Altan rose to his full height and looked up to stare into Wang's eyes. "I wish to take her with me and make her my bride. You may be influential in this little oasis, but as the legitimate ruler of the Southern Provinces, I am your overlord. You will obey my wishes."

Wang bristled at the commanding tone but hid his feelings. No need to start a war that might endanger the gate. Besides, if the universe presented this path to Anila, he should respect it and let her decide, no matter the risks. "I shall talk to her."

"Please do." Prince Altan smiled. "Consider her the thirteenth warrior in the group, the odd one who will bring good fortune to my entire military campaign."

Wang suppressed a gasp of surprise that Altan would be familiar with the ancient legends. What else did the prince know, and what was his final plan?

* * *

Anila fumed, pacing in front of Master Wang in the empty hall of the Temple. She couldn't calm herself. She couldn't believe Master Wang would even bring up the topic. "I am not a prized mare for some king's harem. I am a Chi warrior, following the path of the Protectors of the Celestial Gate."

"I know." Wang nodded. "But I am sending you on a mission with the Protectors to train Prince Altan's new recruits. That's all you are required to do. It will give you an inkling of what being a Protector entails."

"That part, I welcome." Anila sighed. "But I suspect Prince Altan is not the kind of man who takes no for an answer."

"You do not have to do anything you do not wish to do, Anila. And the Protectors will be there to support you." Wang smiled. "I trust you to make your own choices. But also remember that you didn't take any vows yet, and choosing a different path is not a sin."

Did the master want her to accept? "Master Wang, do you think Prince Altan represents my future?"

"No, but I've been wrong before." Master Wang chuckled. "I believe the universe sometimes takes us on a side path for a reason. And this is your opportunity to explore the outside world. All you have ever known is this monastery. There is more to discover out there."

"If you think I should go, I will go." But Anila would never change her mind.

"Consider it your final test before you take the vows."

Her heart beat faster. Master Wang thought she was ready to become a Protector? "Thank you, Master Wang. I will do my best."

"You are welcome. Now, go."

Anila saluted. "Master, what about my nightmare? Did you find out what it means?"

"It was a true vision, Anila. There are no coincidences. Everything is linked. The barbarians' imminent attack is the reason Prince Altan requested Protectors to train his new recruits." Master Wang sighed. "Altan rules the land we stand on, so I must respect his wishes."

"I see..." Anila realized Master Wang may not have a choice either. "We are warriors of peace. We do not want to start a war against our legitimate ruler."

"Exactly. But I also believe this unexpected mission will lead you to your true destiny." The master smiled, looking younger than she ever remembered. "It will bring you the clarity you seek."

"I hope so." Anila bowed, right fist in her left hand. "Thank you, Master Wang."

As she hurried out of the Temple to make preparations, Anila's heart beat faster at the excitement of going on her first mission. It would be an adventure.

Chapter 4

Bayor Khan straightened in the saddle and patted Thunder, his favorite stallion. Perched at the top of a hillock, he surveyed the vast plain of grasslands and rolling hills, with the occasional island of trees. Although the region was once the site of great cities, when the land folded on itself, it buried all traces of civilization. Now, tall grasses and young forests spread across the entire continent, from the northern mountains to the great southern river.

Fast-moving clouds raced across the pale sky, and the autumn rain muddied the steppes. But soon, it would snow, then the ground would turn rock-hard with ice until the spring thaw.

The tall she-wolf at Bayor's side howled, stretching her long dark coat sprinkled with white flakes, like a night full of stars.

Other wolves in the periphery answered her call.

"Calm down, Stardust. It's not mating season. You don't need to go galivanting with the wild ones." He'd known the she-wolf since he'd rescued her from a bear trap as a pup. She never left his side.

Stardust stared at him with golden eyes and emitted pitiful yelps.

"Your wild cousins are hunting for food. You get fed daily. I'd say you are spoiled." Bayor chuckled. "Some would say you are getting a little too fat to run with the packs."

The she-wolf howled, as if in protest.

"Sorry, Stardust. The truth is, you are magnificent... especially with your thick winter coat."

Stardust made happy noises and wagged her tail wildly.

Sometimes, Bayor suspected the she-wolf understood a lot more than he realized.

Since the cataclysmic alignment, the planet kept regulating itself, and the land slowly recovered, but the seasons were more pronounced. Hotter summers and colder winters. At least, that's what the few surviving elders who remembered the world before kept saying.

Bayor never knew that world. He looked to the future and believed in working to build it, not lamenting about what was lost or what happened in the past.

For the sake of his warriors, he must cross the Great River to warmer climates before the deep freeze. Unknown to his people, Bayor's parents had come from faraway, and he was of different blood, but he considered himself one of them, and he wanted them to be warm, sheltered, and well fed... like Stardust.

From the top of the hillock, he had a bird's eye view of his encampment below. Large round tents dotted the perimeter, most of them for his soldiers, others for the steeds, and the many craft-masters and workers who took care of the camp. Round holes in the roofs let out the smoke from the fires. Animal pelts lining the walls helped keep the tents warm.

Pens and enclosures kept milk cows, sheep, and goats safe from predators.

Outside the perimeter, the packs of great wolves would stand guard at night and sound the alarm in case of an attack.

Stardust howled, and he followed her gaze.

Trappers and hunters returned to the camp, carrying gazelles across their saddles and dragging wild boars laid on branches tied into a travois to make them easier to drag. Soon they would roast on a spit over open fires. Large cauldrons already steamed, spreading a delicious aroma of wild rice and beans.

Something with a very large wingspan circled overhead, then hovered over the hill in front of the black stallion. Thunder reared.

"Easy, boy." Bayor patted Thunder's neck to calm him. "This big bird is our friend."

The being landed gracefully. His wide wings shook then retracted, revealing a tall man in black hooded robes. Unlike the horde warriors, he sported a thick, square beard. A large gold plate on his chest and a gold buckle on his belt reflected the faint light of the dipping sun. So did the wide cuffs on his wrists. He was the last of the Gripus, an extinct race of winged men who could fly or walk as they chose.

The man fisted his gold-ringed hand on his heart and bowed. "My Khan."

"Zaal! Always punctual, even after days of absence." Bayor smiled, happy to see his old friend and mentor unscathed.

Stardust loped toward the man, tail wagging, begging for pets.

Zaal patted the she-wolf's head, then tucked his gold-cuffed wrists inside wide sleeves and stepped up to Bayor. "You look in good health, my Khan, getting stronger and wiser by the day. A far cry from the helpless little boy I saved from becoming a hungry tiger's meal all those years ago."

"And I will always be grateful to you, Zaal." Bayor found himself acknowledging this a lot lately, but the man did save his life. "You came into my life at a critical time. Your tutelage, your wise counsel, and your protection made me the leader I am today. Thank you."

"You are most welcome, my Khan. I also enjoy our special bond." Zaal bowed, and all his gold glittered.

Bayor had different tastes in body ornaments, but to each his own. "What news from the south?"

"Prince Altan is on the move, my Khan. He borrowed Protectors from the Temple of the Celestial Gate to train his fresh recruits."

"Really? That's rather bold, even for him!" This was a sure sign of escalation. Bayor had waited long enough. "Then it's time to set things in motion."

Zaal straightened his frame. His square beard and muscular physique, as well as his curly hair and beaked nose, evoked the giant statues sometimes seen at the entrance of ancient Temples... for good reasons. They were his people from long ago. "What do we do first, my Khan?"

"We cross the Great River, my friend. You told me it's so wide in places that one can barely see the other shore. We select such a place near a wooded area, and build the rafts to cross it... away from the eyes of Altan's sentinels."

"Well thought, my Khan. But it will require many boats." Zaal's piercing gaze turned south, far in the distance. "And the current is swift in the middle."

"True. But our army is capable. We have the best craftsmen and experts." Bayor had chosen each one well. "We should also make sure Altan's sentries on the far shore do not spot us as we ferry warriors, workers, animals, and supplies across the treacherous waters."

"Right." Zaal pinched his beard. "Maybe a distraction could direct their attention somewhere else... away from the river bank."

Bayor rejoiced. His old friend never disappointed. "I assume you already have something in mind?"

Zaal smiled and nodded. "Always, my Khan."

"Good. You'll explain it to me over dinner and a horn of strong tika in my tent." Bayor was excited about the campaign. "We'll leave at dawn. Spread the word."

"Yes, my Khan." Zaal deployed his wings, cried to the darkening heavens, then took flight toward the camp.

Bayor gazed at the last sliver of red sun dipping on the western horizon. Soon, very soon, he would bring peace and prosperity to heal this wounded world... before petty provincial rulers without honor destroyed it with their greed, or in their struggle for power.

But for the prophecy to unfold, he must go to the Temple of the Celestial Gate and claim the Celestial Gem, which would confirm him as the sole legitimate ruler of all the land.

* * *

The next morning, before sunrise, after a mug of strong tea, Anila was ready to leave with the Protectors. Unlike them, she wore the sandy garb of an Acolyte, but she adopted the black mantle with the deep cowl that hid their bare skulls, and the sturdy leather boots. She even carried a sharp blade on her hip. From a distance, she would look just like them.

She'd never left the oasis, but she had heard many colorful stories from the villagers and from the newcomers talking about their homeland. This would be her first adventure, and her heart beat faster at the prospect. Her first mission. She must rise to the challenge.

Her favorite white cat jumped on the outdoor table.

"Good morning, Cottonball. How sweet of you to come say goodbye." She scratched the cat under the chin, making him purr. "I will miss you, sweetie... but I'll be back. I promise."

Cottonball rubbed his head on the corner of the woven trunk containing her rolled sleeping mat, clothes, and small weapons. The long poles and spears would already be loaded and waiting in the cart, down in the village.

As Master Wang stepped out of the Temple onto the esplanade and watched her from the top of the stairs, she bowed and saluted him. He nodded back.

She resisted the urge to wipe the tear at the corner of her eye. Master Wang had been like a father figure to her, and she'd never left the monastery. It was her only home. But a Protector never showed weakness.

Speaking of Protectors... the twelve assigned to the mission slipped into the courtyard through a side entrance. Anila had a chill. They glided rather than walked, in a single file, silent despite the sturdy traveling boots.

Anila hoisted the woven trunk on her back, adjusted the straps, and followed at the end of the file. The Protectors went out through the main gate, between the two monumental pillars. Anila glanced back and noticed the master's watchful gaze.

But she must focus on the mission. The steep descent down the cliff trail was easy for her, even with the added weight of the trunk.

When they reached the village, Prince Altan's military camp had been dismantled. Villagers loaded her trunk on a cart with those of the Protectors and the long weapons.

Then, Anila followed her group to the stables. The Protectors saddled their assigned steeds and checked the straps.

"This one is for you." The stableboy smiled as he handed Anila the reins of a white mare, already saddled and ready to go. "She is gentle enough for a new rider."

"Thank you. I appreciate the thought." Anila liked the white mare. She hoped this trek through the desert would give her an opportunity to improve her riding skills. She needed the practice.

"Shall I help you get on her back?" The stableboy stepped closer to give her a boost.

"No, thanks." Anila grabbed the pommel, slid her booted foot into the leather stirrup, and lifted herself onto the saddle with great agility, from years of Tai-Chi practice.

"I guess you don't need help." The stableboy chuckled. "Have a nice expedition." He smiled and walked away to take care of other animals.

In the first light of day, the long caravan started moving along the serpentine road around the dunes. Chariot wheels creaked on the hard sand, birds called as they circled overhead, the steeds whinnied when small creatures scurried away from their path. Burden beasts defecated on the road as they trudged, and no one commented, or even noticed.

Anila was glad Prince Altan rode at the head of the caravan, so she wouldn't have to suffer his presence.

The farther they rode from the oasis she called home, the more Anila realized her life may never be the same. She had never left Temple Rock before and already missed it. She turned in the soft saddle and glanced back. From this distance, the monastery looked more like an austere and forbidding stone fortress perched atop a tall, oblong rock... an island in a sea of sand, with two tall pillars at the eastern end, piercing the sky.

Soon, the sun rose higher and heated the sand. Fortunately, a light breeze cooled the air, carrying the scent of dry sage. Unused to the saddle, Anila couldn't quite find the perfect balance and kept adjusting her position on the mare.

She hadn't seen Prince Altan all morning, and she was glad for it. But now, he had stopped by the right side of the sand road and waited, while the distance between them slowly closed. Then he prompted his beautiful chestnut and positioned him to ride next to Anila's mare.

They now rode side by side, behind the chariots, followed by the Protectors and the soldiers who closed the march. Prince Altan looked at ease and very comfortable in the saddle.

As if to impress her, he made his chestnut do all kinds of subtle maneuvers with a slight pressure of a thigh on the flank, a pat on the neck, a short clicking sound, a gentle twist of the hand holding the reins. Anila couldn't help but admire his riding skills.

"Anila." He offered an easy smile that almost softened his perfect profile. "May I call you Anila?"

"It is my name, my Prince." She'd prefer he didn't call her at all, but she was on a mission with the Protectors. So, she must behave like one and keep the peace.

"Well, Anila," he said her name like a caress. "For your comfort and safety, I would prefer it if you rode in one of the chariots with the other women."

"What?" Anila felt the heat of shame creeping up her cheeks. He must have noticed her inexperience in the saddle. How embarrassing.

"Should I tell the chariot in front of us to stop?" Prince Altan's blue gaze never wavered from her.

"No, my Prince. Thank you. I do not need protection." She slowed her breathing to strengthen her confidence. "A Chi warrior doesn't travel on soft cushions like courtly ladies."

"But as a woman..." The unspoken end of the sentence reeked of prejudice.

"No, my Prince." Anila enjoyed refusing him. It made her feel powerful. "Please, treat me like a Protector and forget I am a woman."

"That would be difficult to forget, Anila... even in these ghastly clothes, and that boyish hair." His blue eyes twinkled with open delight. "I beg you to reconsider."

"Not a chance, my Prince." Anila straightened in the saddle, finding her balance. She liked her comfortable clothes and her short hair. "My rightful place is with the Protectors and the soldiers."

"But it doesn't have to be." Prince Altan offered a slow, patronizing smile. "Remember that, when you get saddle sores. My offer will still stand." He tsked, prompting his chestnut to a fast trot, toward the front of the caravan.

Anila sighed, embarrassed by the incident. She cast a furtive glance at the Protectors riding behind her. They saw and heard the whole exchange, yet they remained impassive, calm, and silent under their black cowls, as if in deep meditation. But she knew better. They were watching and noticing every detail... like spies. Would they report to Master Wang? She would be mortified if they did.

They rode all day, and part of the night. Finally, the caravan stopped in the middle of the road. The attendants unhitched the burden beasts, then unsaddled steeds and camels. Anila followed the Protectors and watched them unbuckle the straps as they unsaddled their mounts then fed them oats. She imitated them, grateful the mare was patient and gentle.

Strident screams erupted from one of the chariots assigned to the ladies. Anila ran to the chariot, opened the back drapes and saw an unlikely scene. Ladies on one leg, atop silky cushions and pillows, grasping the chariot's top frame as if to climb it. Others clutched their throats, eyes wide with pure horror. They all stared at a tiny yellow snake.

"It's all right." Anila gently picked up the snake, careful to avoid the tiny fangs, and admired it. "Look! It's just a baby." Its darker markings hadn't come out yet. "He's more frightened of you than you are of him."

She didn't tell them its venom could already kill, or that it would grow up to be one of the deadliest predators. All creatures had their place in the Chi. Killer snakes were useful, cleaning the desert of the sick and the lame. Anila stepped back and closed the chariot's flap. Then she released the baby snake on the warm sand, and it slithered away into the night.

Servants lit a fire and the caravanners sat in a wide circle around it, to eat fruit, bread, and cheese. The soldiers were laughing, drinking ale, singing to the music of the string instruments, and telling stories.

But the Protectors ate in silence and only drank water, so did she. Then they retired to the periphery to meditate. Anila followed them but secretly wished she could have joined the others in the merrymaking. She had only known quiet and orderly monastic life, and this vastly different philosophy of living could bear studying. But the mission came first. She was here to train Prince Altan's new recruits... nothing else.

Prince Altan did not show his face around the fire, and the refined ladies, probably afraid of wild life, never left their comfortable chariots.

At a familiar purr, Anila turned to see a white cat rubbing its head on her leg. "Cottonball? How did you get here?"

The cat must have boarded the caravan in the village. He meowed and walked away backward, as if he wanted her to follow him.

"Are you hungry? Thirsty?" She rose to her feet and followed the cat.

Cottonball seemed to be leading her somewhere. Then the cat stopped and hissed.

Anila crawled and peeked over the crest of a dune. In the distance, Prince Altan spoke with a tall, hooded figure. Both seemed very secretive, faintly defined in shadows against the thin crescent of the large waning moon and its tiny sister. The cloaked stranger's beaked nose reminded her of the man she saw that night by the cliff balustrade... with an unusually large messenger bird.

She blinked, and when she looked again, they were gone. Only a flapping of wings as a large bird flew into the night sky. Could she have imagined the encounter? Sometimes, the desert played tricks on the eyes and the mind, especially at night.

But Cottonball had seen them first and led her to them. Cats were more sensitive than people. They could see auras and feel the energy in all things. That's how they could detect faraway smoke and predict earthquakes and sandstorms, and sense evil in people.

The cat purred and rubbed against her legs. She knelt on the sand to pet him and noticed crumbs of cheese on his face. He'd found treats and might have hunted a few scorpions as well.

The cat trotted away, then froze in mid-stride, and pounced on a small lizard.

"Don't go too far, Cottonball, and make sure you are back to the caravan when we leave in the morning." She would relish having the cat around to remind her of home.

As she rejoined the group, Protectors and soldiers spread their sleeping mats under the stars on opposite sides of the road.

Anila wondered what the secret meeting of Prince Altan and the mysterious stranger meant. Was the cloaked figure one of the Protectors from the caravan? Or could it be a foreign spy? Or a traitor?

That night, despite her excitement, the soreness from riding, and the many questions churning in her head, Anila fell asleep quickly, exhausted from the long ride.

Chapter 5

Prince Altan, ruler of the Southern Provinces, slowed his chestnut and let the caravan pass him by as he stopped by the side of the sand road. Removing only twelve Protectors from the Temple couldn't be counted as a victory. He hadn't expected Master Wang to be so stubborn... or have Immortal blood.

His powerful new friend, who promised so much in exchange, was not happy about that. He wanted all the Protectors away from the Celestial Gate. But things didn't always go as planned.

Altan also refused to be defeated by a stubborn young woman. A thousand noble daughters would fight each other to death for the honor of bearing his heir. Why did this one resist his advances, despite his most charming behavior?

When he saw her, rod-straight but relaxed on her white mare, he marveled at how fast Anila adapted to the saddle. She had better posture than most of his soldiers. As he brought his chestnut to ride beside her white mare, she turned her head the other way. How vexing.

Altan hated being ignored. He wished he could just slap the young woman into obedience, make her understand the truth of her situation... she would be his and would bear his heir... whether she liked it or not. But she never left the midst of the Protectors. Were they guarding her? He couldn't afford to anger the formidable warriors and would have to get her away from them.

"Anila," he said as gently as he could, patting his chestnut stallion, rendered nervous by the proximity of the mare. "We are approaching our next stop, and you might find it a delightful surprise."

The young woman gave him a haughty look but did not speak. He saw no fear in her amber stare, only determination.

"Aren't you curious?" Altan suspected someone who'd been locked up with monks all her life might be.

Same fierce look. Did she consider curiosity a sin?

Altan might as well tell her. "Within the hour, we shall reach a famous caravanserai, built around an oasis. It's a fortified town in the desert, a favorite stop for the caravans, a safe place to rest the beasts and for the travelers to relax."

"I don't need to relax." She raised her chin, staring straight ahead.

Altan would never admit defeat. "It's also a great place to hear foreign languages, drink, taste exotic foods, trade, gamble, and see rare objects and animals from faraway lands."

Did he see a brief spark in her wide amber eyes? So, she was curious after all. Good. Altan could use that to his advantage.

* * *

Rounding the bend of a dune, Anila rose in the saddle to gaze at the marvel ahead. Prince Altan called it a caravanserai. From a distance, it looked like a gigantic square fortification, with very high walls and stout towers at each corner. The road appeared to pass straight through the arch of the tall gate in the middle of the wall.

The Protectors didn't react, so she slowly sat back on the mare and controlled her excitement.

As the caravan drew closer to the fortress, Anila could see fully armed sentries atop the rampart, gazing into the distance. The sun's rays reflected on shiny blades and spear points. Above the gate, archers knelt, aiming their crossbows at the road.

Again, Anila wondered what kind of danger prompted such military protection in the middle of the desert. Had hungry populations turned to crime to survive? Or was the attack of the barbarians imminent? She shuddered at the memory of her nightmare.

On each side of the monumental gate, two giant statues of square-bearded men with wings flanked the stone arch. Red and yellow banners floated down from the top of the rampart.

The front wall face above the gate stood out, decorated with bird motifs in bright blue and white tiles. Down at the foot of the rampart, vendor stands, shaded from the sun by orange and green awnings, offered a display of souvenirs and cooked foods for hungry travelers. Anila could smell the delicious aroma of vegetables cooking on a grill above an open flame. Her stomach rumbled. She hadn't eaten anything since last night.

On closer inspection, Anila realized this fortress looked old and weathered. It dated from the time before. Its stone walls, like those of the monastery she called home, had endured the cataclysmic alignment. So had the giant statues. She wondered what they represented. She had read most of the Temple scrolls but didn't remember any mention of sturdy people with square beards and wings.

Orders, yelled from the gate, traveled from chariot driver to chariot driver, and eventually trickled down to the tail of the caravan. One chariot at a time, one group of riders at a time, the entire train slowed and eventually halted. The space between each chariot and each group shrank. Camels brayed, steeds snorted and pawed the sand, and saddles creaked all around. At a full stop, the caravan looked much shorter.

A detachment of guards came running out of the gate and deployed along the train, glancing at the animals. Were they looking for signs of disease? A young guard opened the back drapes of a chariot to peer inside, eliciting a flurry of protests from the ladies. He closed the drape quickly, a deep red blush on his cheeks.

Anila suppressed a chuckle.

The guards avoided eye contact with the mounted soldiers, and the Protectors hid their faces under the deep shadow of their cowl. Anila pulled her hood further down over her forehead in imitation.

The inspection seemed rather perfunctory. Then, upon another order yelled from the gate, the guards promptly turned around and folded back. To the right side of the gate, at the head of the column, Anila could see Prince Altan conversing with a man in shiny green robes. Judging by the black hat and the rectangular seal on his chest, he must be a high-ranking official. He also seemed to bow low and with deference to his overlord.

Apparently, traveling with the formidable Prince Altan, ruler of the Southern Provinces, had its privileges. No close inspection or taxes for this caravan.

Finally, the train started again, proceeding through the gates at a snail's pace, then crawled along the wide thoroughfare, lined with mud shacks, and shops, and eateries. After a lifetime in a monastery and the silence of the desert, the noisy crowd of the caravanserai came as a shock.

Never had Anila seen a mix of so many different people speaking so many different languages. Some had very dark skin, others were white as milk, with pale eyes and hair of honey. Many wore robes and turbans, others in leather gear carried various blades. Unfamiliar aromas and sweet perfumes assailed her senses. Music filled the air, and people danced in the squares. Some laughed. Others haggled with street vendors.

Two men stumbled out of a drinking establishment, shouting at each other. Then they started an awkward fist-fight on the square. The crowd formed a circle around them to watch. But four guards quickly intervened and dragged away the culprits. So, maybe the armed guards were here to keep order inside the caravanserai, not to defend it against outsiders.

Anila admired the resilience of the people after the cataclysm. She was glad to see they had not just survived, but recovered and found a way to prosper and live full lives. It would be a shame to have all this progress destroyed by war. From what she read in the Temple archives, during a war, the population usually suffered and paid the price in lives, while the rich and the powerful used them to defend or increase their holdings.

As she squinted ahead, Anila spotted Prince Altan on his chestnut, stopped on the right side of the street, waiting for her group to catch up with him. What did he want this time? He prompted his mount toward Anila's and then rode alongside her mare.

"Anila," he said like a caress. "May I offer you the luxury of princely accommodations while in town, instead of the stable? A clean, private bath, as opposed to the cesspool of the public bathhouse?"

A clean bath sounded wonderful, but Anila's entire being revolted against the purpose behind the suggestion. "Thank you, my Prince. But I will stay with the Protectors, and bathe whenever and wherever they decide to do so."

"Suit yourself, Anila, but if you change your mind, remember my offer still stands." He clicked his tongue, prompting his chestnut to a trot and forged ahead.

Anila enjoyed her victory, a little surprised Prince Altan didn't insist more. Maybe he changed his tactics. But most likely, he feared the Protectors. Good.

The train divided into smaller groups. Prince Altan led the chariots with his ladies and servants toward their luxurious apartments, and the musicians stopped by an inn. Anila followed the mounted soldiers and the Protectors to the stables. There, they dismounted and unsaddled the steeds. She enjoyed brushing the white mare. After the harsh desert, and her kind tolerance for

Anila as her new rider, the animal deserved to be pampered.

Then the soldiers left.

When a shaved monk in white robes walked into the stables, then stopped and looked around, all activity ceased, and all eyes turned to the newcomer. The Protectors formed a circle around the monk.

The holy man in white bowed. "I have a message for the leader of the mighty Protectors."

The Protector in charge stepped forward and saluted, right fist in the left palm.

The monk returned the salute. "My master is the head of the Temple in this caravanserai. He is extending his hospitality to the mighty Protectors during their short stay. We have clean dorms, a private bathhouse, and our cook prepared a feast in your honor."

The head Protector nodded. "Our master told us about your Temple. Thank your master for us and tell him we shall join him shortly."

Anila realized she had never heard a Protector's voice before today. The other Protectors bowed silently in respect and acceptance. She did the same. So, the Temple masters all over the land knew and respected each other. She found it reassuring.

She also rejoiced at the idea of healthy food and a spotless floor to unroll her mat. Temple life was austere, but always clean.

To Anila, a real bath sounded wonderful, since the body was the Temple of the soul. At home, daily washing consisted of a cold splash with a dipper from a bucket... or a dip in the underground river before celebrating seasonal festivals.

This sounded much better.

* * *

The Temple's bath house was made of stone, and the pool steamed, blurring the view as the Protectors undressed and discreetly slipped into the bath waters... silent as always. Anila sank underwater to wash the sand from her hair, enjoying the freeing sensation of being immersed. Her skin tingled all over. She welcomed the relaxing steam after the dry desert.

In the dim light of oil lamps in sconces, everyone's head, neck, and shoulders looked the same. Only Anila had a mop of hair... short as it was. But soon, she would take the solemn vows of the Protectors, earning the right to shave her head.

As she soaked her sore muscles, she realized that for the Protectors, even bathing was an act of meditation, a communion with the natural elements. From the corner of her eye, she noticed local monks in white robes gathering the visitors' dirty garments left on the floor for the laundry. In their place, they set neatly folded clothes and bath sheets on long benches for everyone... even her. She recognized her pile from its sandy color. No black and white for her... yet.

Once clean and refreshed, Anila gathered with the Protectors in the refectory. They were invited to sit on benches around a long table, while the local monks sat on long rushes on the floor to eat. The Temple master joined the Protectors at the center of the table and smiled a lot as they ate and spoke in soft tones.

Monks brought platters of food to be shared. The communal feast consisted of unfamiliar beans, spicy vegetables, and exotic fruit Anila had never tasted before.

The master explained that this monastery was built so monks could live pure lives and meditate, in order to compensate for the sins of others. They helped keep the balance of good and evil. They also clothed and fed the needy, while Anila's monastery's only goal was to protect the Celestial Gate.

After the meal, the Protectors gathered in a small courtyard to speak with the Temple master in private.

A monk in white robes bowed to Anila. "The master needs to speak to the Protectors about Temple business. Maybe you would like to take this time to explore the caravanserai."

Thrilled by the idea of discovering this interesting place, Anila bowed. "I would like that very much. Thank you."

"Only one thing." The monk hesitated. "Our streets are not always safe, despite all the guards. You may want to carry weapons." He chuckled. "But look who I'm talking to. A Protector in training certainly knows how to defend herself."

"Will you come with me?" She could use a guide.

"Sorry, no. I have chores to do here." The monk bowed. "Be safe and enjoy what our caravanserai has to offer." He left quickly and disappeared into a low building.

So, the Protectors didn't want her to listen to their conversation with the local master. They had their own mission. They kept secrets... like spies. So, be it. Anila didn't mind. Freedom called. As she exited the grounds through the small arched gate in the wall surrounding the monastery, she felt as if she could fly. Never before had she felt so free. She could go wherever she pleased, do whatever she wanted. What a pleasurable feeling!

Without the cloak, in the simple pants and shirt of an Acolyte, wearing sword and boots, she was glad she looked like a boy. She didn't want any trouble, and from what she gathered while traveling with the caravan, it seemed that in the outside world, men enjoyed more autonomy than women.

Oil lamps in wall niches lit the narrow streets, dimming the stars. Inscriptions on the walls in several languages, some familiar, some very alien, warned of harsh penalties for thieving, maiming, or killing. It seemed most of these infractions were punishable by death. Not a very forgiving place.

Strange aromas and smoke floated in the air from open windows and doors of inns and eateries. Through a wide-open door, she could see men inside, drinking and laughing. Some gambled with coins and jewels on the table. A turbaned man smoked a water pipe. Another, wearing a toque, hand-fed table scraps to the monkey sitting on his shoulder.

As she turned a corner, Anila came upon a small stage, where people were paraded, with a price written on their foreheads and chains between their ankles. Men, women, and children. They looked alien, some with red skin, others with blue skin, and they all looked sad. Anila read about these people in the Temple scrolls. They were from other planets, left behind with no way to get home when the cataclysmic alignment occurred.

And now, they were being sold... as slaves... to filthy traders haggling on the price. Slavery! Anila's heart dropped in her chest. How barbaric. She wished all people could be free and treated equally. She shrugged her disgust for such practices. She was tempted to intervene but must not. Slavery was part of this world and accepted as lawful.

Besides, she was on a mission with the Protectors and must behave like one... respecting the rules of the lands they traveled. She remembered stories told by young Acolytes rescued by Master Wang... former slaves who'd escaped bondage. She wondered why Prince Altan tolerated such practices. Why had he not banished slavery from the Southern Provinces?

As she walked away from this terrible scene, Anila turned into a narrow alley, where women stood in front of their open doors and smiled at the men passing by. Some of them looked like men dressed like women. One passerby talked to one lady then went inside with her and closed the door.

Anila must have wandered into the district of ill repute. When a powdered woman in a crimson dress showing a lot of cleavage, stepped to her and caressed her cheek, Anila didn't know what to do. Then she remembered she looked like a boy to these people.

"I can give you a night you will never forget, young man." The woman exuded heavy perfume. "I can do things that would make your father blush." The woman smiled and her eyes shone with intensity.

Shocked, Anila stepped back, then she laughed and walked away quickly, ignoring the string of insults the lady of the night launched at her back.

Although she had studied the process of procreation, Anila realized she knew nothing of the pleasures of the flesh... except for a stolen kiss at a summer festival when she was thirteen. It never happened again, but she still remembered the thrill.

Of course, as a future monk, she didn't need that kind of knowledge... yet, some said sexual attraction was a powerful force that ruled the world. Prince Altan certainly had lots of women to share his bed... an entire harem.

She must have made a wrong turn and ended up in a cul-de-sac with straw and manure on the ground and a broom in a corner. That space was probably used as an overflow stable. As she turned around, two burly men blocked her way. They held on a chain a spotted white panther with long fangs. A male. The big cat pulled in her direction and hissed.

Anila stopped, surprised.

"Give us your sword, your medallion, and whatever coins you have in your pockets, lad... or we sic the beast on you!" The rough voice hurried the words... with a hint of fear.

The white spotted panther bared his fangs and growled.

Anila eyed the big cat. White and black... the Tai-Chi colors. Even in the dim light, she could tell the poor beast was thin, his pelt marred by whip scars.

"Do you know that according to the rules of this caravanserai, thievery is punishable by death?" Maybe that would discourage the miscreants.

"We are not thieves. You will give us your goods willingly and graciously... or we sic the beast on you." The man holding the chain let it slide a foot or so.

The panther pulled harder, huffing and hissing.

Anila sat down on the ground and crossed her legs. "Sorry, I do not yield to threats."

"You asked for it, lad." The man loosened the chain and the panther ran toward Anila.

Show no fear. She closed her eyes and found that place of absolute stillness inside her, where she was in tune with the universe. She used her ability to read people to send the panther a message of love and hope. "*We are all brothers and sisters in the Chi.*"

Then she felt a raspy tongue licking her face. She opened her eyes slowly and smiled as she scratched the panther's furry chin.

Then Anila reached for the cat's collar and unbuckled it, freeing the beast from the chains. "Go, run, the desert is your home. Be free and live happy."

The white panther shook his head then head-butted Anila, before slinking away. He leapt up a low wall, then soared to the building roof, and ran along its edge to disappear into the dark night.

Anila rose to her feet as the two burly thieves yelled obscenities, but the panther was gone. Then the two men turned toward Anila. One reached for throwing knives on his chest, and the other for a whip at his belt.

One knife flew at Anila's head, but she dodged the blade. Then she grabbed the broom in the corner and deflected the next two flying knives with it. The other man cracked his whip, and Anila caught the end with her broom and pulled. The whip flew off the man's hand.

Now, she faced the miscreants, holding the broom like a long pole.

They must have seen the determination in her eyes, because they screamed, turned around and ran as if they had seen a horrifying monster. If this caravanserai was considered a safe haven for travelers, Anila wondered what the rest of the world must be like.

She took a few breaths to slow her heartbeat, then she made her way toward more crowded areas. She slowed her steps as she reached a square, then sat on a bench, watching people go by, and listening to their conversations.

In the distance across the square, she saw Prince Altan, with a military escort. He was deeply involved in a discussion with a well-dressed official, too far, and too surrounded to notice her. The business of ruling the land never stopped. She was willing to bet his courtly ladies weren't allowed to roam the streets... then again, they would probably find the underside of society too vulgar for their taste.

Then Prince Altan spoke to a man in a black cloak, wearing heavy gold ornaments.

He had a square beard and a hooked nose. They walked away together, in deep conversation.

Two men sitting next to Anila on the bench talked about the barbarians with fear in their voice and eyes.

"I hear they cut the tongue of those who lie, and the ears of those who spy. They commit horrible atrocities on their prisoners, like maiming and torture by fire and sword," one said.

"I heard that, too. But is it true?" the other scoffed. "No one I know ever saw or met a barbarian... bandits and thieves, on the other hand, are everywhere. What trader hasn't been attacked by thieves?"

After tonight's encounter, Anila tended to agree.

Chapter 6

In the warmth of Bayor's tent, his lieutenants and master craftsmen sat on low stools, in a wide circle around the central fire. The familiar sound of crackling wood and the smell of smoke permeated the air. The dancing flames illuminated the eager faces. A worker poured tika from a gourd into the drinking horns.

Bayor pushed his fur cloak over the back of his heavy chair and raised his horn of strong tika. "To the Chi!"

He could feel the disapproval of his mentor, Zaal, standing behind his chair, but ignored it. His esteemed winged teacher, spy, and confident, did not believe in drinking, nor did he recognize the benevolent force that held the universe together.

The lieutenants, experts, and artisans, some human, others of brightly colored skin, raised their own horns. "To the Chi!"

Stardust, lying at Bayor's feet, howled to be included in the toast. Other wolves outside the camp answered her call. The assembled men and women laughed.

They all drank, and Bayor took a gulp of spirit, enjoying the burn down his gullet, finding it invigorating. He sighed and set the drinking horn on his side tray.

Then he eased his scimitar to the side, leaned forward, and stared at the faces of his lieutenants and crew masters, etched by the dancing flames. "How go the false rumors we are spreading of barbarian atrocities?"

"My Khan." One of the spies rose, flushed with excitement... or from the strong drink. "The rumors are working. The people are terrified. The local lords do not have an army strong enough to face us. They believe we are unstoppable and will yield, rather than lose everything. They will not resist our advance."

"Good. We do not want to kill the innocent. Most of the local lords' soldiers are farmers, and all hands will be needed after we take over the land." Bayor wanted to avoid bloodshed as much as possible. Soon, these people would become his to rule, and he would be kind to them.

Zaal behind him cleared his throat and stepped to stand at his side. The trembling light of the flames accentuated his hooked nose and glanced off his many gold ornaments. "Our only problem is Prince Altan, who resides in the mountains south of the Great River, controlling access to the desert. He is drafting and training new recruits. He hides behind high walls and has many archers."

The lieutenants grumbled in dismissal to look brave, but their unsteady auras revealed their fears.

Bayor rubbed his smooth chin. "How close are we to crossing the Great River?"

"My Khan." His master boat builder straightened on his stool. "The rafts are nearly completed, and we can cross the river in three days."

"Good. According to my calculations, there will be no visible moons by then. We'll cross on a dark night... it's risky in the strong current, but we don't want to be seen." Bayor squinted at his master carpenter. "Where are we with the catapults?"

"All the parts will be ready in time for the crossing, my Khan. We'll carry the sections on flat carts and assemble them when we get to the fortress." The carpenter smiled under his thick moustache and extended his furry boots on the rug toward the central fire.

Bayor lifted his chin to the weapons expert. "Weapon supplies?"

"We have enough arrows for a lifetime, my Khan. Our bows are the best, and so are our blades." The man nodded. "From what our spies reported of our enemy's defenses, we have enough tar and wrecking balls for the catapults to destroy Prince Altan's stronghold."

"Perfect." Bayor hoped he could win swiftly, causing as few casualties as possible. He turned to a woman lieutenant in warrior garb. "How is the general mood among the warriors?"

"They are ready to fight, my Khan, they have been training with spear, blades, and bow, every single day. They are in good spirits, well-fed, well-rested, and healthy. The skill of our riders and the precision of our archers on a galloping steed are unmatched."

"That is true." Bayor turned to a tall, dark man. "Steed master?"

"Every rider has three healthy mounts, my Khan. So, when one gets tired or is injured or killed, they still have two spares." The man nodded. "We have the best mounts and the best riders."

"That's good to hear." Bayor wanted to give his men a chance of winning without dying. He raised his drinking horn. "May we find strength and focus in the Chi and win a swift victory to save this world from those who would exploit it for selfish gain."

All present, except Zaal, raised their horns. "To the Chi!"

* * *

Anila noticed the desert road hardening underfoot and the rays of the red sun softening. Sparse bushes dotted the dry land, and dark mountains rose ahead, blocking the horizon. By then, the caravan had shortened, since they'd left musicians and merchants behind at the caravanserai.

Anila rejoiced at contemplating the end of the long trek. As the ground sloped upward, the burden beasts struggled pulling the chariots up the incline. The mounts needed rest, and so did she. Even the Protectors and the soldiers behind her seemed to slump in the saddle.

Soon, the ground turned to rock, interspersed with patches of greenery, even a few wooded areas. Anila could smell the moisture cooling the air, as the red sun hid behind clouds. Many insects buzzed around the animals, causing them to blink and flip their tails.

From a distance, Prince Altan's stronghold hanging on the rocky slopes, halfway up the mountain, looked like a fortified city ensconced between cliffs and giant boulders. Tall walls filled the gaps between the natural rock. A sturdy construction from before, that survived the cataclysm, no doubt. The current sparse population wouldn't allow for quarrying monumental stone or building great walls.

Soldiers walked the ramparts, and light glinted on their sharp metal blades. Anila noticed the two giant winged statues flanking the main gate... like at the caravanserai. Were these winged men imaginary guardians from the local folklore? Or did they exist in the past? Many alien races had left the planet when it was in jeopardy. But she'd never read about winged men in the Temple scrolls.

The caravan entered through the arched main gate, under the watchful gaze of guards in red armor, carrying spears and swords. Anila also noticed archers on the rampart above the gate, similar to those at the caravanserai. Again, she wondered about what prompted such protective measures. Who in their right mind would dream of attacking these walls?

Past the open gate, many small buildings lined the streets of the enclosed city, some made of stone, others of clay bricks... but what struck Anila was the gloom that seemed to cover the entire town like a heavy lid. No street vendors, no noisy eateries. At their approach, skinny people in drab clothes looked down and averted their eyes. No one talked. No sunshine, no bright banners or color anywhere, even the sky looked gray.

Prince Altan, now waiting on the right side for the caravan to pass, looked upon his people with open satisfaction. He must feel very safe inside his gloomy stone fortress... but his people didn't share his good fortune.

Prince Altan noticed her looking at him and reined in his chestnut to turn in the direction of Anila's mare. "So, Anila, what do you think of my home? Could it become yours as well? It's a very safe place to live."

Anila didn't plan to live here any longer than necessary. "Safety is subjective, my Prince. When anything is possible, no place is really safe... only in your mind does it seem so." She already missed the monastery. "This place is quite a contrast with the desert and the caravanserai. So far, all I see here is gloom.”

“Wait until you see my castle. It’s a haven of luxury, comfort, and opulence.” Prince Altan sounded proud of it. “My ladies are eager to return to their sumptuous accommodations.”

“I have no doubt.” Anila remembered the precious fabric of the bright dresses, the delicate jewels, and the fancy shoes of Prince Altan’s ladies.

Some barefooted children in rags begged the soldiers for scraps of food. The soldiers kicked them away, yelling expletives.

Anila took a slow breath to suppress the disgust on her face. “Why don’t you share your wealth with the less fortunate who work hard to generate it for you? Don’t they deserve decent food and warm clothes?”

“My dear Anila.” The patronizing tone grated. “In order for society to work, we must respect the natural castes among people. Some are born to serve, some to work hard, and others, like you and me, are meant to rule.”

“I do not wish to rule.” Anila struggled to keep her voice down. “In the monastery, everyone contributes and everyone is treated equally, like members of the same family who love and help their less fortunate members. In the Chi, we are all brothers and sisters... even the animals.”

"The Chi?" Prince Altan huffed. "My dear, you should refrain from making such comments in public. They only show your lack of refinement and experience. People may laugh at you. Furthermore, in respectable society, women are meant to be seen and admired for their beauty, not express their opinions in matters better suited for men... like politics."

"My Prince, as a Chi warrior, I could never agree with such principles." Anila wanted to say more, but remembering she was on a mission, she stopped herself.

Prince Altan pressed his lips together as if to stop a stinging reply. Then he made his chestnut rear and turn around, to stare at the dozen Protectors riding behind her. "I am aware of Master Wang's revolutionary ideas of equality, but while in my home, I expect you all to keep your political views to yourself. I am your overlord, and I expect you to respect my views."

Anila managed not to react. Would he cast her out for her insolence? No. If he did, the Protectors would leave with her, and Altan couldn't afford to lose them.

The leader of the Protectors nodded his assent. Not that they would ever converse with strangers. They were always quiet and secretive. Becoming one of them might prove difficult for Anila, who struggled to keep her opinions to herself.

As they reached the stone castle overlooking the fortified town, it looked as if it were hanging off the cliff. Then she realized most of it had been carved into the rock wall. Green gardens on terraces, with purple and yellow flowers and sparkling fountains, decorated the grounds. It seemed the nobles did enjoy a lovely place to live.

Anila didn't understand why some should delight in such luxury while others toiled and suffered. Not that she wanted any of that luxury. She didn't. According to ancient wisdom scrolls, too much of it might corrupt the soul.

Prince Altan halted his stallion. The chariots proceeded ahead, while Protectors and soldiers stopped behind him. He turned to the Protectors. "You may follow the soldiers to the stables and check your accommodations."

The head Protector nodded his assent.

Prince Altan smiled at Anila. "I would offer you private chambers in the palace, but I sense you might refuse them."

"You would be correct, my Prince." Anila struggled to smile but couldn't. "The accommodations reserved for the Protectors will suit me just fine."

"Remember that my offer will stand if you change your mind." Prince Altan turned to the Protectors and calmed his impatient chestnut with a pat on the neck. "I expect to see you all in the main hall tonight, for the festivities in celebration of my return... with my future bride."

Anila bristled at the imperative tone and the implications. It wasn't a request, but an order. How she hated it. Still, she managed to keep her tongue.

The head Protector nodded to Prince Altan, who kicked the chestnut's flanks, then trotted ahead to catch up with the chariots.

* * *

Later that night, after a cold bath and a fresh set of clothes, Anila joined the Protectors to attend the courtly celebrations. As they approached the great hall, string music floated in the air, along with the aroma of roasted meats and baked sweets.

Anila had never tasted meat, but she knew the smell from when the villagers at home butchered a pig or an ox on special occasions. Light from many candles on the high chandeliers spilled through the wide openings over to the terrace and across the courtyard.

As she walked into the richly decorated ballroom with the Protectors, fully armed and silent in their loose black pants and white tunics, the music and conversations died. Elegant men and ladies, standing or sitting around the ballroom, stared at them and gasped in shock.

Even the servants passing trays of food and drinks froze in surprise. Anila casually sensed their mood and they were truly shocked. Had they never seen warriors

104

before? Shaved monks? Or did they disapprove of weapons and simple clothes?

Anila recognized the harem ladies to one side, in fancy dresses the color of spring grass, yellow leaves, and red fruit. They giggled and whispered comments behind their fluttering fans. Others stared in open condemnation at the swords, shaved heads, tattoos… and even at Anila's short hair. They obviously found the Protectors uncouth, and unworthy of the palace halls.

A white cat jumped off the lap of a harem woman and trotted his way to Anila across the marble floor.

"Cottonball!" Apparently, he had charmed the ladies and traveled with them in great comfort. Smart cat. Anila dropped down and picked up the feline, who smelled of floral perfume. She scratched the soft fur under his chin and was rewarded with a loud purr.

Then Prince Altan made his grand entrance, dressed in blue silk with silver threads, silver dragon plate on his chest, holding an ornate staff. A drumroll and a fanfare of trumpets exploded as he walked into the hall.

Cottonball hissed at him, leapt off Anila's arms, and raced out of the ballroom… confirming her suspicions that the prince had a dark side. Cats were never wrong about that.

Anila attempted to read the prince's state of mind but couldn't. Even his aura remained dark and unreadable, as if he shielded himself from her on purpose. So sneaky... But she must keep the peace, although she couldn't help being suspicious of this smooth-talking man who wanted to claim her as his bride. His unbridled ambition raised its snake head at every turn.

Prince Altan walked straight to Anila and took her hand to kiss her fingers.

She struggled not to resist, but she hated his insistent contact.

Finally, he let go of her hand. "Anila, you are a beautiful woman. Why do you insist on dressing in the drab threads of a peasant? Even your choice of jewelry is dreadful."

Anila's hands went to her red jasper pendant, but she muzzled her objections. Her pendant had sentimental value. It also helped her focus her Chi.

"When we are wed, you will wear courtly dresses for public appearances, and definitely a wig... until your hair grows long enough to dress it up." He signaled a foot lackey. "Take Anila to the dressing room where the ladies prepared suitable clothes for her."

The lackey bowed.

But Anila didn't move. "Sorry, my Prince, but my clothes are fine. This is who I am. This is what I wear. And I like my hair short. If it offends you, I shall remove myself from your presence. But I will never change to accommodate a man's taste."

"We'll see about that." Prince Altan scoffed. "And as the future mother of my heir, you will also have to stop that fighting nonsense. Here, in civilized society, physical work and combat training are for the lower classes, not the nobility."

Anila was too shocked to respond. She also suspected, from his muscular fitness, that Prince Altan had received ample physical training beyond riding his chestnut. She finally found her voice. "I beg your pardon?"

"How dare you refuse my orders in public!" Prince Altan struck his staff on the floor, bringing the room to total silence. "As I mentioned before, you should refrain from expressing your opinions in matters of importance. Only men in charge can make rules for the proper conduct of women."

Anila could feel the heat rising to her cheeks. She was about to explode when she caught the side nod of the head Protector, motioning to Anila that they were leaving.

Anila stepped back from Prince Altan. Without a word, the Protectors formed a tight circle around her. They all turned on their heels and glided out of the ballroom, with Anila in their midst, leaving Prince Altan in stunned silence, alone on the marble floor.

Anila was grateful for the presence and support of the Protectors. She released a frustrated breath as they exited the palace and crossed the courtyard in the direction of the stables. She also noticed the brisk mountain air. It already felt like winter here.

In the small room by the stables where they spread their sleeping mats, the Protectors retrieved their cloaks for warmth and sat in a circle. Anila joined them. Despite their stoic faces, she could tell they were upset.

The head Protector cleared his voice. "We need to review our situation. I have noticed signs that Prince Altan is respected and feared, but not loved. He also has a temper. Does that present a conflict for our mission?"

Another Protector, a woman, nodded. "I can sense his thirst for conquest and power, not harmony, not peace."

Another Protector joined the conversation. "These people smile at those they hate. Lots of hatred going around. They all envy each other's wealth or status, and they judge and criticize each other."

Anila agreed. "Prince Altan only wants to marry me because he says I have Immortal blood, and he wants to reinforce his status with an Immortal heir. He only cares about power."

"I also noticed little things in the reaction of his people," another woman Protector said. "They bow to him, but there is fear in their eyes. Underneath the polished façade, I can sense selfish and ruthless tendencies."

Another Protector nodded. "I've met men like him before. They are usually brutal and abuse their people, but Prince Altan hides it behind a smile."

Anila was surprised that the Protectors expressed such strong personal opinions, and she was delighted at their solid moral compass matching hers. "But what can you do about it?"

The head Protector pinched his lips. "Maybe we should contact Master Wang and ask for guidance."

Anila shook her head. "I know what Master Wang will say. Last I spoke to him, he hinted that he didn't trust Prince Altan either, but since the prince oversees the lands where the Temple stands, the master had no choice but to obey his command. Master Wang doesn't want to start a war against the legitimate ruler of the Southern Provinces."

"I can understand that." The head Protector nodded. "But can we, in good conscience, train a tyrant's army?"

Anila sighed. "You should decide for yourself what to do. No one can challenge you and win. You are the mighty Protectors."

"It's not that simple, Anila." The head Protector narrowed his eyes at her. "We must finish the mission... train Prince Altan's recruits. That's what Master Wang ordered us to do, despite the fact that he didn't trust the prince. The master must have his reasons. Sometimes destiny takes you to your goal on a side road, or a long detour.”

“That’s what Master Wang said to me before we left.” How Anila missed the peace of the monastery. Castle life just didn’t suit her. She hated the superficial crowd in the palace. She refused to be part of it. And she hated the politics.

“So, it is decided.” The head Protector pinched his lips and nodded. “We shall start training the new recruits, but observe and gather more information.”

Wait and see... all right. Anila nodded her assent with the rest of the Protectors. She admired them for their sense of honor, keeping to the mission and remaining calm and serene despite their personal objections. She could learn a lot from them and would follow their example.

Chapter 7

On the shore of the Great River, Bayor inhaled the brisk night air from the height of the lookout tree platform, rigged with ropes. He detected the fresh fish smell as he gazed through his long-view lens upon the horizon, south, across the swift water.

A faint red glow rose in the distance, far behind the mountains. He could almost smell the smoke of the burning woods. Zaal never disappointed. He'd created a distraction big enough to shift Altan's focus, call the attention of his sentinels, and mobilize his men.

Returning the lens to his belt, Bayor glanced down below, at the sloshing water's edge, as people, animals, and supplies already boarded the first floating platforms. The master boatbuilder instructed the warriors pushing the rafts through the shallows, showing them how to steer with the long poles.

On land, more warriors assembled the last logs, tying them together with fibrous rope of intertwined and braided long grasses. From a distance in the dark, the disassembled catapults on their rafts looked like floating trees and debris.

In a sudden gust of black feathered wings, Zaal dropped in midair in front of Bayor and hovered. He remained almost invisible in the dark night as the clouds blocked the stars, and a black cloak covered his gold ornaments. "It is done, my Khan. Everyone south of the river is being called to combat the fire attacking the woods."

"Good." That would keep Altan's men busy.

"Burning a village or a small town would have been more dramatic, my Khan. And more damaging to their morale." Zaal's tone indicated he would have preferred it.

"I refuse to kill innocent people." Bayor was tired of repeating it. "I just hope the animals who call that forest home had the good sense of fleeing at the first whiff of smoke."

"I'm sure they did, my Khan." Zaal's superior tone grated. "Be at peace. The morning rain will extinguish the blaze anyway."

"Good. All we need is enough time to cross the Great River undetected." And unscathed... but Bayor didn't say the last part. No need to introduce negative thoughts. He must keep the morale of the horde as high as possible.

Zaal slowly flapped his wings, creating a cool breeze. "What do we do after the crossing?"

"We'll disappear into the foothills between the mountains. The warriors will take the path to Altan's fortress. Meanwhile, the workers, animals, and the supply train will take a different path, to pitch the tents and set up camp on the gentle slope you spotted, on the other side of the mountains."

"Glad you are taking my advice for the campsite, my Khan." Zaal's grin accentuated his hooked nose over the square beard.

Bayor felt good about his plan. "Altan's sentries won't be able to see us until we cross the last mountain pass, but we'll attack his fortress in the middle of the night, when everyone is asleep."

"Aren't you afraid your men will think a night attack from the shadows is for thugs and assassins? It might insult their honor and tarnish their reputation." Zaal's smooth voice implied Bayor was wrong.

"Reputation doesn't matter as much as doing the right thing, Zaal." Bayor sighed. "You should know that since I told you to spread these horrible rumors about us."

"Yes, my Khan. I'm sorry." But Zaal's tone remained patronizing.

"All my warriors know they are brave. They have nothing to prove." Bayor meant it. Besides, Zaal didn't know everything about him either. "A surprise attack at night will save lives."

"Very well. As you wish, my Khan." Zaal nodded, then turned around in midair and flew away, south, across the Great River.

A gust of wind brought the familiar smell of rain. A storm was brewing high above. Good. The clouds would provide more cover for the horde.

Down below, on the muddy shore, the stable masters herded steeds toward square rafts with a railing all around. Bayor hoped the animals would survive the crossing unharmed. In the pitch dark, he couldn't see the turbulent current in the deepest part of the river, but he knew it was there and presented a dangerous challenge for his army.

Although the crossing seemed to be going well and on schedule, Bayor worried.

The master boatbuilder ran to the foot of the lookout tree. "My Khan, almost everyone is on the river. This is your raft. It's time for you to cross."

"Thank you." Bayor whistled, and Stardust and Thunder came running toward the tree.

Bayor climbed down the rungs of the rope ladder and took the black stallion's bridle to lead him to the water and upon the raft.

Thunder protested, pounding both front hooves.

Bayor calmed the beast with a reassuring pat on the flank. "It's all right, Thunder. I'm coming with you."

Stardust seemed to enjoy this new adventure. She had no problem leaping onto the raft. Her heavy landing upset the balance, but she deftly avoided the hooves of other animals, who quickly recovered as well.

The wild wolves would remain behind. Unlike Stardust, they feared the river... maybe for good reason. Bayor could sense their unrest. They howled despite the moonless sky.

Soon, an entire flotilla of rafts, carrying Bayor's warriors, workers, steeds, weapons and supply chariots, drifted across the current, toward the southern shore. Gusts of wind assailed the passengers. The temperature dropped and a cold downpour drenched everything.

Bayor heard the commotion before he could focus his gaze and see the trouble on the rushing waters. Half way across the river, two rafts, carrying workers and supplies, hit the turbulence. Someone fell in and was carried away by the swift current. One raft hit another and broke in two. Then the grass ties loosened, freeing the logs that quickly rolled and dumped their loads of people and supplies, threatening to hit other rafts in their path.

Stardust also noticed and howled her distress. The wolves, left on the northern bank, howled back at her in the night.

Bayor wanted to howl, too, but he must remain strong for his people. There was nothing to be done for the unfortunates. He was too far away, and they had already vanished in the night under the downpour.

Going after them would jeopardize the other rafts.

He strained his eyes but could only see blackness and rain. He reminded himself his people could swim. So could the animals. He hoped they would land farther downriver and survive. They might even rejoin the convoy in the morning.

Then his heavy raft, loaded with men and steeds, struggled in the eddies of rushing white water. The skilled boatman swore under his breath but kept the raft steady enough as the steeds whinnied in sheer panic. Eventually, they reached calmer waters and crossed to the other side.

When his floating platform hit the southern bank, heavy rain battered the muddy terrain. Bayor was glad to see almost all the rafts had made it intact with their loads of animals, people, and supplies.

As his army regrouped to travel, warriors on one side, and the supply train on the other, Bayor walked away from the activity to thank the powers that be for a successful crossing.

"I am grateful for the protective power of the Chi." He took a knee and looked up, welcoming the rain on his face. "O mighty warriors and animals who perished in this dangerous current, I grieve for you and feel responsible for your passing into the spirit world. May your peaceful souls rise and find your departed loved ones in the Chi."

"Are you speaking to the dead?" Zaal asked haughtily as he alighted next to him and folded his wings. "Have I taught you nothing?"

Bayor rose and wiped the mud from his knee, resenting the rebuke. "I am honoring the souls who traveled back to the Chi to join our ancestors. We are all brothers and sisters in the Chi."

"There is no Chi." Zaal wiped rainwater from his gold breastplate. "How many times do I have to tell you? My own people were once worshipped as benevolent gods and thought to be all-powerful and omniscient. But believe me, they were no such thing."

Bayor shook his head. "It doesn't mean the Chi doesn't exist. I have seen too many instances of miraculous healings and wishes answered. Our thoughts shape our reality as the Chi pervades everything. I can feel it in my bones."

Zaal huffed. "The universe was not created, but is the result of a dumb accident. Nothing about it is kind, and life flourishes in spite of the harsh conditions of the universe. The strong rule, the weak and the destitute die young, there is no Chi, and nothing beyond death."

"How can you be so cynical?" Bayor narrowed his eyes at Zaal. "Did you ever observe the magnificence of the world around you? Did you ever witness the miracle of birth? Nature is filled with inexplicable feats of survival despite bad odds."

"Only because you choose to see these things as miracles," Zaal railed. "But my people are not born like yours. They hatch from the eggs of the Great Mother. And no, I've never experienced that sense of wonder. There is no Chi."

For the first time, Bayor considered his teacher's words with distrust. He refused to believe the universe was heartless and cruel. "How could you or anyone be certain the Chi doesn't exist?"

"I have lived a very long time, my Khan. I know a lot of things hidden from simple men." Zaal turned around, deployed his wings, and flew up and away in the downpour.

Bayor, too, knew many secrets hidden from simple men... and the existence of the Chi happened to be one of them.

* * *

Military life in Prince Altan's castle started early, but the Protectors were the first to rise, long before dawn. Anila enjoyed following their monastic rituals, ablutions, meditation, tea, Tai-Chi form, weapons training. It reminded her of life in the Temple. Only after completing her own daily routine, was she ready for the task Master Wang entrusted to her - training Prince Altan's new recruits.

Anila observed the lot gathered in a large courtyard. Only men. Not a single woman among them. The red armor of plaited, interwoven leather, boiled to hardness into a mold, may not protect them from the barbarian's curved blades.

Worse, most of these recruits couldn't stand straight and struggled with their weapons. One held his spear at the wrong angle. Another dropped a sword, the blade clattering on the stone paving. Another stabbed his neighbor's foot by mistake. It was obvious they had never handled a sword or a spear.

Some had the sturdy constitution of farmers, probably drafted against their will. Others, lean and muscular, seemed proud, probably volunteers hoping to distinguish themselves, bring honor to their family or village, and enjoy a glorious military career, getting rich from plunder.

All of them had the wrong idea about what military life entailed, like being forced to fight through impossible weather conditions, fatigue, hunger, being sent to slaughter for no good reason... Not that Anila had ever experienced it, but she had read many scrolls on the condition of soldiers at war. These men could not even read.

As Anila walked between their ranks, she evaluated their strengths, weaknesses, and personal abilities to sort them into proper classes to become archers, riders, spearmen, or swordsmen. Then the Protectors would take smaller groups aside to teach them that particular skill.

But right now, she must tell them of the Chi. Even a limited understanding of the energy moving through the universe could help them, so they could learn and improve quickly in their martial discipline... if they believed.

"Attention!" Anila projected her voice far and wide.

A general gasp filled the yard. The recruits just realized from her voice that she was a woman. They straightened somewhat, but many struggled with their armor and their arsenal.

"Are you a girl?" a young man snarled. "We don't take orders from women."

"Half of the Protectors who came here to instruct you are women." Anila scanned the young faces one by one. "Do any of you want to confront them about this in person?"

A mild murmur from the recruits confirmed they feared the Protectors.

"Good. I didn't think so." Anila took a deep breath and projected her voice so they could all hear. "A strong warrior learns to gather and channel the Chi, and fight with energy, balance, and fluidity, rather than muscles and brute force."

All the faces staring at her frowned. In lack of comprehension? It was as if she had spoken in an unknown language. A demonstration might work better. She assumed a stiff horse stance, legs apart, knees bent, fists clenched.

"You!" She pointed her chin at a tall, sturdy man. "Come running from the side and push me over."

The recruit shook his head. "I could never shove a woman!"

Anila made a serious face. "I gave you an order, soldier. Execute it. Now!"

The young man looked mortified and slowly came to the front.

"Now, run and push me over!" She managed to say it with authority.

The young man took a deep breath and then started running.

Under the strong push, Anila tumbled sideways, then rolled over in one smooth motion, found her feet, and stood back up, facing her opponent. "That's what happens when you use your muscles instead of the Chi. You lose your balance and you fall. On the ground, you are vulnerable. To fight efficiently, you must stay on your feet."

The recruits remained silent, glancing at each other with worry in their eyes.

"Now, see the difference." Anila assumed the same stance, but relaxed, soft knees, soft elbows, hands open, feeling the flow of the Chi, rooting herself into the ground. Then she motioned to the sturdy young man. "Now, do the same thing as I am relaxed and using the Chi instead of my muscles."

The young man took a running start toward her. Anila, rooted her feet deep in the ground like a tree, focused on the strength of the Chi flowing through her. At the moment of contact, she sent a small jolt of energy radiating outward around her body. The young man went flying far and wide, falling hard on the ground, much farther than she intended. Oh no! Was he hurt?

The new recruits emitted a collective gasp.

Anila felt bad for not controlling her Chi better. "Are you all right?"

The young man rose, massaging his hip, red-faced, looking down at his feet and grumbled. "I'm fine."

His comrades laughed, increasing his humiliation.

One raised his hand. "It's not fair! You are using Protector magic!"

Another stepped forward. "Why don't you use your magic to win the war for us, instead of making us fight?"

Anila shook her head at the ignorance of these men. "There is nothing magic about what I just did. I only used the natural forces existing all around us. Anyone can do it if they meditate, focus on the Chi, and train daily."

The young man she had thrown shook his head. "I could never do that."

"Yes, you can. Any of you can. You just have to practice." Anila scanned their faces. "You all heard stories of mothers who lifted a heavy cart, or a fallen tree, to pull their child from under it. They don't have brute strength. In moments of great peril, our body remembers to use the Chi."

The young men mumbled to each other. Most of them had heard such stories.

"But in order to do that at will," Anila paused for emphasis, "you must have the perfect posture, balance, be relaxed, and be aware of the energy flowing around you and through your body. You also have to believe you can do it and focus your mind. You cannot be distracted."

"What has the mind to do with anything?" The tone was belligerent. "We are going into battle against butchers. Brute force is the only way."

"Wrong!" Anila stared at the uncomprehending faces. "You have much to learn."

"Like what?" A voice from the back.

"When a skilled archer releases the arrow, he follows it with his gaze and guides it with his mind, making sure it hits the target." She made eye contact with the first row. "That's why they never miss."

The recruits glanced at each other, frowning.

Anila allowed herself a silent sigh. These recruits were worse than first-time students at the Temple, because they did not believe. It would take a lot of work to get them in fighting shape. They would never be ready on time to fight the hordes.

Anila shivered. Maybe that was a good thing. Sometimes, right and wrong seemed blurred... and non-violence could be a challenge.

* * *

From the top of the rampart, by the hazy red glow of the afternoon sun, Prince Altan surveyed the recruits training in the largest yard. Each Protector instructed a different group. He couldn't distinguish one Protector from another. They all looked alike.

He hoped these masters of fighting would impart their secrets to his troops so that they could win him the crown. Altan was the obvious choice by blood, as his ancestors had ruled long ago. But now was his time. He wouldn't let an uncouth barbarian like Bayor Khan steal his claim to the throne.

Without their hooded mantles, he could see the Protectors' heads displayed a large round tattoo on the back. How distasteful... especially for the women. Good thing Anila hadn't taken vows yet and didn't wear such ugly marks on her skin. He hoped she'd soon renounce the idea of becoming a Protector... in any case, Altan would use his influence to make certain she never did.

Then he spotted her, teaching a sword class. Even with her sandy garb and short-cropped hair, she almost looked like one of the monks. She had the same silhouette, the same posture and movements. He would

124

have to take her away from their influence. The sooner the better.

The style of her sword movements seemed unfamiliar, not the technique he'd learned as a child... more fluid. Different sword, too, straight, and double-edged. The woman saluted, sword in hand, and her recruits did the same. Despite being a woman, she had earned their respect. Strange...

"Class dismissed!" Even her tone of voice sounded rough.

The recruits scrambled away.

Altan climbed down the rampart stairs and met Anila in the courtyard. "How are these new recruits doing?"

"My Prince, they have a lot to learn." She sheathed her blade with brisk precision, then wiped a sweaty brow.

Altan cringed inside. "Are they that bad?"

"Worse." She shook her head. "Most of them never held a blade in their life."

"Probably not." Altan forced a smile. "But the Protectors will whip them into shape in no time at all... right?"

"Not just the Protectors." She huffed. "I'm doing my share."

"Yes." Altan sighed. "And to be honest, I find it disturbing that you are so skilled with a sword." He would make sure she didn't have access to weapons after he married her.

"Why does it bother you, my Prince?" Anila snatched her black cloak from a bench, threw it over her shoulders and donned the hood. Now, she looked like one of the Protectors. "You hired us for that very reason. We are the best at what we do. We are Chi warriors."

"Yes... but my future queen will have no need for fighting skills. They are considered rather uncouth at court." Altan realized he must soften his tone to win her cooperation. "My queen will always be protected inside my walls. And the castle is an impregnable fortress, guarded by many soldiers."

"I have no intention of marrying or becoming queen, my Prince." Her strong statement was infuriating. "I'm a Protector in training and will never need protection."

"Shouldn't you consider your duty for the good of the land?" Altan made an effort to smile. "As a young woman of Immortal blood, you must understand the importance of breeding with another Immortal to perpetuate the Celestial bloodlines."

She straightened her tall frame. "To my knowledge, I have no Immortal blood, my Prince."

"But you do have noble blood, Anila. Without a doubt. As an Immortal myself, I can sense it inside you." How long would Altan have to tiptoe around the young woman?

"But even if I did, I wouldn't want to pair with you, my Prince." She walked away from him, too quickly for him to follow without looking desperate.

Altan fumed as he watched her glide away and disappear around a building. Too bad he couldn't force her to do his bidding... not as long as the Protectors were around. The woman's stubborn streak would drive him mad.

* * *

That night, as she meditated on the rampart before bed, Anila became aware of a strange presence. The moonless night and the clouds above made it particularly dark. But Anila focused her mind and eyes. She had a glimpse of Altan on the rampart, a short distance away, with the strange man in the black cloak again, just as he had been in the desert and in the caravanserai.

They whispered close to each other's ears as if sharing secrets.

Anila suspected Altan had many ambitions and ulterior motives in wanting her as his queen. But according to the prophecy, in order to rule the entire continent, he should be claiming the Celestial Gem from Master Wang at the Temple. Did he try? Did Master Wang refuse?

Then the strange man seemed to take flight. With his own wings? He definitely had wings. How odd! But she must have imagined it. It couldn't be true. People could never fly... yet, giant statues of ancient people with wings flanked the caravanserai gate and the entrance of Prince Altan's castle. Could it be more than local legends?

That night, after she lay down, safe among the Protectors, Anila had another vivid dream about the barbarian invader named Bayor Khan. For some reason, he didn't seem as scary as before, but strong and magnificent...

Chapter 8

Bayor patted Thunder's neck as he emerged with his army on the other side of the high mountain pass in the pitch-black night. Accustomed to the dark, he had an overhead view of Altan's town and castle far below the high cliff, asleep, quiet, streets and ramparts bathed in the faint glow of sparse oil lamps. Only a few sentinels, tired and sleepy by now, manned the walls... and they all faced the front gate, not the high ridge behind and above them.

"Do not make any noise until I give the official signal to attack." Bayor kept his voice low. "Do not harm the civilians, but feel free to scare them into hiding. Only kill the soldiers who resist and lock up those who don't. Find Prince Altan and bring him to me alive."

His lieutenants acknowledged his orders with muffled grunts.

Bayor pointed to the flat open area outside the town gate, probably used during the festivals and as training grounds. "Set up the catapults over there. From now on, keep the men, the animals, and the wheels quiet."

It seemed to take forever to descend the steep slopes in near silence. Even the wild life grew silent, and Bayor hoped Altan was asleep and would not notice it. Somehow, his highly trained warriors managed to remain invisible and unheard. Even Stardust seemed to understand the need for stealth, sniffing the ground like a predator on a hunt.

Under the cover of darkness, two hundred of Bayor's fighters deployed atop the cliffs above the castle, and another two hundred around the base of the walls and boulders surrounding the fortified town. The catapults, blackened with pitch, remained invisible to the sleepy sentinels guarding the front gate.

As Bayor whispered, his orders traveled from warrior to warrior. The archers posted on the cliff readied their bows, while other warriors dropped down ropes and slid silently toward the castle roof. Another contingent climbed down the sides of the rock face and deployed at the top of the ramparts, while others surrounded the outer base of the walls, ready to scale them with hooks and grapples.

Soon, signs of silent struggle on the ramparts indicated the warriors had neutralized the sentinels. Now, they were free to infiltrate the fortress and open the main gate for the rest of the horde.

A wolf howl pierced the night. It was the signal from his men that all was in place, ready for the attack. Stardust answered the call. Silly girl. There were no wolves south of the Great River.

Bayor shot a flaming arrow in the sky, giving the signal for the rest of the army to advance, and for the catapults to fire. Fireballs flew through the air to land on the ramparts, damaging the walls and lighting fires. Castle guards ran in all directions, yelling and seeking cover.

Flames surged as the stone balls doused with pitch ignited roofs and wood piles. Screams, alarm gongs, and horns resounded throughout the fortified town.

While Prince Altan's soldiers and archers ran out of their barracks and rushed to man the ramparts, Bayor's stealthy warriors already opened the gate. Hundreds of barbarians rushed inside the walls, brandishing blades, screaming like savages, and poured through the streets in the direction of the castle, neutralizing resistance as they advanced.

Good. Time for Bayor to proudly ride through the main gate and cross the town, to claim his victory in the castle.

* * *

Prince Altan awoke in the middle of a nightmare with wolf calls and loud bangs shaking the walls and the ground. Then the sound of a horn and a frantic gong confirmed his fears. A persistent drumbeat spelled a message saying that invaders had breached the walls.

"How is that possible? Invaders in my home?" Altan jumped out of bed, ignoring the protests of the two naked women still in it, and reached for his clothes.

"My Prince!" General Torino rushed into his bedroom without as much as a knock. "It's the barbarians. It's Bayor Khan and his army of louts and criminals."

The two women in his bed gathered the blankets tight around themselves to hide their nudity.

Altan tied up the strings of his trousers. "How did they get inside?"

"Stealth, my Prince, like lowly thieves and snakes and night creatures. Nothing honorable, believe me." Torino could barely catch his breath.

Altan grabbed his boots and sat to pull them on. "It's time for the Protectors to earn their keep. Where are they?"

"In the small room next to the stables, my Prince." Torino shuffled his feet. "But I doubt they'll fight for us. They made it clear repeatedly since they joined us that they wouldn't get directly involved."

Altan reached for this sword belt in a clinking of blades and cinched it on his hips, then he seized his staff and straightened his frame. "We'll see about that."

The short walk to the stables was punctuated by screams of ladies in distress, fireballs landing in the manicured gardens, and the sound of arrows whistling overhead.

When he barged into the room assigned to the Protectors, Altan couldn't believe the sight. Twelve monks and Anila, sitting immobile, legs crossed, eyes closed, indifferent to the tumult around them. A white cat hissed at him and vanished into a dark corner.

"What is this I hear?" Altan felt the heat of anger mounting to his cheeks. "How dare you refuse to fight?"

No reaction from the meditating monks.

Unbelievable! "You would let the barbarians destroy my home and kill my men, without lifting a finger to defend them? What kind of Protectors are you?"

Still, no reaction.

"This lack of loyalty is treason of the highest degree, and punishable by death." Maybe that would change their mind.

Still, no reaction.

Altan was tempted to draw his sword and lop off a head to make an example, but he knew that the Protectors wouldn't let it happen, and he would end up dead. He was no match for their skills and didn't intend to lose his life just to make a point.

He brandished his staff. "This is the symbol of my power, a divine reminder of my noble blood, of my right to govern and order any of my subjects into submission."

Still no reaction from the stubborn Protectors.

Unwilling to tempt fate, Altan changed his approach. "Fine. I will let the barbarians kill you where you sit... or, maybe they will make you decide to fight."

The head Protector opened his eyes and stared at him but did not move another muscle. "My Prince, we shall not kill for you. We are not yours to command. Fight your own battles."

Altan fumed. "Anila! You are not one of them. As my subject and my future bride, you must obey my orders."

The young woman opened her eyes. "I am not yours to command either, my Prince. I belong with the Protectors, and I shall not fight for you."

Altan growled in frustration. "You are a bunch of traitors and cowards. After this is over, I will decide your fate. You will be tried and executed for treason!"

Ignoring his threats, the Protectors closed their eyes, including Anila, and returned to their meditation.

Altan marched out of the room and realized the barbarians were advancing on the palace and greatly outnumbered his men. He raised a chin to his general. "Torino, make sure we still have a castle when the sun rises."

"Yes, my Prince." The general saluted and turned around.

But since the walls had been breached, Altan knew his soldiers were doomed and the battle was already lost. He wasn't going to wait for defeat. He ran in the opposite direction, toward the stairs leading down to the cellars... and to the secret passages connecting to the caves underneath.

Altan always had an escape plan, a safe exit in case of trouble. He had survived many battles without fighting. And he knew where to get help to rule another day.

* * *

Bayor ascended the steps and sat on Prince Altan's throne, while Stardust settled at his feet. He couldn't believe how easily he had taken the stronghold. Some might say it was too easy, but he was glad the casualties were few.

As he looked around the room, the dancing flames of the chandeliers glinted on way too many silver decorations, princely busts, as well as silk rugs and tapestries.

"My Khan! The fortress and the castle are entirely ours." The female lieutenant bowed. "Altan's soldiers are locked away in the underground prison, and the civilians, including the nobles, are unwilling to resist, too happy to remain alive."

"Good." Bayor smiled, satisfied his rumors of bloodthirst and cruelty had worked.

"But our warriors found no trace of Prince Altan anywhere, my Khan." The lieutenant shook her head. "No one has seen him."

135

"Or they don't want to tell you where he is." But Bayor suspected the higher-than-mighty Prince Altan had fled in the face of danger. He would never risk his life. No matter. "Where are the Protectors I've heard so much about? Did you kill them or take them prisoners?"

"Not exactly, my Khan." The lieutenant cleared her throat and hesitated. "They are meditating in their quarters and refuse to fight."

"What?" Bayor chuckled. He should have guessed that Chi warriors would remain neutral. "Why not? They are supposed to be the fiercest fighters in the land."

"A young warrior provoked them to prove his valor, but nothing made them move... not threats or insults, not even the prick of a blade." The lieutenant paused. "I made him stop the taunting, of course."

"They didn't react at all?" Bayor liked them already.

"They seem to be in some sort of trance, my Khan." The lieutenant looked confused.

"A trance?" Bayor found the notion interesting.

"Come see for yourself, my Khan." The lieutenant pointed outside. "They are in a room next to the stables."

Formidable warriors who refused to fight and were in a trance? Curiosity got the best of Bayor.

He rose from the throne and Stardust sprung up on all fours, friskier than ever. "I want to see that with my own eyes. Lead the way."

When Bayor entered the small room where the monks sat on their sleeping mats, backs straight, legs crossed, and eyes closed, he still couldn't believe it. He walked the length of the room, inspecting each one while Stardust sniffed around.

The lieutenant remained at the door, as if out of respect.

The Protectors looked like monks, shaved heads, Tai-Chi tattoos, serene faces, completely immobile. They were one with the Chi. Bayor knew that feeling. He let his mind venture inside their heads. They exuded love for all life. He knew that feeling, too. They were fearless, peaceful, serene, in harmony with the entire universe. And their clear and vibrant auras reflected the purity of their spirit. He was glad they refused to fight his army, because despite their tiny numbers, they might have won.

Then Bayor noticed one in particular, who wore sand-colored clothes... a young woman, younger than the rest. He ventured into her mind but couldn't read her thoughts. Pure Immortal blood? How surprising!

She wasn't one of the Protectors. She had cropped dark hair and wore a simpler garb under the dark mantle... and a white cat curled up in her lap. The small feline looked asleep, and completely unfazed by the presence of the she-wolf. How odd!

* * *

Anila came out of her meditative state but kept her eyes closed for a few seconds. She felt an unusual presence in the room, but since Cottonball didn't move or hiss, it wasn't evil.

She opened her eyes slowly and stared into the yellow eyes of a furry face... a very large wolf face. She stilled her heart and took a slow breath, struggling to remain one with the Chi. When she raised her gaze, the fierce barbarian warrior she'd seen in her nightmares stood behind the beast. "Bayor!"

The wide aura bathing his rough exterior was bright blue, like that of Master Wang. He offered a kind smile that softened the angular black markings on his face.

"I fear you have me at a disadvantage, young lady." Bayor's northern accent matched his baritone voice and his strong physique. "You know my name, but I do not know who or what you are."

Anila glanced sideways at the Protectors, but they remained undisturbed. A woman warrior stood just outside the small room. Cottonball stretched and opened his eyes, but he didn't react to the large wolf or to the barbarian Khan... good. Definitely not evil. Still...

She took another slow breath to calm her mind. "My name is Anila, I am a Protector in training, and this is Cottonball, one of the Temple cats who followed me here."

The barbarian chuckled. "I am Bayor Khan, ruler of the barbarian hordes, and this is Stardust, the she-wolf who follows me everywhere."

Stardust sniffed the cat on her lap and Cottonball purred, stretched, rose to his paws and stretched again. Then the cat bumped his head against the she-wolf's leg and walked away purring. That would be normal animal behavior in the monastery, where the Chi was strong, but they were a long way from it, although the Chi was strong around the Protectors as well.

Bayor lowered himself on one knee, and even at that level, he looked formidable. There was a special light in his mesmerizing green eyes, but no threat. Not at all what she would expect from a conqueror... and he smelled like sage.

He slowly reached for her pendant.

Anila forced herself not to react to the intimate gesture. No one had ever dared hold her pendant.

The barbarian caressed the stone, as if fascinated by it. "Where did you get it?"

"It's a family heirloom." Anila swallowed a lump in her throat. "The only thing I have left, from the parents I never knew."

"Who were your parents?" Bayor frowned. "What happened to them?"

"No one knows... I assume they died in the great cataclysm. I was found and raised at the Temple of the Celestial Gate by Master Wang."

"Very interesting." He let go of the stone, rose to his full height and smiled. "Would you like to see what a barbarian encampment looks like?"

Although curious, Anila checked herself. "I am on a mission with the Protectors. I must remain with them."

"Must you?" Bayor's green gaze scanned the room. "With no recruits to train, I suspect your mission is cancelled."

"Still..." Anila noticed the Protectors were out of their meditative state and listening. She turned to the leader.

The head Protector gave her a slow blink, indicating it was okay.

Bayor must have seen the blink. "The Protectors are invited as well, if they are interested."

The head Protector bowed. "Due to the recent shift of power, we have important decisions to make... but they do not concern Anila, and she is free to go with you if she wishes."

Anila couldn't believe the Protectors would let her go alone with the barbarian. Didn't they care about her safety? Did they trust him? Or did they think her capable enough to defend herself against his horde?

Then she remembered Master Wang's comment about different paths and keeping an open mind. Were the Protectors following Master Wang's instructions?

Bayor offered his hand to help Anila get to her feet.

"No, thank you." Anila had never needed help from anyone. Ignoring the offered hand, she sprang up in one fluid motion. "But I wouldn't mind seeing this camp of yours. How far is it?"

"Not too far, but you'll need a mount." Besides the accent, there was something kind and trustworthy in his voice... not unlike Master Wang.

"Fortunately, my mare is next door." She liked him, but could she trust him? She tried to read Bayor's intentions but couldn't. That was unusual for her.

Fascinated by the barbarian and more than a little curious, Anila realized what that special thing about him was. The fascinating green eyes, the bright aura, the fact that she couldn't read his mind... he must have strong Immortal blood!

Chapter 9

Anila rode alongside Bayor into his encampment, Stardust loping at their side. She counted at least a hundred very large tents, round and bundled with pelts and ropes, as well as many covered chariots. They occupied a vast strip of grassy land on the lower slopes.

Red and yellow banners with a Yin-Yang symbol fluttered in the breeze from the pointed top of most tents. So, his people knew and valued the power of the Chi. The Protectors would appreciate that, but she was glad they declined to come and remained in Prince Altan's fortress.

Anila enjoyed her newly found freedom... and Bayor's company. She still couldn't get used to the idea that this fearsome barbarian had strong Immortal blood, but he never said he did, and she didn't dare ask. Still, he had a bright aura, and she could sense the unusual strength of his Chi... like an invisible net of energy surrounding him. All the Protectors had it, but she'd only seen this level of intensity in Master Wang.

Even by morning's first light, the barbarian camp buzzed with activity. Several kinds of people lived and worked there, some with pale skin, others with dark, red, or blue skin. Some tended to the large birds of prey perched on long rails. Others brushed the steeds, sharpened tools on a stone wheel, milked the mares and the goats, corralled the sheep.

Unlike Prince Altan's people, they smiled as they worked. Men and women cooked on campfires, stirring stews in large vats that spread the aroma of lentils, rice, meat, and enticing herbs.

The clean carcass of an entire ox was steaming on hot stones with a fire lit underneath. The aroma spread as the meat sizzled. The cooks stuffed more hot stones inside the carcass, then covered it with grasses and heavy blankets. Having never tasted meat, Anila couldn't imagine cooking or eating an entire ox.

Bayor must have noticed the direction of her gaze. "It will be fully cooked by sundown, in time for tonight's feast, when we celebrate our victory." He smiled. "You are invited, of course."

"Thank you. I look forward to it." Festivals were scarce at the Temple, and Anila suspected the barbarian celebrations would be quite different and interesting.

The hammering of a forge filled the air, along with smoke. The blacksmith intoned a rhythmic song as he struck the red-hot iron.

Anila couldn't help but admire the perfect organization all around the camp. "Everyone seems to have a specific place and a task. It reminds me of the Temple of the Celestial Gate."

"Really?" The barbarian sounded amused.

She reined in her mare to avoid a young warrior in full battle gear, long hair gathered on top of the head, carrying an armful of arrows. The woman smiled at Anila and nodded her thanks. Another woman warrior? She remembered the female officer who accompanied Bayor to the Protectors' sleeping quarters.

Anila was impressed. "How big is your army?"

"Big enough." Bayor halted his black stallion and pointed to the far edge of the camp, to a green strip of land. "Over there are the training grounds."

Anila gazed in that direction, amazed at how fast the riders raced their steeds, standing high in the saddle, shooting arrows at faraway targets. Others stood up on the beast's bare back at a full gallop and shot the bow without losing their balance. Some turned in the saddle to shoot backwards.

"Impressive!" She knew from experience that this kind of skill took time. "How much training does it take to learn that?

"A lot. But that's all they do." No bragging in the voice whatsoever.

Anila couldn't hide her admiration. "I've never seen a bow small enough and light enough to shoot from the saddle... and the range is remarkable."

"Because it's not just made of wood. We use several elements, like horn, wood, and sinew, layered and bonded together with hoof glue to give the bow its special shape, flexibility, and enough tensile strength for a far reach."

"Clever." Anila was also curious about his obvious knowledge of the Southern Provinces. "Since you and your horde never set foot south of the Great River before, how did you know to make your camp here?"

"I have my ways of getting information." Bayor turned in the saddle and smiled at her. "Just because I come from the far north doesn't mean I don't know everything about this land. I make it my business to learn about my future empire and its people."

"Your future empire?" Anila couldn't help a chortle. "You seem pretty sure of yourself. You have no doubt you will be emperor?"

"Doubt, like fear, is the enemy." He straightened in the saddle.

"But how did you know about this particular location for a camp?" Anila sensed he kept many secrets... like Master Wang.

Bayor tsked and his stallion resumed walking. "Let's say... I have access to excellent maps."

Anila also prompted her mare forward. She remembered seeing a few maps at the Temple, but none detailed enough to show a possible camp site for an entire army. "Ancient maps from before the great cataclysm?"

"Among others." He remained vague and tight-lipped about it.

Fine. Of course, he had no reason to trust her with his military secrets. "You know, people around here are under the impression that you practice torture, sorcery, and black magic. They say you show no mercy, use snake poison, conjure fire-breathing dragons... and you have a reputation of cruelty to everyone... even your own people."

He nodded. "That's the way I like it."

"But it's not true!" She didn't see any evidence of that when the barbarians took Prince Altan's fortress. "Your warriors do not indulge in carnage but behave with honor."

"We do value honor." He glanced at her sideways. "But I want my enemies to fear me."

"Why? Doesn't fear bring evil?" That's what she was taught, but she sensed no evil in him.

"To them, yes." He turned in the saddle to face her. "Fear can also be a formidable weapon if wielded properly."

"Really?" Anila frowned. The black markings on his face alone would scare the bravest soldiers. Although... the angular lines started to peel off at the corners. She could now see they were painted, not tattooed. She also realized in the early light that under the warpaint, Bayor was much younger than she first assumed. She wondered how he looked without the paint.

"Anila, you are staring. Is there something on my face, or should I be flattered?"

She averted her gaze and felt heat creeping up her cheeks. Was she blushing? Her heart beat faster. She couldn't help herself. "Sorry. That was rude."

He chuckled. "Don't worry, I'm used to it. Strangers always stare. Does my appearance scare you?"

"No... I mean, not anymore." She now found his imposing presence rather exciting, but maybe she shouldn't be so honest.

"So, I did scare you before, didn't I?" He laughed. "When was it? Tell me."

"The first time I saw you in my dream, several days ago... but I had a few more dreams since then." She said dreams as she no longer considered them nightmares. "That's how I knew who you were when I saw you."

"Interesting." He half-smiled, and his green eyes narrowed upon her. "And what was I doing in your dreams?" The slow remark brimmed with unspoken suggestions.

"Most recently, we were galloping together across vast expanses of rolling hills and tall grasses with your army." As she recalled the powerful image, her heart skipped a beat, but not from fear.

"So... what do you think of me now?" He looked straight ahead, offering his strong profile.

"I think you are kind to your people, and a good leader." She averted her gaze and glanced around. "Despite what I heard, I see no sign of cruelty here either. Your people work hard, but they seem healthy and happy. They smile, and the blacksmith was singing as he worked."

He squinted into the rising sun. "You want to know why my people are happy?"

"Sure." Happiness was different for different people. Anila found hers in the Chi.

"It's because they are free!" He proclaimed to the wind. "They also have full bellies, and they are all treated fairly... workers and warriors alike. None of them were drafted, so, they follow me by choice. They work hard and are rewarded for it. There are none more loyal."

"I see..." Anila glanced down at Stardust. "Some also say you travel with ghostly birds of prey and sleep with great wolves. I saw the birds in my dreams, and here in the camp, too, but I only see one wolf here... and she seems quite tame and friendly."

Stardust howled at the mention of wolves, then wagged her bushy tail.

Bayor burst into sonorous laughter. "That part is true. The golden falcons help us hunt and sometimes fight with us along with the eagles. The packs of wolves travelling with the horde are our friends, but unlike Stardust, they are wild. We throw them kitchen scraps, but mainly, they hunt for themselves."

"So why do they follow you if you don't feed them?" Anila found it strange. It didn't follow the natural laws of survival in the wild. "Do they hope to eat your sheep?"

He smiled. "No. They never enter the camp."

"Then why do they follow you?" Anila wanted to understand.

"Our presence disturbs their prey into making mistakes, and all the activity in the camp scares the worst predators. So, the wolves feel safe sleeping on the periphery. At night, they howl at the first sign of unusual activity, sounding the alarm like sentinels."

Anila tried to imagine what kind of predators would threaten entire packs of wolves. Maybe bears, tigers, panthers, lions? "Where are the wolves now?"

"We left them north of the river. They fear the swift water and for good reason." Bayor gazed into the distance, toward the southern desert. "Besides, they wouldn't be happy crossing the sand dunes... even in winter... no suitable hunting grounds for them. They need the abundance of feathered or furry prey found in the northern wilderness."

Anila's nightmares seemed so long ago. There was much more to the barbarians than their scary looks and brutal reputation of ferocious atrocities toward the conquered... and their leader seemed to be a strong Immortal. "Where are you going next?"

"South." He smiled and his face softened.

"Across the desert?" Was he looking for the Celestial Gem? "Are you going to the Temple of the Celestial Gate?"

"Maybe." He obviously didn't want to talk about it.

To change the topic, she pointed her chin to the wide blade hanging from his belt. "I'm not familiar with your kind of sword. It's quite curved and wide at the end, with only one edge and a diamond-shaped tip. It must be fashioned that way for a specific fighting technique."

"It's a scimitar." He drew the wide curved blade and turned his wrist slowly, letting the first rays of the red sun bounce on the shiny metal. "When striking down from the back of a steed, it offers a better angle and deeper cutting sweep."

"I see..." Anila shuddered at the bloody images coming to mind. She wondered how many enemies he had killed in combat but dared not ask.

He sheathed the scimitar and drew a shorter blade. "But for fighting in close quarters, we favor the dagger. Its length and sharp double edge are most deadly."

Anila couldn't help but admire the work of art on the blade and handle. "It's beautifully crafted."

"Forged from a special metal fallen from the sky. It will never shatter." He sounded proud. "Our metal workers are the best in the land."

"I noticed your stirrups are high up and made of metal, not leather like ours." She pointed to his feet. "And your boots have thick heels."

"Yes." He nodded. "Together, they offer better stability when standing up in the saddle to shoot the bow." He glanced at her, and the sun illuminated his green eyes. "It also allows the riders to turn around and fire arrows backwards to their pursuers."

"Impressive." So many different techniques Anila never knew existed. She wanted to learn them all.

"Are you hungry? Thirsty? May I offer you breakfast in my tent?" The smooth tone of his baritone voice made her blush.

Was it a mistake to accept? Could breakfast mean something different in his culture? She didn't care. She wanted to know more about him and his people. Curious about visiting his tent and hungry from the delicious food aromas floating around the camp, Anila nodded. "I missed my morning tea. I could eat something."

"Good. It's very close." He prompted his stallion in a different direction.

She followed him, enjoying the ride.

As they rode at a slow pace through the camp, Anila noticed a small group of workers practicing Tai-Chi between two tents. She recognized the familiar form she enjoyed at the monastery. It made her feel safe.

"Here we are." Bayor dismounted in a clicking of weapons and then handed the reins to an attendant, who walked away with the stallion.

Another attendant took the reins of Anila's mare as she dismounted.

From up close, the round tent seemed very high and wide, the size of a big house. Bayor held up the flap to let her inside, but Stardust rushed in first.

Anila ducked under Bayor's arm and stepped into a different universe. Pelts and furs lined the walls and the floor. A central fire kept away the morning chill, and a hole in the top allowed the smoke to escape. Oil lamps and wax candles provided a soft glow.

The she-wolf went straight for a comfy bed next to a large chair covered with furs, on an elevated step.

Anila pointed to it. "Is that your throne?"

"I have no need for castles or thrones. This is just where I sit in council."

Anila was reminded of Master Wang's green chair at the Temple, unpretentious, yet formidable.

"But let us not stand on ceremonies." Bayor gestured to a low wooden table with sheepskin cushions on each side. "Please, sit."

Anila lowered herself to the sheepskin pillow and found it extremely comfortable... more than she cared to admit. Was it a sin to enjoy comfort? At the monastery, the floor mats of the refectory were thin. Even the sleeping mats didn't cushion the bones from the hard stone floor.

"Did your people invent that small bow that's so efficient? Or did they borrow the idea from some other tribes?"

An attendant walked in, carrying a platter of red berries, apples, nuts, dry cheese, and clotted cheese.

Bayor slid the tray in front of her. "Our ancestors from before perfected that bow long ago. The survivors of the cataclysm remember the technique and are teaching it to the new generation... my generation."

So... he didn't know the world before. He must be about Anila's age. "How do you happen to know so much?"

"I was lucky to have a great mentor... Zaal. He's a wise and knowledgeable teacher." He nodded. "My parents died in a horrible accident. Their mounts were spooked and they fell from a high cliff into a gorge. Then their bodies were trampled by a herd of wild beasts stampeding at the bottom. I was still a child at the time. I barely remember them..." Something caught in his voice. "But Zaal was always there."

"How sad to lose your parents so young." Anila could relate to being orphaned. "I never knew mine."

A servant brought a tray of steaming dumplings, and strips of roasted meat then set it on the table. Meat? Anila never had meat, but it wouldn't be polite to refuse it.

Another serving girl brought two bowls of lentil stew, along with flat bread in a basket. And a young man with four mugs hanging from his fingers balanced a kettle of hot tea, and a pitcher of goat milk on a tray. Although they behaved with great respect, they did not bow or use grandiose decorum around their ruler.

Anila stared at all the goods on the table. "There is enough to feed ten people here. Are we expected to eat all that?"

Bayor served the tea. "My warriors are not children, or monks fasting and meditating all day. They train and work hard. They need sustenance."

Anila straightened her back. "At the monastery of the Celestial Gate, everyone trains hard as well. Protectors, teachers, Acolytes, all of them spend a lot of energy. But we do not eat much. Only on festival days do we indulge a little... usually with baked goods or sweets."

"It's probably because you live in the desert, where the food choices are limited." He served milk for both of them.

"Maybe." Anila didn't realize the Temple's resources were so meager. "Yet, I never felt deprived, and never went to sleep hungry."

"I believe life is meant to be experienced to the fullest, with all the senses, appreciated, and relished. I want to take pleasure in everything. The air we breathe, the company of Stardust, the delicious foods we eat, the excitement of weapons practice." He speared a piece of meat with his dagger and chewed it with gusto.

Anila managed not to gag at the smell of meat and chose a piece of bread and cheese.

"I especially like riding Thunder at a full gallop in the rain." He took a sip of milk.

"I have never experienced rain." Anila didn't know what to think of his strange philosophy. "There are other things to be enjoyed, like the connection to the Chi, the beauty of the desert at sunset, and the peace and serenity of monastic life."

"True. But I prefer a stimulating conversation... or the love of a beautiful woman like you, Anila." His green eyes stared into hers and lingered.

Anila had a delicious frisson at hearing him saying her name. No one had ever said it with such adoration. "You find me beautiful?"

"Of course, you are a gorgeous creature, Anila." His green gaze never left her. "All these bountiful gifts of nature make life worthwhile. It would be a sin not to enjoy them all."

"But what about duty and sacrifice, what about righteousness? What about protecting the weak and the helpless?" Anila had mixed feelings. Her upbringing emphasized those values. "What about the Chi? The Protectors sacrifice everything to focus on their sacred duty to guard the Celestial Gate."

"That is honorable, but I believe you can serve the greater good just as well without renouncing all of life's pleasures." He took another sip of goat milk.

Before Anila could respond, a tall man, with dark skin and a square beard under his hooded cloak, barged into the tent. "My Khan. Sorry to interrupt."

"Zaal!" Bayor smiled. "Is everything all right?"

"I need a word with you, my Khan. It's important." The man straightened his muscular frame and pulled back his cloak. The thick gold on his chest and wrists reflected the dancing light of the candles. So did the gold ornaments on his belt and scabbard.

So, this was Bayor's famous teacher. Anila felt as if she had seen him before, but she would remember someone wearing that much gold... although the black cloak might have concealed it. She tried to read him but couldn't. Strange. Did he have Immortal blood as well?

"Duty calls." Bayor rose and smiled at Anila. "After you finish your meal, meet me at the training grounds. If you are interested, I could show you some of our fighting techniques."

Anila was about to burst with excitement but struggled to hide it in front of Zaal. Bayor had guessed what she wanted, and she didn't even have to ask. "I shall meet you there in a little while, my Khan."

He chuckled. "No need to stand on ceremonies with me. Just call be Bayor."

"Thank you, Bayor." Saying his name so familiarly gave her goosebumps.

As the two men left the tent, Anila noticed something strange and somewhat familiar in the tall frame, the beaked nose, the walk, and the posture of the man named Zaal.

Could he be the mysterious figure she'd seen on the terrace at the monastery? Or maybe he was the one speaking in secret to Prince Altan in the desert at night, and at the caravanserai... or the one who seemed to fly away on Altan's rampart? Could there be others who looked like him, or was she imagining things? She couldn't be sure of anything. All her sightings happened at night in the shadows.

Bayor obviously loved and respected Zaal, but could his mentor have a darker side?

Anila couldn't help picturing Zaal with wings. Was it just her imagination? Or did beings with wings truly exist?

* * *

Bayor sighed his frustration, struggling not to burst with outrage as he paced Zaal's tent in front of the black banner with a gold griffin, the symbol of the extinct Gripus race. He resented his commander's suggestion. "I refuse to march on the Temple of the Celestial Gate at the head of the entire horde. The Temple is an island of peace and wisdom, and Master Wang is a brother in the Chi."

"That again?" Zaal straightened, smoothing his gold breastplate. "My Khan, how many times do I have to tell you? The Chi is an illusion!"

"Zaal, please, do not insult my beliefs. My entire horde rides under the banner of the Chi." Bayor struggled to control his frustration. He refused to throw away a lifetime of trust and mutual respect over this disagreement. "Just because you cannot experience the Chi, doesn't mean it doesn't exist."

"But, my Khan, what if Wang refuses to give you the Celestial Gem?" Zaal's dark eyes stared back over the hooked nose. "What then? You need that sacred stone, in order to realize the prophecy, and to consolidate your claim as the legitimate ruler of all the land. That gem is the key to your peaceful takeover. Only with it can you be accepted as the uncontested ruler."

"I know..." Bayor took a slow breath. "But Master Wang is highly respected and wise. I wish to visit him alone, as a friend, not treat him as a potential enemy."

"My Khan, if you fail to convince him, you'll need your army to fight his Protectors." Zaal's gold cuffs caught the sunlight from the opening in the tent roof. "I understand he has hundreds of them guarding the gate, and each of them is lethal."

"Forget it." Bayor couldn't believe his esteemed mentor would advocate such an aggressive approach. "I refuse to declare war upon the most revered holy man in this land. His Temple is dedicated to the Chi. It's a place of peace, harmony, knowledge, and wisdom. I want my ascent to the imperial throne to be peaceful, not bloody."

"You are naïve, my Khan, probably due to your age and inexperience." Zaal cast Bayor a stern glance. "There is no such thing as a conquest without bloodshed."

"I beg to disagree." Bayor raised his voice. "And as the sole leader of the horde by virtue of my Immortal family line, I alone make the decisions here. The horde will remain here, and I shall only take a dozen warriors on the desert road."

Zaal pinched his lips and took a step back. "Your word is law, my Khan."

"Thank you." Bayor retrieved a measure of calm. "I believe diplomacy, not military threat, is the best strategy in this case. I don't want my reign to start with a massacre."

"You may not live long enough to regret your stubbornness, my Khan. Trusting Wang could get you killed." Zaal deployed his wings and hovered, then took flight straight up, through the wide smoke hole in the canopy of his tent.

Bayor smashed his fist on the heavy table to vent his frustration. His ideas and Zaal's had come into conflict quite often lately. Bayor seriously questioned the counsel of his commander. Why did his esteemed mentor consider Master Wang a potential enemy?

Still stunned, Bayor walked out of Zaal's tent and whistled for Thunder. Then he took a deep breath and released it slowly to calm his mind.

The black stallion came trotting at the call and whinnied with excitement.

"Good boy." Bayor patted the shiny neck, then vaulted upon Thunder's back and prompted him toward the practice grounds.

He smiled at the thought that Anila was waiting for him there. He truly enjoyed her company.

Chapter 10

The enormous crater, dug in the stone of a high plateau and surrounded by unscalable cliffs, resonated with the joyous flapping of majestic wings. Gripus wings! Three dozen pairs of them. Zaal and his brethren hovered, stirring the air all around, spreading the scent of well-groomed feathers. Zaal's brethren were all tall and muscular like him, all male according to his race, with square beards, long curly hair, and the blackest eyes over beaked noses.

The afternoon sun glinted on the polished gold of their breastplates, belt buckles, rings, and wide arm cuffs. Some also wore gold shin plates. The more the better. Gold sustained their longevity and kept them in good health through the millennia.

In the presence of his own people, Zaal felt a strong sense of belonging and pride, even if it was a small group, marooned on this lowly planet millennia ago as a meager clutch of eggs.

This crater was their home, their nest. Now, it served as a secret meeting place for winged beings, away from human eyes and ears. It was in this very place long ago that the Great Mother had laid her eggs so they would be safe... the only reason his clutch had survived the purge.

But the abandoned hatchlings didn't wither or die. Relying on strong instincts, they learned to fly on their own, hunted for food, grew, and thrived in the wild. When they reached adulthood, they ventured among the natives and blended with the local populations to learn.

There, they found the remains of their own civilization preserved on Temple walls and in scrolls. The people of this planet hated the Gripus and had exterminated their older brethren or driven them back into space. Zaal and his clutch siblings survived for millennia, hidden among their enemies.

Now, with the recent discovery of ancient Gripus technology preserved in a cave, the isolated clutch brothers had made contact with their home planet. Their fortune was about to change. Zaal could barely control his excitement.

The large banner, black with a gold griffin, the symbol of Gripus pride, hung from the rim, halfway to the bottom, undulating in the cool breeze. Zaal was proud to serve his noble race, superior in so many ways, yet scorned and reviled in the far past. Now, the locals considered the Gripus extinct and irrelevant, even forgotten.

But not for long. Soon, those who ruled this arrogant little planet would understand their place and bow to his superior race... the Gripus race. Even the so-called Immortals would bend before his kind... like the holy Master Wang, hiding behind his mighty Protectors.

The Great Gripus, his entire body covered in glittering gold, looked like a glowing angel in the afternoon sun. He hovered in front of the black banner with the golden griffin symbol. As he raised his arms, the assembly cheered.

"Brethren!" The strong voice of the Great Gripus echoed and bounced on the walls of the crater. "After millennia of isolation, we were finally able to contact our home-world, and now, we have their warm and supportive response. Today, we are few, but we control the powerful. And tomorrow, we shall be multitude and rule this planet unchallenged."

All the Gripus in the crater cheered and flapped their wings, hovering up and down... including Zaal.

"We shall restore our temples and be worshipped as gods once again!" The words of the Great Gripus spread like a healing balm on old, festering grudges... millennia of humiliation, while pretending to serve inferior beings.

A loud ovation acknowledged the statement.

The Great Gripus waved his beringed hands, asking for quiet. "Envoys, make your reports. Zaal, you speak first."

Zaal hovered further into the circle and cleared his throat. "As the esteemed savior and mentor of Bayor Khan, ruler of the barbarian hordes, I have his trust and his respect. He listens to my counsel. And since he made me Commander of his armies, I have the obedience of his lieutenants and tribal chieftains."

The gathered Gripus nodded and mumbled their approval as they hovered up and down.

Zaal waited for the appreciative flapping of wings to abate. "Bayor Khan brought his barbarian hordes from the northern mountains, across the great plains, and crossed the Great River into the Southern Provinces, almost unchallenged. Yesterday, he took the fortress of Prince Altan with minimal losses on each side."

"Perfect." Satisfaction rang in the voice of the Great Gripus. "What did he do with Prince Altan's army? We shall need it, as well."

"Prince Altan's soldiers are safe, Great Gripus, locked up in the prison under the castle." Zaal had made sure of it.

"Including Prince Altan?" Derision tainted the Great Gripus' voice.

"No, Great Gripus. I'm sorry. Prince Altan escaped during the battle." Zaal bowed in apology.

"Not surprising." The Great Gripus motioned to another envoy. "Zilon? Prince

Altan is your charge. Do you know where he is?"

Envoy Zilon batted his wings and flew inside the circle. "I have Prince Altan under control, Great Gripus." The envoy's smooth voice resonated through the crater. "He fled his castle before the invader through escape tunnels in the rock. He is hiding in a natural cave with all the creature comforts. He supports our noble cause and is eager to lend us his army... under one condition."

"What does he want in exchange?" The Great Gripus sneered.

"The imperial crown, of course." Envoy Zilon's derisive tone sent ripples of laughter through the assembly. The circle twinkled with blinding flashes of gold in the afternoon sun.

"Fine!" The Great Gripus sighed. "Promise him anything he wants. We are not interested in administering the land anyway. We only want the gold for the benefit and the glory of all Gripus. And Prince Altan will dig it for us."

Zilon bowed. "Of course, Great Gripus. We are not meant for menial work. Let the so-called nobility oversee the extraction for us."

The Great Gripus turned to Zaal. "Please, Envoy Zaal, continue your report."

Zaal nodded. "Tomorrow, Bayor Khan will start across the desert toward the Temple of the Celestial Gate, to claim the Celestial Gem from Master Wang."

"Good." The Great Gripus caressed his gold belt.

Zaal chuckled. "He believes the gem will allow him to rule without bloodshed."

"It doesn't matter what he believes," the Great Gripus snarled. "As long as we control the horde and Altan's army, we can control the entire monastery complex and the Celestial Gate."

"My only concern is..." Zaal pinched his beard. "Bayor Khan doesn't want to take his entire army. He seems hesitant to shed the blood of Master Wang and his mighty Protectors."

"Not even to become ruler of all the land?" The Great Gripus angled his head in false concern. "We do not care who rules the land, Bayor the barbarian, or Altan the blood prince, as long as the human emperor does our bidding."

"I understand, Great Gripus." Zaal bowed. "But I fear even the imperial crown will not motivate Bayor Khan to fight the Protectors, destroy their Temple, or kill Master Wang." He paused. "I apologize for my failure to convince him otherwise."

"No matter, Zaal. You did well. Tell me... can the Protectors be turned to serve our cause?" Silence followed the question of the Great Gripus. "Or maybe they can be seduced... or fooled into working for us."

"Not likely, Great Gripus." Zaal always told the truth to his brethren. His bond of love and obedience to the clutch and the

Great Gripus was unbreakable, and he always found forgiveness and protection for his failures. "The Protectors are loyal to a fault and very perceptive. They claim to be one with the Chi and draw their intuition and their strength from it."

"Then they are gullible dupes." The Great Gripus exploded into a deep belly laugh. "The Chi is but an illusion."

"I know..." Zaal lowered his head to show his respect. "But the Protectors are lethal and unmatched."

"Unmatched among the natives, maybe..." The Great Gripus caressed his shiny breastplate. "But they have never confronted our kind."

"True." Zaal knew the great advantage of flight for a warrior. "Especially if we have access to our own weapons. I heard the transmission from our home-world mentioned a stash preserved in an underground vault by our predecessors."

"It's true. These weapons do exist." The Great Gripus nodded. "They may not be in perfect working order, and it might take some work to recover them, but I have a plan."

The Gripus assembly cheered.

Zaal flapped his wings, then regained his calm. "As soon as Bayor Khan leaves to cross the desert, I will be in command of the barbarian horde left behind. And I will have full control of Prince Altan's fortress."

"Wonderful. Well done." The Great Gripus smiled at Zaal. "You will have Prince Altan's soldiers released, and you will gather them under General Torino's command. Then you will lead the barbarian hordes across the desert to march upon the Temple of the Celestial Gate. Meanwhile, General Torino will follow, at a distance, with Prince Altan's army, toward the same destination."

"It will be done, Great Gripus." Zaal bowed, excited by the prospect of regaining supremacy for his race.

Soon, the humiliation Zaal had suffered for millennia from the natives and for two decades from Bayor Khan would end. All this time, bowing and coaching and smiling, while he should have been worshipped as a god.

He would find immense satisfaction in killing the young upstart himself, once he outlived his usefulness... or if he dared turn against the Gripus, like his parents did.

Zaal remembered with glee the shocked expression on their royal faces when he spooked their mounts with his wings. They all fell, twisting and screaming, all the way down the gorge into the horns and hooves of the stampeding herd below... then he'd unleashed a tiger on their young heir to become his savior and the family hero. But now, Bayor, too, was becoming cumbersome.

* * *

As the red sun lowered on the western horizon, Anila squinted at the wooden target far away, wondering if the arrow would fly that far. Bayor said it would, and he was watching her intently, and so did the she-wolf.

Adjusting her bow stance, Anila checked her balance, emptied her mind, and focused on the Chi. The evening breeze carried bird songs and the smell of the campfires. With the mountain on one side and the down slope on the other, she looked over the flat expanse of the training grounds, almost deserted by now. She enjoyed being alone with Bayor.

Then she took a deep breath, raised the bow, pulled, aimed, and exhaled slowly as she released. Her mind remained focused on the long arrow as it flew far and straight above the grass. It hit the target dead center and planted itself halfway in.

Stardust howled her approval.

"Yay!" Anila whooped with joy. "This bow is very powerful… and accurate."

"Only when a skilled archer focuses on the Chi to guide the arrow all the way." Bayor laughed. "Obviously, you are very familiar with the flow of the Chi."

"Of course. That's part of our training with Master Wang. Like the Protectors, I'm a Chi warrior."

169

"I'm glad to hear it." At the sound of a horn, Bayor turned around toward the camp, a short distance away.

Stardust straightened her ears and sniffed the air.

"What is it?" Anila didn't want this moment to end. She truly enjoyed Bayor's company.

"The victory feast is about to start." He raised an eyebrow. "Will you be my guest of honor?"

Anila wanted to go, but wasn't sure it was the correct etiquette. "Are the Protectors who remained in the fortress invited as well?"

"Yes, but they sent word that they would not join us." Bayor extended his hand to take her bow. She handed it to him. He returned it to the rack.

"I'm not surprised the Protectors declined your invitation. Don't be offended. They never attend these celebrations. Not even the Temple festivals. They consider them frivolous." Anila fell silent, remembering a long-ago kiss under the stars.

"But you are not a Protector... so you are free to attend, right?" Bayor's green gaze searched her face.

Anila realized she wanted very much to stay with him and have fun. Especially since he mentioned he was leaving the next morning. "The Protectors may not approve... but you are right. I'm not one of them... yet."

"Good!" He flashed a devilish grin. "Besides, it would be rude to refuse an offer from the man who indulged you all day around his camp, feeding you, and showing you his secret fighting techniques." Bayor's green eyes sparkled as he offered his arm.

Stardust wagged her tail.

Anila took his arm, enjoying the contact of his strong muscles under the soft black wool. She felt as if she could fly. Freedom was intoxicating. Together, with Stardust, they walked across the green grassy expanse, toward the encampment proper, and the delicious aroma of cooking food. They reached it, just as the last rays of the setting sun gave way to the dancing flames of the bonfires.

Then the happy tunes of flutes and tambourines traveled on the evening breeze, and Anila felt the sudden urge to dance. Not that she would know how... but today, she felt exceptionally light on her feet.

* * *

As he sat with the warriors in a wide circle around the fire, Bayor admired Anila's lovely face, illuminated by the flames. He couldn't get enough of her energy. She appreciated and admired everything new, always positive in her comments. Unlike the population at large, who judged his people on appearances, she looked at him with an open mind, and an insatiable thirst for knowledge.

Both children of the cataclysm, they must be the same age, but he felt older... probably from the burden of leadership thrown upon him at a young age. Thankfully, Zaal was there to guide and protect him after his parents' untimely death. Despite his natural aloofness, Zaal had been the only pillar of strength and wisdom in his life.

Anila took a sip of mead and smiled. "This drink is so bubbly and refreshing."

"Careful, it also has a kick. The fermentation in it tends to blur the lines of propriety. Excess leads to drunkenness, and drunk people do not make wise decisions."

"I read about it... but I never knew it tasted this good." She took another sip.

"Have some food. A full stomach helps keep a clear mind." He reached for a passing tray and handed her shredded meat and rice wrapped in a flat bread. "Try this. It's my favorite. Do you like spicy mutton?"

"I don't know." She took the wrap and looked at it, the warm light of the fire illuminating her amber eyes. "We don't eat meat of any kind in the monastery, as all creatures are related in the Chi. But when travelling, we must respect the customs of the places we visit."

"That's an excellent policy." Bayor chuckled. "And when I visit the Temple of the Celestial Gate, I promise to conform to your customs as well."

"That's fair. We also use spices, but on vegetables." She took a bite and chewed it thoughtfully. "This is delicious." She closed her eyes. "Thank you, brother sheep, for nourishing our bodies. May your spirit find peace in the Chi."

Bayor refilled the horn Anila handed him, then he offered a handful of meat to Stardust, who lay at his feet. The she-wolf gulped it in one swallow.

"Good girl." Bayor patted the wolf's head and was rewarded with a lick on his hand.

Warriors passed around trays of wild berries, apples and nuts... also steamed roots, goat cheese, and milk. Anila tasted almost everything, nodding and making comments for each discovery.

Toward the end of the meal, the warriors passed around the gourd of tika.

"What's that?" Anila's eyes rounded in question.

"Tika. It's a very strong drink, and I'm not sure it's a good idea." Bayor chuckled.

"I want to experience everything." She smiled. "I'll soon return to the monastery and may never have a chance again."

"Who am I to protest?" Bayor couldn't imagine living like a monk. He happily filled her horn.

She sipped and winced then coughed. "This one has quite a bite."

Bayor chuckled. "I warned you." Hearing a familiar footstep, he turned to see

Zaal walking toward him with a serious face. He immediately rose. "Is there a problem?"

Zaal bowed. "No problem, my Khan. Only a suggestion."

"Speak." Bayor knew from experience that suggestions from Zaal should never be ignored. He trusted his mentor's judgement.

"Maybe we should send feast food to the warriors guarding the castle. And..." He hesitated. "And maybe to the prisoners as well."

"To the prisoners?" Bayor squinted. "Haven't they been fed?"

"Yes, my Khan. But roasted meat, delicacies, and mead might keep them in your good graces. Eventually, you want them to become part of your own army, so you want them to like you, be healthy and in a good mood. Don't you?"

"I didn't think of it that way. I don't even know if they would enjoy our food choices, but I trust your advice." Bayor smiled. "Great suggestion, Zaal. Please, see to it."

"It will be done, my Khan." Zaal bowed and stepped back then turned around and walked away.

Anila, who had witnessed the exchange, stared at Zaal's retreating back. "I know you have great respect for him, but for some reason, I don't trust him."

Bayor sat down, took a sip of strong tika, enjoying the burn warming his throat. He petted Stardust before responding. "I don't always agree with Zaal, but his knowledge is vast, and he has been looking out for me since childhood. His loyalty is beyond any doubt."

She narrowed her amber eyes at him. "Are you sure?"

"He's always been right... so far." Bayor hesitated to express his doubts about Zaal's strange behavior of late... like his suggestion to bring his entire army to the Temple of the Celestial Gate... and take on the Protectors if Master Wang refused to entrust him with the Celestial Gem.

The music of flute and string instruments rose louder and started a new and devilish tempo with tambourines and drums. Warriors applauded and a few entered the circle to dance in friendly competition.

Bayor saw an opportunity to teach Anila something new. He rose and extended his hand. "Do you dance?"

"I never have. I only practice Tai-Chi. Despite its gracefulness, it's not a dance but a deadly martial art." She took his hand.

"So is this dance. Each move mimics weapons training." He pulled her up to her feet. "Let me teach you how warriors dance after a victorious battle."

She rose and observed the warriors stomping their feet, brandishing their swords, twirling, then doing flips in the air, landing back on their feet. "That's the same acrobatics archers did on their mounts earlier on the training grounds."

"Exactly. It's good practice, and it's fun, too. Watch." Bayor executed a back flip, twisted in the air, and landed on his feet. "It's all in the height of the jump and the twist."

"I practiced many jumps over a person, an obstacle, or a pole in weapons training, but I never practiced this particular kind of back flip."

"Then this is your chance." He extended his arm behind her waist. "Try it. I got you. My arm is supporting your waist. I promise I won't let you fall."

She gazed into his face with her wide amber eyes. "I do trust you."

"Good." Bayor skipped a breath at the trust in her eyes. "Ready?" He braced himself to catch her if she fell. "Go for it."

She flipped with such grace he almost let her go, but he kept his arm out to support her arched back then caught her waist to prevent a hard landing. "You almost did it on your own."

She smiled and gazed up at him, so close, as if unwilling to free herself from his hold, her face flushed with the victory of her first try. "Almost? Really?"

"Yes, really. Try it again." Her close proximity made Bayor's heart beat faster. "Just a little more height in the back jump, and you'll land perfectly."

"If it's all right with you." She stepped away then leaped again, and this time the twist was almost perfect.

"That was even better. You are very flexible and strong." Bayor couldn't contain his joy at her success and took her into a bear hug. "Congratulations!"

She leaned against his chest. He relished her contact and her trust. Then she looked up at him with her wide amber eyes, and his heart skipped a beat. He wanted to kiss her, but it wouldn't be right to take advantage of an innocent young woman.

She smiled sadly. "I wish you weren't leaving tomorrow."

His heart melted. He reached and pushed back a short strand of black hair from her forehead. "Maybe you and the Protectors could travel with us, since I'm going to the Temple of the Celestial Gate. Your mission here is over anyway, isn't it?"

Her big eyes lit up with hope. "That's a great idea. I shall ask the Protectors tonight."

Chapter 11

Prince Altan paced the length of the sumptuous carpet covering the rock floor of his secure cave, deep under his occupied castle. How humiliating to be caught unprepared in the middle of the night... by a filthy barbarian of all people. It was the Protectors' fault. They must have informed the enemy and plotted against their legitimate ruler. No wonder they refused to fight for him. When all this was over, he would have them executed.

Candles and oil lamps illuminated the wall portraits of his Immortal ancestors, whose blue eyes seemed to judge him with unflinching stares. Did they consider him a coward for fleeing before the horde that breached his fortress and neutralized his soldiers?

At least Altan still lived, and they were all dead, despite having Immortal genes. Violence and politics often mixed. The barbarians would have executed him and paraded his head on a pike. Savages!

Altan shuddered at the very thought. He valued his life too much to risk it. Honor was for the simple-minded. He believed in strategy. Staying alive and free was a good strategy. A dead Immortal could never rise to power.

He turned to the wide opening in the rock, a large terrace overlooking a dark precipice. The faint moonlight bathed the rocky landscape, and a cool breeze carried the smell of wet grass. Soon, it would be dawn. When would Envoy Zilon return? The alien Gripus made many promises, but could he deliver?

Of course, Altan had failed in his mission to lure all the Protectors away from the Celestial Gate to fight the barbarians. Master Wang only loaned him twelve. The rest of that exceptional martial elite remained at the Temple. The Gripus didn't like that... it complicated their plans, but what else could Altan do?

The sound of flapping wings made him turn to see Envoy Zilon alighting on the terrace overlooking the cliff. Reflections of the oil lamps and candles glinted on the gold of his belt and breastplate as he landed.

"So, what did your brethren say? Do we still have a deal?" Altan hoped this set back wouldn't compromise his plans. He couldn't wait to be crowned emperor.

Envoy Zilon walked inside, onto the silk rug and retracted his wings. "The Great Gripus agreed to your demands, my Prince." He bowed. "But as soon as you are back in charge, you must reopen the old mines and see that the gold is extracted at an efficient rate… it will require intensive labor.”

“Let me worry about the labor.” Altan was born for the imperial throne, and he would do whatever it took to secure it… even enslave his subjects, if that’s what it required.

“Efficiency is of the greatest importance, my Prince. See… gold is essential to our way of life, our health, the health of our home planet, and to boost our technology.”

“I see…” Altan preferred silver to gold, but maybe he could get his hands on some of their fancy weapons. He’d read about them in ancient scrolls and could use them for his personal protection, and also for his imperial elite guard.

“Of course, we shall leave the ruling of the land, the extraction, and the delivery of the refined gold to you, my Prince.” Zilon bowed. “Also, we wouldn’t mind reopening the old temples where the Gripus used to be worshiped.”

Altan could tell from the Envoy’s tone that being worshiped would give him great pleasure. So, the Gripus had a weakness other than gold. “I can reopen the few temples that are still standing… and the preferred offerings would be… gold?”

“Perfect.” Zilon smiled wide under the hooked nose, and gold blinked on his teeth. “Of course, since you failed to get the Protectors away from the Celestial Gate, we need your army to march on the Temple to force Master Wang's cooperation... control of the gate is crucial to our plan."

A few months ago, Altan would have sworn the Celestial Gate was only a myth... but the Gripus said it was a piece of alien technology that opened to other worlds. "If I still have an army, feel free to use it. But whatever soldiers survived are now prisoners of Bayor Khan."

"We are working on this detail right now, my Prince." Envoy Zilon smiled. "After we take over the monastery, you can take possession of the Celestial Gem."

"The Celestial Gem is real?" Another myth shattered.

"According to my fellow Gripus, it is." Zilon bowed. "Although, it's only mentioned in ancient scrolls, and no one has ever seen it."

"Then I should definitely acquire it... even though I am the only choice for the imperial crown." Altan couldn't take any chances.

"Definitely, my Prince." Zilon nodded. "The gem is a powerful symbol. It gives the bearer uncontested authority to rule all the land."

"Good. Let's march on the monastery." Even a small shiny symbol could elevate Altan's status.

"Master Wang is in for a big surprise." The jubilation in Zilon's dark eyes was unsettling.

"Be careful..." Altan resented Wang for withholding the Protectors. He also hated him for not forcing Anila to welcome his advances. But once he became emperor, Altan could impose his will upon anyone he chose. "The high and mighty Master Wang is smart and stubborn."

Envoy Zilon smirked. "If he resists, we are prepared to use force."

"What about his Protectors? Can you defeat them?" Altan considered the Envoy with new respect.

"With your army and our special weapons... definitely." Zilon's silhouette against the candlelight looked predatory.

"Then do with Wang what you will." Altan did not easily forgive humiliation. "You can kill him for all I care."

"It might be necessary, my Prince." Zilon bowed again. "As soon as we take control of the Celestial Gate, the imperial crown and the gem will be yours. Then all you have to do is deliver the gold."

"That won't be a problem." Altan smiled inwardly. Gloating would be unseemly for a future emperor. "Just one more thing."

"Yes, my Prince?" Zilon's suave voice carried a hint of annoyance.

"There is a young woman named Anila. She is with the twelve Protectors who came to the castle." Altan savored the moment. "I want her captured and delivered to me... alive."

"Your wish is my command, my Prince. If that is all, as you say, we have a deal." Zilon turned toward the open terrace over the cliff, deployed his wings, then flew away like a giant bird.

Altan smiled widely as he watched Zilon blend with the night sky. Best deal he ever made. The few gold mines would quickly run dry. The Gripus would have to find other planets to deplete... After they left through the gate, Altan would still be emperor, still young, thanks to his Immortal blood. By then, Anila would have given him an heir.

Then he would destroy the gate and proclaim himself the hero who rid the land of the flying Gripus. He would order their statues destroyed, and would replace them with statues of himself, to be worshiped in the temples. Why not?

* * *

In the early dawn, Anila riding her mare, and Bayor on his black stallion, led the short column as they rode south, followed by the twelve Protectors, a dozen barbarians, and a chariot of supplies. No servants, no cooks. Just warriors.

Anila inhaled the desert breeze carrying the fragrance of dry grasses. Birds of prey flew overhead with happy cries to salute the sunrise. Small creatures scurried over the sand.

She enjoyed this ride more than on her way in because Bayor was beside her. She cast a glance his way. Without the war paint, he was very handsome, with a straight nose and strong chin.

"Thank you for this barbarian saddle. It's very comfortable, and the sheepskins are softer to the mare's back." She looked down at her foot. "You are right, the metal stirrups make a big difference for stability and balance. I like them."

"You are welcome." Bayor motioned with his chin toward her saddle. "I've never seen a cat ride on a mare before."

"I couldn't leave him behind in that horrible castle with those awful people." Anila petted Cottonball, curled up in front of her on the wide saddle. "And who could believe a she-wolf would lope alongside a warrior's mount?"

He smiled... with dimples. "When Stardust was a small pup, she used to ride inside my coat."

"I would have liked to see that. The formidable Bayor Khan riding with a puppy on his chest." Anila smiled back and wondered if he had chest hair.

Cottonball and Stardust exchanged furtive glances, but neither of them seemed aggressive toward the other.

"Look at those two." Bayor pointed his chin to the cat, then the wolf. "They know they are brother and sister in the Chi."

Anila couldn't help but appreciate Bayor's familiarity with the Chi, and his loving attitude toward his stallion and the she-wolf. He accepted everyone just the way they were. Even her. He didn't try to change her but expanded her horizons. She wanted to learn more about his culture... and about him.

"Where did you learn about the Chi?" She wasn't aware the knowledge was widespread. In her experience, it was kept and taught only by Immortal masters to a handful of monks, in their monasteries.

He squinted into the rising sun and his green eyes reflected the light. "My parents believed in the Chi and taught me about it as a child. But I was too young to understand it."

For Anila, awareness of the Chi had always been there, since she grew up in the monastery. "So, when did you realize the Chi was real?"

"Much later." He gazed far away at the horizon. "Several years after my parents' death, I discovered a cache of scrolls in the walls of our home. From it I learned about my ancestry... who and what I was. It also explained Tai-Chi forms to develop my connection with the Chi, for the full realization of my true destiny."

"Destiny?" Anila did not believe in destiny. She wanted the freedom to choose her own path. "Then what?"

Bayor's jaw clenched. "When I asked Zaal about the Chi, he laughed, telling me the Chi was a myth, and it didn't exist."

"He doesn't believe in the force that holds the universe together?" Anila found it odd for a wise and knowledgeable mentor.

"No." Bayor's shoulders sagged. "Most people don't believe in things they can't see and touch."

"I noticed." Anila remembered the reaction of Prince Altan's new recruits. They called her skill magic and it scared them. "So, what did you do?"

"I didn't tell Zaal about the scrolls, for fear he would take them away from me or destroy them." Bayor sighed and his black stallion snorted. "Instead, I practiced Tai-Chi in secret, and soon I could feel and control the energy flowing through my body."

"Then you knew it was a real thing." Anila still remembered the first time she felt the Chi. "I was so energized and excited the first time, I thought I could fly."

"It's a powerful feeling." Bayor nodded. "I kept practicing, then I started teaching it to my best warriors, so they could use the Chi to strengthen them in battle."

"And now even the workers practice the form. I saw them do it in the camp." She chuckled. "I bet, Zaal doesn't like that."

"No. But as the unchallenged ruler of the hordes, whatever I say goes. He can't stop it, so he just makes fun of the Chi and anyone who practices Tai-Chi." Bayor seemed so at ease in the saddle.

Something still bothered Anila. "Zaal is a strange fellow, with his square beard, beaked nose, and flashy gold. Isn't he?"

"You noticed?" The amused tone said there was a story there.

"He reminds me of the winged statues at the entrance of Prince Altan's fortress, and at the gate of the caravanserai." Anila squinted in the sun. "Am I wrong to picture him with wings?"

"You are not wrong." Bayor laughed. "You are very perceptive."

"Am I?" Excitement about new knowledge bubbled in Anila's chest. "Who or what is he?"

"Zaal is a Gripus, from a long-ago celestial race." Bayor stared at the sand road ahead. "He has lived for many centuries and is probably the last of his kind on this planet."

"Really?" Anila enjoyed learning from Bayor. "Tell me more about his race."

"All right." Bayor patted his stallion. "The Gripus came to this planet many millennia ago to mine gold."

"There must have been other alien races on this planet as well. Like the Immortals who started the imperial bloodlines." Anila remembered the slave market. "There are also blue people and red people I saw in your camp, and at the caravanserai." The fact that those were sold as slaves made her shiver with disgust.

"Yes." Bayor nodded. "The Gripus left thousands of cycles ago, but a few of them remained stranded on this planet." He cast her a side glance. "The blue and red people you saw came to this planet long after that. They were left behind when all the space visitors fled before the cataclysmic alignment, over two decades ago."

"Why did they leave?" Could the space faring people be cowards? "Couldn't they have waited a few weeks in space?"

Bayor shook his head. "They expected the destruction to be complete. They did not believe the planet would remain livable afterwards... so they returned home."

"But many of us survived, and the planet is stable again... now we can rebuild." Anila took a deep breath of fresh air. "Do you think these celestial visitors might want to come back, now that it is safe?"

"Some of them might... others might not." The black stallion balked and reared when a snake crossed the road in front of his hooves.

Stardust jumped back with a squeaky cry.

"Easy, Thunder." Bayor kept his balance and restrained his mount with great skill.

Anila chuckled. "Don't worry. They are more afraid of you than you are of them."

Anila's mare remained calm. Raised in the village at the foot of the monastery, she was accustomed to the desert creatures. As for Cottonball, he barely opened one eye from his nap. "What else do you know about the winged men?"

"Interestingly enough, that race is only male." Bayor cast her a side glance, as if expecting a question.

"Only male?" Curiosity got the best of Anila. "How do they reproduce?"

"Their all-powerful Great Mother lays the eggs. But the nature of the Great Mother and the fertilization process are a total mystery. She is not born from an egg like the males."

"Eggs? Like birds? Strange..." Anila wanted to know more. "What else do you know about them?"

"Although very advanced and knowledgeable, the Gripus were not liked when they reigned supreme. They oppressed the local population, who revolted against them. That is why they had to leave, and their sojourn on this planet was erased from the records." He sighed. "Only a few statues and temples survived the purge."

"So, could this mean that Zaal might be evil? Like the ancient Gripus?" Anila still didn't trust him, although she couldn't explain why.

"Zaal is the exception." Bayor smiled and his green eyes sparkled. "When I was very young, I was attacked by a tiger."

Anila held her breath. "A tiger?"

"Zaal forced the tiger back with his scimitar, flapping his wings to scare him back." Strong emotions nuanced Bayor's voice. "Then he snatched me and carried me up in the air, back to my home. He saved my life."

"Where were your parents when this happened?" Leaving a young child alone so close to dangerous wild life seemed irresponsible.

"My parents had just died a few days earlier, when their mounts were spooked and they fell off a high cliff." Bayor's face froze as he seemed to remember the loss.

"I'm sorry about your parents." Of course, Anila never had any, so she could only imagine his pain.

"So, with no one else to educate me, since Zaal possessed ancient wisdom and knowledge, he remained at my side for protection, and became my surrogate parent, my only teacher and mentor." Bayor glanced down and sighed. "Now, he is my trusted aide, informant, and Commander in charge of the horde when my duties call me away from the camp."

"That's a lot of responsibilities." Anila gazed around at the desert. This was all she had ever known, but there was an entirely different world out there, beyond the sea of sand. "What was it like, growing up in the north?"

"We call it the top of the world, but the pole is completely frozen. Only a few bears and small prey live there." He turned in the saddle and a wide smile lit up his face. "We prefer the mountains and the rolling grasslands where we move the herds and flocks to different pastures, according to the seasons."

"Raised in the desert, it's difficult for me to imagine vast expanses of grass." Although, Anila did remember the meadows below Prince Altan's fortress.

"As a child, in spring and summer, I rode through the plains under the big blue sky with total abandon." His green eyes sparkled at the memory. "In winter, when everything is frozen, we stable the small flocks and let the herds migrate south. And we remain inside by the fire. But in the spring and fall, sometimes I enjoyed just standing in the pouring rain."

"Rain... I wonder what it feels like." Anila couldn't imagine a downpour, although she'd read vivid descriptions.

His deep green gaze searched her face. "I could take you with me and show you all those things."

Anila realized she wanted to go with him. But what about her duty to the monastery? Could she renounce the goal she'd been seeking her entire life... especially when she was so close to achieving it?

Bayor turned his gaze ahead, toward the sand road. "We also have forests, lakes, and rivers, where hunters and fishermen find an abundance of prey and fish."

"You kill a lot of animals for food." She shuddered at the thought.

"We have to in order to survive." His face turned serious. "We cultivate what we can, but we move a lot, and nothing grows except grass on the steppes."

Again, Anila realized how small and limited her monastic life had been. She remembered Bayor's acrobatics of the night before and the feats of his warriors in the saddle. "Will you teach me to shoot a bow while riding?"

"Sure." He chuckled. "Given your familiarity with the Chi, you will master it in no time."

"And will you teach me to swing the scimitar?" She hoped he would agree.

He laughed. "And what else? How to throw knives? Axes? Spears?"

"That would be great." Excitement bubbled inside her.

"When we stop for the night, I will start teaching you." He shook his head. "I'm sure you will excel at all of them."

Anila glanced back at the Protectors riding behind them. They remained watchful and quiet as always, but she knew they noticed everything. She let her mind drag behind her to sense their mood. To her surprise, they viewed her curiosity about other martial arts favorably. Good.

She was glad Bayor treated her as an equal, although, sometimes, she wished he was more than a friend. Somehow, she

trusted him, and she hoped he trusted her as
well.

* * *

Envoy Zaal waved at the barbarian
warrior standing guard in front of the metal
gate leading to the vast prison complex
under Prince Altan's castle. "Open the gate."

"Of course, Commander." The guard half
bowed and opened the gate.

"Give me the key and tell the other
guards to return to camp and prepare their
mounts for a long ride." Zaal noticed the
surprise in the guard's eyes. "We are leaving
camp tomorrow."

"Where are we going, Commander?"
The guard handed him the key.

Zaal snatched the key. "You'll know like
everyone else when I announce it to the
horde. For now, just do what I tell you."

"Yes, Commander." The guard turned on
his heel and marched away.

Zaal walked along the corridor and
stopped in front of a small cell. "General
Torino!" Zaal forced a jovial tone. "How did
your soldiers enjoy the food last night?"

The short general straightened but his
eyes wandered furtively. "To tell the truth, I
didn't have any. I wasn't certain it was safe
to eat. From what I heard, the barbarians
wouldn't be above poisoning an entire army.
But the men took a chance and liked it fine.

Surprisingly they woke up and are feeling good this morning."

"Great. I'm glad they are in a good disposition." Zaal reminded himself to smile. Humans trusted a friendly smile.

"Then again, you don't look like a barbarian." General Torino squinted at him. "And you don't dress like them either... except for that wicked sword."

"I am not a barbarian!" The statement came too strong. Zaal controlled himself. "My blade is a scimitar. I have information and a proposition for you and your men, and instructions coming directly from Prince Altan."

"Prince Altan? Why would he speak to you?" The general's face turned pink with excitement. "Where is he?"

"Your prince is safe in his underground escape room." Zaal let the words sink in. "He made a pact with my people."

"Your people?" Suspicion again tensed General Torino's dark face. "What kind of pact?"

"In exchange for our support to his rule, we made an alliance." Zaal chose his words carefully. "You are to march with your army upon the Temple of the Celestial Gate."

"Finally, some action!" General Torino seemed happy about it.

Zaal measured his words. "You will depart one day behind the barbarian horde, who is leaving tomorrow to attack the Temple as well."

"Both armies against the Protectors?" The short general squinted at Zaal. "And why should I believe you?"

"I have the key." Zaal exhibited the heavy key he borrowed from the jailer and turned it slowly in the air. "I will open all the cells immediately. The barbarian guards are leaving the fortress. You have two days to organize and arm your troops. You leave on the second sunrise."

"You are freeing us right now?" Incredulity rounded the general's dark eyes.

"Immediately." Zaal managed a smooth smiled. "This is your chance to please your Prince. He will join you shortly. When Prince Altan becomes emperor, you will be in charge of the most powerful army in all the land."

"What about the Protectors who came to the castle?" That worried tone again.

"They are gone, on their way back to the Temple." How Zaal enjoyed manipulating simple humans.

"Good." Torino sighed with relief. "But... you expect us to fight the Protectors in their own fortress?" Torino sounded excited and afraid at the same time.

"Yes, but you won't be alone." Zaal hid his disgust of the petty general. "The barbarian hordes will attack ahead of you. They'll do the hard work, and you'll reap the benefits of victory."

"In that case, open the gates. You have my full cooperation." Torino smiled with missing teeth... the vagaries of human warfare.

"You are making the right decision, General." Zaal opened Torino's cell then handed him the key.

Soon, all the gates to the large and smaller cells were open. The soldiers, as well as other prisoners in civilian clothing, came out, surprise on their faces. The group marched out, on their way to the castle esplanade.

Zaal walked ahead of them, making sure no barbarian warriors lingered inside the walls. None remained. Good. The horde warriors took his order as if it came from their Khan. This augured well for his plan.

On the esplanade, the news of the new campaign was travelling fast. The soldiers took it with enthusiasm, but Zaal detected some uneasiness among the fresh recruits.

He couldn't resist asking one of them. "Why are you not glad to be free?"

"Free?" The young man spat on the ground. "Prince Altan took us from our homes, our villages, our families. Now we have to fight the Protectors for him? They are invincible. He is sending us to our death."

"Why are you afraid of them?" Zaal couldn't understand why everyone seemed to fear the monks.

"They use magic. They can't be defeated." The young man's eyes rounded in pure fright. "They will kill us all with one thought. They use the Chi."

"The Chi?" Zaal snorted. "You have been fooled. There is no such thing as the Chi."

"Yes, there is," another new recruit insisted. "We have seen it in action. It's powerful. No one can win against them."

General Torino approached the small group. "What kind of talk is that? Your words are those of a coward. I could have you court-martialed for sedition and put to death, soldier!"

The young recruit stepped back and stared at his feet. "Sorry, General."

Torino nodded to Zaal then returned his attention to the young man. "You are lucky we need all hands on deck for this campaign."

"Yes, we do." But Zaal had the nagging feeling that these fresh recruits might create trouble. They seemed convinced that the Protectors couldn't be defeated, due to some unholy power. Ridiculous.

Zaal left the group and climbed the steps to the rampart. Once out of sight of Altan's people, he flew away, in the direction of the camp. He hoped Bayor's lieutenants and chieftains would be as easy to manipulate as Torino and his soldiers.

* * *

In the Command tent, Zaal sat in Bayor's chair. After stating his orders, he stared at the faces of the lieutenants and tribal chiefs. "I understand your hesitation to take the entire horde across the desert. But new information indicates that our beloved Bayor Khan is in great danger from the Temple. He is walking into a trap, and we must go to his rescue."

"What information? How did you get it?" The female warrior squinted at Zaal.

Zaal couldn't let a puny female lieutenant question him in front of the others. "I have my ways... let's say the Temple of the Celestial Gate has fallen under the influence of another feudal lord, who wants to eliminate the competition for the crown to rule all the land."

"What feudal lord?" The woman wouldn't quit.

"Does it matter?" Zaal noticed the lieutenants squirming uncomfortably on their stools.

The chieftains glanced at each other. The large birds standing on some shoulders ruffled their feathers and blinked, shifting from talon to talon. Zaal couldn't afford to lose control.

He rose and made his voice menacing. "Do you contest the word of your Commander?"

Lieutenants bit their lips, and chieftains cast side glances at each other.

The insolent female straightened her back and sustained Zaal's gaze. "Sending the entire horde across the desert when Bayor

Khan specifically told us not to do it, is suspicious at best. Besides, it constitutes a major disobedience. It's also detrimental to the health and the wellbeing of the horde. I want to make sure we are doing it for good reasons."

Zaal couldn't let the horde turn against him. The natives of this planet had cast away his kind long ago. "I am Commander of this horde, and I only have Bayor's interest at heart. Anyone knows that. If I say his life is in danger and we must go help him, we must. If anyone else doubts my word or my motives, speak now."

The female lieutenant glanced around the circle. "My objection stands."

"Anyone else?" Zaal walked slowly outside the circle of lieutenants and chieftains. "What would Bayor Khan do to a traitor who refuses to obey a direct order?"

"The code says the penalty is instant death," another lieutenant whispered. "But Bayor Khan would never do it."

"Yes, he would. And so will I." Zaal swung his scimitar in one smooth stroke that decapitated the rebellious female lieutenant where she stood. A geyser of red blood spurted, then the head flopped on the rug.

A gasp filled the tent, then silence. Fear widened the eyes of the high-ranking men and women. Would they attack him? No. Too much doubt on their faces.

"Let this be an example." Zaal stared down the lieutenants one at a time. "Any other objection?"

No one dared protest. Good. "At dawn, our entire force will leave the camp and start across the desert with minimum provisions. Workers, craftsmen, and animals will remain behind for when we return victorious."

"Yes, Commander." Lieutenants and chieftains nodded and rose, then left Bayor's tent in silence.

Zaal didn't trust them. He would spend the night on a high perch, hidden, to observe any clandestine activities, safe from their traitorous blades.

Chapter 12

Anila glanced up when a golden eagle shrieked overhead, circling in the blue sky… not a native bird but a horde hunter. She truly enjoyed riding the white mare in the cool desert breeze, among the scent of dry sage. With Cottonball curled up on her saddle, Bayor riding at her side, and the she-wolf keeping the pace of the steeds, she experienced a sense of belonging… like being part of a family.

Of course, the dozen Protectors riding behind her, silent but always present, reminded her the desert was her home. She belonged here with them… although she didn't feel so connected to the Protectors anymore. She had come to think of the barbarians as her favorite tribe. She felt guilty about it. By following her heart, was she unfaithful to Master Wang and the Protectors?

At a small junction in the sand road, Bayor raised one arm and halted his black stallion. "We go left."

Anila considered the narrow, secondary path that might lead to an isolated oasis, but she couldn't hide her surprise. "On the way

North, Prince Altan's caravan kept to the main road."

Bayor nodded. "This shortcut will get us there faster."

"Really?" Anila wondered how he'd learned about this minor road. He seemed to know much about the desert... for someone who'd never been there.

"This trail also avoids the caravanserai. We do not need supplies, nor do we want to trade." Bayor grinned. "The citizens there might also be spooked at the sight of my warriors."

"I imagine they would be." Anila remembered the unspoken fear in the people's eyes at the mention of the barbarians. Even though they'd washed away the face paint, Bayor and his warriors still looked fearsome. "The stories circulating about the horde are horrifying."

"I know." Bayor cast her a side glance. "I'm the one who ordered Zaal to spread those rumors, so the civilians would run away and hide as we advanced. If they didn't resist, we wouldn't have to kill them."

Strange strategy, but nothing about Bayor was what Anila expected from a barbarian. He could be frightening and kind at the same time. He lied to avoid bloodshed. He knew the world and how to influence it, but he did it with love, to build a kinder society.

That night, like the night before, they camped under the stars. No tents, just a wide circle with sentinels atop the dunes, watching to keep the steeds safe from predators. Used to the nomadic life, the barbarians seemed very efficient and organized, quick to build fires and cook.

Anila had also noticed how quickly they'd cleaned up the camp site in the morning, leaving no trace of their passage. The Protectors, while remaining silent, had observed and copied their techniques.

The barbarians also observed and imitated the Protectors, who scrubbed their hands with sand before touching the food. Anila found it refreshing that such warriors from different cultures could set aside their ego and learn from each-other. It gave her hope. The strongest people were those who could adapt.

Before darkness spread, Anila joined the barbarians in their daily weapons practice. Stardust followed the practice up close, while Cottonball observed from a distance, comfortably curled up atop the supply cart.

When it came to throwing knives, axes and even spears on a board propped against the supply cart, Cottonball jumped out of the way. But Anila never missed the target, surprising the horde warriors.

Bayor seemed proud of her. "You excel at all our favorite disciplines."

"Thank you." The compliment warmed her inside. "Also thank you for teaching me how to take good care of the mare."

Anila has never shot arrows from the saddle, but after observing the barbarians, she couldn't wait to try. After a few misses, due to the movement of the mare, she quickly found her balance, remaining level in the saddle even at a full gallop.

Bayor, who had observed her with keen interest, brought his stallion closer to her mare. "You are doing well. Maybe, it's time to learn the scimitar technique."

Anila tingled all over at the idea. "Definitely. I'd like that."

"First, you ride forward in my saddle, so I can guide your arm and make you feel the movement, rather than explain it." His green eyes never wavered.

Heat rose up Anila's throat when Bayor lifted her atop his stallion. Her cheeks burned at the full contact of his body against her back. He was so close... He smelled of sage and spices.

Then he braced her waist with his left arm, gave her the scimitar and prompted the stallion. When he took her sword hand in his, swinging the blade with her, her heart beat faster as they moved as one. She could feel the flick of his wrist, the turn of his waist, and the full arc of the strike. The scimitar sliced down on each side of the galloping stallion, and with each strike, Anila felt warm all over.

She wanted this journey to last forever. She couldn't wait to learn more from Bayor each day.

The Protectors retired to meditate after the evening meal as usual, while the barbarians brought out the gourd of strong tika. But Anila stayed with Bayor as the warriors drank, sang, and danced around the fire.

One night, after the merrymaking abated, Bayor looked up from petting Stardust and gazed into Anila's soul. "I know the Protectors are celibate, but did you ever think of having a relationship... maybe when you were younger?"

Anila felt the heat rising to her cheeks again. She never had to answer that kind of question before. How embarrassing... but she would never lie. "Once, as a teenager, I had a crush on a young Acolyte."

"Are you even allowed to have relationships in the monastery?" His smile accentuated the teasing tone.

"Relationships are not forbidden to Acolytes, but they can be a distraction and get in the way of their progress." It had proven true for Anila. She could still feel the shame.

Bayor leaned back against the chariot wheel, hands under his head. "What would a romantic relationship even look like in such a place?"

Anila hesitated. His deeply personal question stirred something in her soul. She lowered her voice. "It was mainly stolen moments of private conversations between practice sessions. Then once, on Festival night, we kissed under the stars." Anila gazed up into Bayor's green eyes and the warm feeling came upon her again. "It was a long time ago."

"What happened next?" His tone turned inquisitive.

But only the truth could set her free, so she wouldn't shy away from it. "I was sad when the young man decided to leave the monastery. He asked me to leave with him, but I wanted to become a Protector more than I wanted this relationship. After his departure, I felt miserable for a while, but I was also glad to refocus on my training and follow my true path."

"And now? Do you still want to become a Protector?" His green gaze searched her face.

Anila froze. "Truth be told, I'm not sure anymore."

The realization was troubling. Was this strong yearning for Bayor just to test her sense of duty? Should she follow the sacred path, or trust her feelings?

* * *

At the end of the next day, Bayor slowed Thunder and shaded his eyes to stare in the distance, at the forbidding promontory... an oblong ridge rising among the sea of dunes. Atop its flat crest, the Temple of the Celestial Gate looked more like a stronghold than a holy place. The ancient fortress at the top of a high cliff featured two monumental pillars at one end, visible from many miles... the famous gate... a marvel of space engineering in a world still in its metallurgic infancy.

"Not what you expected?" Anila broke his train of thought. "I know it looks austere from faraway, but my happiest childhood memories reside in this place."

"I can't imagine spending my entire childhood at the top of that rock." As a child, Bayor would have found it constricting. "I spent my youth riding across the plains, enjoying the wind in my hair."

"I probably would have enjoyed that, too." Anila's amber eyes turned dreamy as she stared upon the fortress. "But I didn't get to choose. Still, I like the peace of monastic life, the physical training, studying the many scrolls in the vast library, and I love this place and all the people and the creatures in it... especially the cats." She petted Cottonball on her saddle, and when she raised her gaze upon him, her eyes sparkled in the reddish sunshine.

Such a wild, natural beauty... with a pure soul. Bayor hoped she wanted him as much as he wanted her. She would make a magnificent queen.

"So, is Master Wang well loved, then?" Bayor didn't expect that, judging by the stern behavior of the Protectors.

"Of course. Everyone loves him." She seemed shocked that anyone would doubt it.

"What kind of man is he?" Bayor should have asked that question days ago... but he was distracted by her captivating personality. She was always on his mind. Together they could rule an empire and start a new dynasty of Immortals. After he obtained the Celestial Gem, Bayor would ask Master Wang permission to propose to her.

"Master Wang has Immortal blood for sure. How much? No one knows, but he is old and can look very young. From what I've seen, I suspect he might be a pure blood."

"Really?" This would facilitate his negotiations with the master.

"Master Wang is very knowledgeable and powerful. But he is also kind and compassionate, a good teacher, and the only father figure I've ever known." The admiration and love in her voice said a lot about the man who earned such praises.

"I can't wait to meet him." Bayor smiled inside. He'd made the right call coming as a friend. He felt good about this. Obtaining the Celestial Gem from Master Wang might prove easier than expected.

The sun was descending toward the horizon when the small group reached the village at the base of the rocky promontory. Bayor must hurry. He turned to his warriors. "You will remain below with the steeds and the chariot. Anila and I will climb to the Temple with the Protectors."

The barbarians acknowledged his orders with fake grunts and true smiles. Of course, they'd rather sing, dance, and drink around their camp fire, than follow the stuffy rules and meditative silence of a holy place. But Bayor would welcome the peaceful experience. His soul needed some quiet. He had important decisions to make.

In the reddish light of the evening sun, Bayor and Anila climbed on foot, accompanied by Stardust and Cottonball. They followed the twelve Protectors up the cliff, along the steep trail, toward the fortress that housed the Temple complex.

Bayor couldn't help but admire the strategic aspect of the location. Any army trying to come up the rock could be defeated from above with arrows, throwing down boulders, explosive jars, fire... It was safe from ground attack.

Anila seemed more excited with each step. Her amber eyes gleamed in the sunset. Cottonball jumped out of her arms and ran ahead, leaping from rock to rock, obviously happy to be home. As for Stardust, the she-wolf seemed perfectly at ease among the gray rocks, and even blended with their dusty color.

For warriors in the prime of their shape, it didn't take long to reach the top. Then the Protectors glided inside the courtyard and vanished among the shadows of narrow alleys between stone buildings. So did Cottonball. But Stardust, who'd rushed ahead, now sat in the middle of the courtyard, waiting for him.

Anila hurried through the gate then stopped and turned back to him as well, all smiles, excitement filling her lovely face. "Come meet Master Wang."

Then she seemed to realize where she was, took a slow breath, and sedately turned around and walked across the courtyard, in the direction of the Temple.

Bayor stepped between the two gigantic pillars of the Celestial Gate and halted, his heart pounding. He closed his eyes, savoring the moment with awe. He could feel the strong Chi of the place. The powerful vibration harmonized with the energy powering the entire universe. This was the place where his ancestors had entered this world.

Although born on this small planet, Bayor had learned from his family scrolls that he was a pure Immortal, a child of the greater universe. And the Celestial Gate was his only hope ever to see the world his parents came from and meet his extended family. Tears escaped his eyes. His best friend on this planet had been Zaal... but he wasn't family, never warm, never loving, and lately he'd become enigmatic, and even defiant.

But the scrolls said Bayor's destiny was to rule the entire planet, and for that, he needed to acquire the Celestial Gem. This symbol would legitimize his claim to power, and give him control over other rulers, as well as access to the Celestial Gate. With

Anila at his side, he would start a new dynasty.

Bayor opened his eyes. At the top of the stairs on the terrace in front of the Temple, stood a tall man in white robes. His wide aura flared blue as he watched the newcomers. Bayor followed Anila across the courtyard toward him in the fading daylight. The holy man's youthful appearance and luminous aura marked him as a pure Immortal... and a very strong one at that.

Anila's blue aura also glowed brightly, like the pure Immortal he already knew she was. He sincerely hoped she would agree to be his queen.

Would Master Wang see him favorably? Or would he contest his claim to the gem? Would he agree to let Anila go? Time for Bayor to realize his destiny and take his rightful place among his peers.

* * *

In the last ray of twilight, Wang watched Anila and the visitor coming toward him across the courtyard... a barbarian, judging by his leather gear, black hair gathered on top, and his scimitar... although his face was clean of war paint. It could only be the famous Bayor Khan the Protectors informed him about in their last message... a lethal warrior with a kind heart and a strong spirit... who seemed to have enchanted Anila.

Despite her monastic garb and the dark Protector cloak, she looked different. Judging by her radiant aura and the happy bounce in her steps, Anila truly enjoyed the man's company.

As for the barbarian Khan, his bright aura not only marked him as a strong Immortal, but a definite pure blood. He also exuded truth and compassion, with a fierce and loyal she-wolf loping at his side. What a refreshing sight! But was he strong enough?

When they reached the top of the wide stairs and stopped, Wang saluted and bowed. "Welcome back home, Anila." He turned and bowed to the young man. "Bayor Khan, ruler of the barbarian hordes, welcome to our humble monastery."

"Master Wang..." The barbarian returned the salute. He was tall. His green gaze, deep and serene, indicated wisdom beyond his years... but according to the Protectors, he also had rogue tendencies. Definitely not an acetic monk. "It's an honor to finally meet you, Master Wang."

"The honor is mine, Bayor Khan." Wang smiled. "We need to speak in private."

"Yes, we do, Master Wang." The barbarian seemed eager.

Anila saluted both men. "Bayor, Master Wang, if you don't mind, I will go to the dorm and clean up before dinner."

"Good." Wang dismissed her with a wave of the hand.

The young woman flashed a smile at the barbarian, then turned around and hurried down the steps and out of the courtyard as Bayor's gaze followed her retreating back with longing. The great wolf did the same. Did both of them miss Anila? Interesting.

Wang sighed. Was this a good sign or a bad one? "Follow me. I assume you came for an important reason." He led the way inside the Temple, hoping the young man would be worthy. "I've heard good things about you."

"You have?" Bayor sounded amused. "So, the Protectors are spying for you and remain in constant contact... How?"

"Never mind." Wang led the way through the dimly lit Temple, where the scent of incense wafted. "It's part of their job."

"What is their job?" The young man's curiosity had no bounds.

Wang glided past the meditation rug, toward a low table and two small stools. "The Protectors' mandate is to protect the Celestial Gate. This also means detecting threats, being informed, and prepared."

"I understand." The young barbarian sounded self-assured. "Like every capable ruler, I also use informants."

Wang nodded. "And I understand that you are not above spreading false rumors."

"It's part of the job." The young man chuckled. He had a strong jaw. "You seem to know a lot about me."

"I know why you are here." Wang indicated the low table and stools. "But you are not the first one to claim the Celestial Gem."

"Prince Altan claimed the gem, didn't he?" Bayor laughed. "When I invaded his fortress by surprise, he fled like a coward." He sighed. "Good thing, too. His soldiers surrendered, and I didn't have to kill them."

"Actually, Prince Altan didn't seem to know about the gem when he came here." Wang sat and motioned for Bayor to sit facing him.

"Really?" The young man sat down with uncommon grace. No fear, no doubt, no shame or regret marred his aura. In the light of the oil lamps, he looked even younger. The great she-wolf lay down at his feet.

Wang adjusted his white robes around his legs. "I can tell you are a pure Immortal, but from what family exactly?"

The young Khan reached inside the fold of his tunic and pulled out a medallion that was resting on his chest. A jade medallion with a Yin-Yang symbol engraved upon it. He ducked under the string and handed the stone to Wang. "I have seen the same design on a different stone, worn by Anila."

Wang took the round jade and examined it. "Yes, it is the same design." He caressed the medallion, and his fingers tingled with its power. It was genuine. "I thought your family was extinguished in the great cataclysm."

"My parents survived the cataclysm, but they died in a horrible accident shortly after, when I was very young. A few cycles later, I discovered hidden scrolls explaining who they were and what I was." The young man took a calming breath. "The scrolls also talked about my destiny to rule this planet."

Wang hid his surprise. This could change everything. "So, you've been preparing for it."

"I followed the teachings of the scrolls. I meditated and trained in the Chi, but I had to do it in secret." Some regrets altered the young man's voice... and weakened his aura.

"Why in secret?" Wang knew secrets could be dangerous.

"Well..." The young man stroked his smooth chin. "My mentor, teacher, and father figure, says the Chi is nonsense and illusion."

"That is unfortunate." And potentially dangerous, too. This young man had to overcome many obstacles.

"Unfortunate, yes." The young Khan nodded. "But my mentor encouraged me to rule and lead my people south, to conquer all the land. He'd heard of the prophecy of the Celestial Gem and advised me to come here and claim it."

"I see. And today you are asking for the Celestial Gem, to consolidate your future rule." But Wang wondered about the mentor's motivations. Many in that position had ambitions of power and greed.

"I'm hoping taking the reins of power is the right thing to do." Bayor Khan shook his head. "There is much iniquity in this land. Some places still practice slavery, others consider women as chattel, and superstitions abound. Ignorance reigns. It is time for this planet to make peace and retake its place in the greater universe."

"I agree." Wang pursed his lips. "But the Celestial Gem is not a magic piece of rock that bestows power."

"Is it space technology?" The young barbarian seemed to know a lot of things.

Wang shook his head and chuckled. "Not exactly. But the Celestial Gem is even more precious... and complex."

"Then what is it, Master Wang?" So much curiosity in the deep green eyes.

"The Celestial Gem is not an it." Wang had never told this secret to a single soul, but now was the right time. "The Celestial Gem is actually a she."

"She?" The barbarian frowned.

"Yes, she... A special Immortal female, genetically engineered to rule this world with wisdom and compassion... She will need the love, support, and protection of another pure Immortal... to safeguard the continuity of the new imperial line."

"Anila?" Bayor's eyes rounded in understanding. "Anila is to become the future ruler? The all-powerful Empress?"

Wang nodded. "Yes... Anila... but she doesn't know who or what she is, or that she is destined to rule this planet. Yet, only she can rule, and only she can choose her Immortal companion.”

* * *

Bayor remained silent, impassible on the surface, in shock at the revelation. Then he closed his eyes to gather his thoughts. This couldn’t be happening. How could he have misread the scrolls? He wanted to wake up from this nightmare.

When he opened his eyes, Master Wang was staring at his aura with the characteristic unfocused gaze. With so many emotions agitating it, Bayor’s aura must be an open book.

Master Wang refocused his gaze and raised one hand in entreaty. “It takes a special man to support a ruling woman without claiming power for himself.”

Bayor took a deep breath. “I have always ruled the hordes, Master Wang. Power and authority always came naturally to me. My people all but worship me.”

“Because you are charismatic, they know you care about their welfare, and you protect them best, because you see what others cannot.” Wang sighed. “Such is the burden of an Immortal.”

“Yes, it is.” Bayor let his shoulders fall. “But I fear the hordes may not accept another ruler, and I may not have the right temperament for what you ask.”

217

"Because you like to rule." Wang nodded. "I know it's a lot to ask."

"Yes." Bayor felt a great void inside, a great sadness.

"I feel no anger or resentment from you." Master Wang took a deep breath. "Would it help if I told you your pendant is the proof that you and Anila were destined for each other in the original plans for this planet?"

"Because both pendants have the same design?" Bayor shook his head. "The Yin-Yang is a common symbol among Immortals."

"Yes. But if you look closely, you'll notice the subtle indentations of the edge." Wang trailed his finger on the rim, then handed him the jade medallion. "Your two pendants were made to interlock together."

Bayor felt empty, defeated. "If Anila is the supreme Empress, I will have to renounce my claim to the imperial throne and submit to her rule as her vassal."

"Yes... I'm afraid you will have to." Master Wang's blue stare never wavered.

"Thank you, Master, for trusting me with this secret." Bayor let go of all his hopes in a deep sigh. "But although I love Anila with all my heart, and I want her to be safe and happy, I'm not certain I am the right man for this task."

Wang smiled. "I understand it's a lot to take in, and you are tired from the journey. Take your time, young man. Think about it.

You are welcome to spend the night as my guest. We'll talk again in the morning."

"Thank you, Master Wang." Bayor bowed from his sitting position and saluted. "But I wish to rejoin my warriors in the village for the night."

Stardust, lying at his side, straightened her ears. Bayor gave her a scratch on the back of the head, and they rose together.

"Be careful on the way down." Master Wang stood up from his stool. "The steep trail to the village is treacherous at night."

"That's all right." Bayor didn't care about the dangerous climb. He needed space to think. "There is a half-moon in a cloudless sky, and Stardust can see well enough for two. I need to eat and sleep with my warriors tonight."

"I understand." Wang nodded. "I hope you make the right decision."

Bayor bowed again. "Thank you, Master Wang, for your time and your trust. I shall return in the morning."

* * *

Wang watched the man and the great wolf walk away, out of the Temple and into the night and shuddered. He liked Bayor. But as he tried to foresee the possible futures, a dark cloud covered his mind. Something wasn't right. He could sense trouble and danger coming his way, but from where?

He signaled to the Protector standing at the back door like a shadow holding a spear.

The shadow glided toward him and took a knee. "Master?"

"Have a Protector team physically man the gate at night until further notice. I want all the Protectors in full alert. I feel grave danger coming our way."

"Understood, Master Wang. Full alert." The shadow glided away in total silence.

Wang hoped he was wrong as he feared the worst.

Chapter 13

That night, Anila couldn't find sleep. She should be happy to be home, to return to her training and her peaceful routine... but something was missing. Her quiet monastic life now seemed dull. Even the food tasted bland.

She turned on her thin mattress but couldn't help thinking about Bayor. She missed him. She couldn't wait to see him again and hoped she would have the chance to at least say goodbye.

She dreamed of riding beside him in tall grasses with wind and rain on her face, sharing new adventures on the green plains and across rolling hills, his strong, honest face and his deep green eyes scrutinizing her intently.

In her restless sleep, as she tossed and turned, a black cloud hovered over her mind. Then, the cloud was flying with swift black wings and shooting lightning bolts that set the monastery on fire. She could hear distress calls from children but was unable to help them.

She started awake in a cold sweat. Silent darkness reigned. Dawn came later these days. Everything seemed calm and serene all around, but if she went back to sleep, the nightmare might return. So, she rose silently and left the dorm to seek solace in her Tai-Chi form.

Standing atop the great wall, she scanned the dark sky. As always, the desert night twinkled with friendly stars... no menacing cloud with wings. Maybe the nightmare was just a bad dream.

She inhaled the cool air scented with sage and became one with her surroundings. The fragrance of spiced tea wafted in the air. Kitchen duties started long before dawn. The birds in the Banyan tree were still asleep. Only night creatures chirped in the desert.

Anila relaxed her muscles and softened her knees. Making herself heavy, she rooted her bare feet to the stone and sank into the form, letting the strong energy of the place flow through her and guide her movements as she gathered and shaped the Chi. She always found peace in the slow, meditative motions.

A hot pinpoint sensation pricked Anila on the back of the neck. Someone was watching her. She closed the form and turned around, overlooking the courtyard. There, in the darkness preceding dawn, she recognized the powerful silhouette of Bayor, with Master Wang, Stardust, and Cottonball, observing her intently.

"Bayor!" Her heart skipped a beat. She felt warm all over despite the chill.

Was he leaving already? She hoped not. She hurried down the narrow steps lining the wall and ran toward him. Then, remembering where she was, she slowed her breathing and her pace. When she reached the small group, she saluted. "Master Wang... Bayor. Isn't it early, even for you?"

"Come to the Temple, Anila. We have to talk." Master Wang sounded very serious and motioned for her and Bayor to follow him.

Stardust and Cottonball loped alongside them, like inseparable friends.

Anila found Master Wang's cloak-and-dagger attitude rather peculiar. She cast side glances at Bayor, but he avoided eye contact. He looked somber and stared straight ahead. Nothing remained of his former sunny disposition.

She unfocused her eyes to see his aura. Not as bright as before. He was troubled, confused, unhappy.

Did Master Wang refuse to give him the Celestial Gem? Why would he refuse? Weren't Bayor's goals noble and legitimate? Anila thought he would make a perfect emperor, just, kind, and fierce to protect his people.

Master Wang entered the Temple, dimly lit by wavering oil lamps, and led them to the meditation rug. "Sit."

They sat in a small circle, including Stardust and Cottonball. Both cat and she-wolf remained calm and silent, as if respectful of the place.

Anila couldn't wait. "Master Wang, is something wrong?"

The master took a slow breath and his blue gaze rested upon Anila and Bayor. "I fear we are facing great danger... soon."

"What danger? Prince Altan was defeated." Yet, Anila had a scary dream... but her dreams didn't always manifest in the real world.

"It may not be Prince Altan..." Master Wang stared down at the rug. "But something is threatening us. I'm not sure what it is. It seems my ability to see the future is failing me. I believe the time of the prophecy is upon us."

"The coming of a new ruler who will bring peace and prosperity to this planet?" Anila rejoiced. Bayor would be perfect. Finally, some important change for the better.

When she glanced at Bayor, he looked miserable, avoiding her gaze. Why?

"Yes." Master Wang stared at Anila. He didn't look happy either. "But first things first. There is something you should know about the Celestial Gem."

"What about it?" Anila's heart beat faster at the idea of getting reliable information.

"Bayor knows this." Master Wang glanced at Bayor, then returned his blue gaze to Anila.

She couldn't figure out why both seemed so gloomy.

"The Celestial Gem is not a stone, but a special individual, genetically engineered by Immortals to become the absolute ruler of this planet when the time comes, and start the new imperial line." The master's shoulders dropped.

Anila gasped. Her heart thudded. She had no idea what to do with that revelation. "This is a big secret. Isn't Bayor the future emperor? Why are you telling me?"

"Because this secret pertains to you, Anila. You are the Celestial Gem, entrusted to me before the cataclysm, until you were old enough to rule." No emotion whatsoever on the master's shaved face.

"No." Anila found it difficult to breathe. She didn't want such a responsibility. She wasn't the right person to rule. "It cannot be me."

"But it is you, Anila. You are the Celestial Gem." Master Wang smiled, kindness softening his surprisingly youthful face. "Your medallion is the DNA seal proving you are the future ruler of this world."

Anila's heart raced as she glanced at her red jasper medallion, then stared at the Yin-Yang symbol carved upon it. "This?"

Bayor dug inside his tunic and pulled out a similar medallion, but carved in jade. "I have one, too, although I am only the heir to an old Immortal family, not specifically bred to rule."

"But I don't want to rule." Power and politics never appealed to her. And despite having enjoyed her youth in the monastery, Anila realized she was not really fit for ascetic life either. She found this revelation confusing. "Master Wang, what does this mean?"

"It means you are destined to be the ruling empress over the entire planet, and Bayor was destined, a long time ago, to be your consort when you start the new imperial line."

"What? No." Anila resented being ambushed. "I just want my freedom." She wanted to choose her own future. Master Wang had failed her. "You knew this all along? Why didn't you tell me this a long time ago?"

"I didn't want you to feel trapped or be influenced by prophecies and legends." Master Wang sighed. "Besides, I believe destiny can be altered."

"Great! Let's change it, then." If Anila had power and free will, maybe she could decide not to rule at all. "If I have authority, I have the final choice. I can choose to remain free of political obligations. Maybe, Bayor can rule instead of me, yes?"

"It's not that easy, Anila. You are the Celestial Gem, not him." Master Wang glanced down at his hands. "And Bayor declined the offer of being your humble consort while you reign supreme."

Bayor adjusted his sitting position and lowered his gaze, as if he couldn't look into her eyes.

"You refused to be my consort?" Anila gasped, as if stabbed in the chest. "Why? I don't understand."

"I'm so sorry, Anila." His voice caught. He cleared his throat. "The conditions are all wrong. Besides, my warriors are loyal only to me. They will not obey a stranger's orders."

"But we would be great together as a couple." Anila felt as if the ground had opened under her. "You made me feel things I never felt before. With you, I can be myself without reserve. I could see myself as your life mate."

"I, too, enjoy your company immensely, Anila. I do care for you... a lot..." The pain in his green eyes was difficult to watch. "But you must understand that I am and will always be a ruler, not a follower... not a consort."

A sneaky feeling snaked into Anila's mind like a poisonous vine. "Did you know I was the Celestial Gem when we met? Is that why you were kind to me... to secure your rule?"

"Absolutely not. I thought the gem was a mere relic, a symbol of power." Bayor straightened his frame, and his face hardened. "But as soon as I saw your medallion, I knew you were a pure Immortal. My attraction to you is genuine. You are beautiful and exciting. You make me feel alive, and I considered you the ideal mate for me... while I ruled."

"So, what's the problem?" Were all men that obtuse and complicated?

"It seems you are destined to rule above all, including me, and I cannot be your humble shadow." His face softened as he gazed into her eyes. "Anila, I know myself. I am a ruler and I need to rule, whether it's a horde, a continent, or an entire planet. It's in my nature to protect my people, and that will never change. I would make a poor consort, unhappy, and possibly resentful. It would never work between us under such conditions."

Anila realized no one could ever be happy against one's very nature. She struggled to hold her tears. "I understand."

"Do you? Really?" His shoulders relaxed. He seemed relieved.

"Of course, I do. You have a fierce, independent spirit. You cannot be my obedient mate, just as I could never be Prince Altan's dutiful brood mare." But it broke her heart that they would not have a future together.

"I wish the circumstances were different." His smooth forehead creased in a plea. "Can you forgive me? Please, don't hate me."

"I could never hate you for being truthful." Anila tried to smile, but sadness filled her heart. "You are a very good man, Bayor... and I will be very sad to see you go."

Memories of her former pain when her first crush left the monastery flashed upon her mind. She held back bitter tears. She felt abandoned... again.

"You are both good people." Master Wang took a deep breath. "And as long as Anila is safe, this world stands a chance... But I suspect dark forces are assembling in the shadows. I already alerted the Protectors, and we should prepare for some kind of attack on the monastery."

"An attack?" Anila remembered her nightmare. "Last night I dreamed of a dark cloud with flapping wings, flying over the monastery and raining lightning and fire upon us."

"A black cloud with wings?" Master Wang's face froze.

"Master, what does it mean?" The frightening images surged in Anila's mind again.

"It means... the Gripus are back." Was it fear in Master Wang's eyes?

"The Gripus?" Anila never trusted Zaal.

"The Gripus?" Bayor frowned.

"Yes." Master Wang took a deep breath. "The winged abominations did a lot of damage to this planet once, but they have been gone for millennia."

"Not completely gone." Bayor straightened his frame. "I happen to know one, my mentor, Zaal."

"Your mentor is a Gripus?" Master Wang looked as if he'd been punched in the stomach.

"But..." Bayor seemed at a loss for words. "He told me he was the last of his race on this planet."

"A Gripus is never alone. He always has his clutch brothers helping him." Master Wang rose and paced the meditation rug. "They function like a military unit... and they live for a very long time... as long as they have access to gold."

Anila was mad at Bayor. "I told you not to trust him."

Bayor shrugged. "How was I to know?"

Anila remembered her various night glimpses of strange beings with beaked noses and gold ornaments. She shuddered. "I may have seen one at night flying off the monastery cliff... just before Prince Altan's visit." Anila frowned. "And again, in the desert, at night, convening with Prince Altan... and maybe once more at the Caravanserai, then on Altan's ramparts. Always at night."

Master Wang shook his head. "Wherever there is one, there are always many more. And in the night sky, no one can see them fly."

"My Gripus mentor, Zaal, saved my life as a child. I've always trusted him. He commands the horde in my absence..." Bayor's green eyes rounded at the realization. "But he has been behaving strangely of late."

Anila could not resist. "I never liked him."

"They must be plotting something big." Master Wang rubbed his bare chin.

"How could Zaal fool me my entire life?" Bayor sounded shocked.

"Do not blame yourself, Bayor. You were an innocent child when Zaal gained your trust. The Gripus are skilled at fooling people." Master Wang pursed his lips and took a deep breath. "We must prepare for the worst."

Bayor stared down at his hands. "Zaal wanted me to bring the entire army here. Now, it all makes sense. And with the horde under his command, he could bring my barbarians to bear on this monastery."

"They are probably on their way here right now." Master Wang sighed.

"I should go stop the horde. Tell them to turn back." Bayor looked angry.

"Or not." Master Wang's eyes clouded. "Let them come. The Gripus do not know we guessed their plan. When the horde arrives, you can retake control. They can help us fight the Gripus."

"I approve." Bayor's brow rose. "When do you think the Gripus will strike?"

The master narrowed his blue eyes. "From what I read about them, they like to attack at night, when they can blend with the dark sky."

Anila nodded. "It was night in my nightmare when I saw the attack."

Master Wang straightened. "Prepare the Acolytes for battle, Anila."

"Yes, Master. I'll unlock the chests containing the live blades. We'll also grease the crossbows, gather the arrows, and sharpen swords and spears. Today, we'll practice the bow."

"Good, Anila. Thank you." Master Wang raised one finger. "And fetch the cask of black powder I keep in the cellar. You remember how to pack it in clay jars with a wick, and how to make it explode?"

"Yes, Master Wang." Anila swallowed the lump in her throat. Black powder was dangerous to handle.

"Teach the Acolytes how to do it as well." Master Wang pursed his lips. "The villagers should hide in the caves with their families, so should the youngest students."

"I'll see to it, Master." She bowed. "Anything else?"

Bayor cleared his throat. "I will order my dozen warriors in the village to come up to the fortress. They are the best archers and can help the Protectors in an aerial assault."

"Good." Master Wang nodded. "Coordinate with the Protectors."

"I will." Bayor straightened. "I will also post a watch on the rampart for signs of the horde. They may be days away, but we have the fastest mounts."

Master Wang smiled. "Thank you, Bayor. I appreciate your help."

The morning call of the loud gong rang throughout the compound, making the very stone vibrate underfoot. Soon, the monastery would be buzzing with activity.

Anila rose and saluted both men. "If that's all, may we all be safe in the Chi."

As she turned away from Bayor, her heart ached with regret. What a terrible shame that she could never be with him. In different circumstances, they could have been so happy together.

But great danger threatened the monastery. She must silence her selfish dreams and prepare for battle. Her first duty was to protect her home and the people she loved.

* * *

After a day of preparations, Bayor watched the midnight sky full of stars from the top of the great wall. Stardust at his side emitted soft puppy sounds to be petted, and he obliged her.

Not a single cloud over the desert. All sorts of unfamiliar creatures chirped and sang and howled at the halfmoon. At least, it wouldn't be pitch black if the Gripus attacked tonight. But Bayor knew how difficult it was to see a flying man in the dark... almost impossible... as if they could become invisible.

His dozen horde warriors also watched the skies. They hadn't protested being summoned to the Temple fortress, but he could tell they resented the bland monastic food and the strict rules of silence. However, they did warm up at the prospect of battle, especially alongside the famous Protectors. They considered it a great honor.

He still couldn't process the fact that his traitorous Gripus commander would lead the horde against the Temple of the Celestial Gate. Would Bayor have to fight his own warriors? He hoped not. He loved them like family. What a mess!

He'd been duped by Zaal all these years. How could he have been so blind? What did it say about him as a ruler? Maybe Bayor was meant to be a lowly consort after all, although his warrior pride would never allow it.

Even Anila mistrusted Zaal from the start. And she foresaw the Gripus threat in a dream. Bayor hoped Anila and her friends would not suffer for his mistake.

He noticed the desert creatures had fallen silent. Like the calm before the storm. He motioned to the leader of the Protectors and cupped his ears. "Listen."

The shaved silhouette nodded, and a series of silent signs coursed along the wall, from Protector to Protector.

Was it the horde? Was it the Gripus? Where would the danger come from?

As hard as he squinted into the darkness, Bayor couldn't see anything out of the ordinary... not in the desert, not in the sky. But nature never lied. The stillness said it all. Even Stardust froze, waiting. The enemy was here, but where?

Then a strange vibration filled the air. The stone under him trembled, and a thundering rumble shook the entire complex. It came from inside the courtyard. The two monumental pillars came alive with light. Strange lightning coursed along the written words in an archaic script that seemed to change and rewrite itself over and over.

The gate! The Celestial Gate was opening!

Were the Immortals of legend coming back to help?

The Protectors seemed as surprised as Bayor. All turned toward the opening gate and stared in awe as the fabric of space and time split, and light came through it from another part of the universe.

In a loud flapping of black feathers, an army of winged soldiers poured out of the opening, flying hard and fast, clouding the night sky over the monastery.

"Aim and fire at will!" Bayor and his twelve archers came to bear.

So did the Protectors. Soon, the sky whistled with a thousand arrows. A few Gripus fell from the sky. But the enemy above fired steadily with lightning strikes on the Protectors and on Bayor's archers. The Gripus soldiers surging from the open gate rose above the monastery and blended with the night. Only the lightning flash of their deadly weapons betrayed their position.

* * *

"They are here!" Anila motioned to the Acolytes manning the big drums on the rooftop. "Pound the battle drums!"

How did the Gripus manage to open the gate?

The drums sounded for battle, and the gongs rang, sending coded messages to Protectors and Acolytes all over the compound.

Acolytes came rushing out of the dorms, taking a knee, loosing arrows into the sky. A Gripus fell to the ground, wounded, bleeding pure liquid gold! Then two more landed next to him in a frenzy of wings and black feathers. Acolytes rushed in to fight them with swords, but the Gripus weapons shot constant repetitive fire, like lightning bolts.

"Take cover! Don't sacrifice yourself!" Anila had never seen such deadly weapons. Crouching behind a stone bench, she pulled out of a basket one of the explosive clay pots. Making certain the Acolytes had retreated behind the walls, she lit the wick with an oil lamp and threw the small jar in the corner where the three Gripus had fled.

The loud explosion filled the corner of the yard with fire. The three Gripus flapped their wings to take flight, but their wings erupted into flames, and they fell back down, screaming like wounded eagles and contorting in pain. The smell of burnt feathers and smoke filled the air.

Anila suddenly understood what the horrors of war described in the scrolls truly meant. Experiencing it was horrible. She had never seen such suffering or heard such desperate cries. And the smoke gripped her throat. She found it difficult to breathe. How could she ever be a leader if she lost focus in the middle of carnage? She must calm herself and concentrate.

From the corner of her eye, she spotted Master Wang, running toward the gate, toward the flow of Gripus soldiers pouring out of it. His aura radiated righteous wrath, white with blue rays coming out of it like arrows. Anila had never seen that kind of aura around him before.

As the Gripus became aware of him, they fired their weapons at him, but Master Wang's aura somehow repelled the energy of their weapon fire, and he kept advancing.

As he reached the gate, Master Wang extended his arms, and a white beam of pure energy surged out of his open hands. He was using the Chi as a weapon! Anila saw him strike one pillar with lightning, and the gate suddenly closed. A few Gripus, caught between the pillars as the rift in space closed, were cut in half, their front half plummeting to the blue tile like dead birds.

Then the Gripus in the sky peppered the Temple grounds with merciless fire. Acolytes ran for cover, stone exploded, and trees caught fire. The Protectors, imitating Master Wang, used their Chi to form a protective shield above the complex.

Remembering a long-ago class, Anila focused and joined their collective minds, lending her ability to gather the Chi to their purpose. But soon, the shield collapsed under the constant pummeling of Gripus firebolts.

The battle now raged between the ground and the sky. Archers aimed and released arrows. Gripus shot lightning strikes at those below, and not everyone could escape their deadly fire. Several Gripus landed and fought on the ground, engaging Protectors and Acolytes.

Anila could no longer use her black powder jars, as friends and enemies were fighting everywhere. She engaged the first enemy on the ground. No fear.

She rushed him and grabbed the hand holding the weapon. A slight twist and the Gripus lost his grip. The weapon fell with a soft thud. Before the Gripus could regain his balance, Anila drew her sword and sliced his arm, then she stabbed his heart.

Sickening gold blood poured and pulsed, showering her.

Master Wang summoned light from his fingers to light up the night sky, revealing the enemy above. Good. At least, the archers could see their targets.

As she looked for her next opponent, Anila glanced up and saw Bayor on the wall above with Stardust. A familiar Gripus was hovering close to him... Zaal! And the Gripus aimed a firebolt weapon at Bayor!

Anila seized one of the bows leaning against the wall. In one smooth motion, she grabbed the arrow, notched it, pulled the bowstring, took a deep breath, aimed, and released.

Chapter 14

In the chaos of the night battle atop the great wall, Stardust growled, staring at a spot above and behind Bayor.

He turned around and looked up toward the flapping of wings. The Gripus hovered, weapon aimed at him, a slick firebolt the size of a knife, light and shiny.

Zaal! He'd never seen that look of hatred on his mentor's face before. His trusted friend of so many years had morphed into a coldblooded monster.

"Stardust, hide!" He didn't want her to get hurt.

The she-wolf retreated into the shadows but still stared and growled.

An arrow whistled close. Bayor ducked as the arrow flew past him, aimed at Zaal's chest.

Zaal deflected the projectile with one bare hand and sneered.

"You can do that?" Bayor had underestimated his mentor's skills.

The floating Gripus laughed, and his gold breastplate caught the red glow from the fires below. "Finally, I get to show you who I really am, you puny, arrogant

Immortal. You think you are a such a great warrior, but you are only a mouse facing a tiger."

Bayor's bow and scimitar looked primitive next to Zaal's firebolt. He reached for an arrow on his back.

"Don't even think about it." Zaal slowly raised the barrel of the firebolt to Bayor's head. A tiny blue light blinked on it. "Touching that arrow will bring you instant death."

Bayor froze. He could hear Stardust growl in the shadows and calmed her with his mind. The she-wolf wanted to protect him, but she was no match for Zaal's weapon.

Bayor focused on the Chi to give him strength... like it did for the Protectors, like it did for Master Wang. He slowed his breathing and stilled his mind. Maybe talking would provide a distraction and buy him time. "Why are you doing this?"

"Because I can." No apology, no guilt, no remorse in Zaal's strong voice.

"If you hate my kind so much, why did you save my life all those years ago?" The smoke made it difficult to breathe.

Zaal scoffed. "I didn't do it for you. I only did it to take control of the horde."

Bayor shuddered. Maybe Zaal, in his arrogance, would reveal a weakness. "How did you control the horde? I am their Khan. They obey me, not you."

"There are ways to make them obey." Zaal grinned and smoothed his beard with one hand, the other still aiming his weapon at Bayor. "Did you know I killed your parents?"

"You what?" Bayor couldn't hide his shock at the news. How could anyone be so cruel? "Why?"

"You wouldn't believe how easy it is to spook a mount when you flap large black wings in front of their eyes... it was so much fun watching the stallion and the mare try to regain their footing at the edge of the precipice." Zaal chuckled. "The small rocks dislodged by their hooves fell over the edge, as if joyously drumming their impending demise."

How could he find that joyous? "You are despicable."

"Your parents gripped the reins and tried to control the steeds, but they only made things worse. I flapped my wings some more. The mounts screamed as they lost their footing, and so did your mother when they all fell backwards, pell-mell... all the way down the cliff." Zaal paused and smiled. "The stampede of horned cattle at the bottom of the gorge was not a coincidence either. It was a perfectly orchestrated accident."

Bayor felt stabbed in the heart. Hot anger rose through him, but he remembered the Chi and took a slow breath, exhaling his negativity. His emotions quieted somewhat, but his fingers itched to grab that arrow, while Zaal still held his firebolt steady.

How could anyone be so vicious? Bayor realized the depth of the betrayal. "What did my parents ever do to you?"

"They knew about my kind." Zaal jeered. "They refused my services and said they could never trust a Gripus. That our long-ago reputation was well founded, and no native or Immortal should ever trust us."

Bayor understood his motives but couldn't fathom the cold-blooded malice. "Then you saved me from the tiger."

"Oh, the tiger attack didn't happen by chance either." The dark sheen in Zaal's eyes reflected pure evil. "I lured the tiger to pick up your scent."

"What? Why?" Bayor knew, but still hoped to distract Zaal.

"To become your hero and savior, of course, and secure my place as your trusted mentor." Zaal's evil grin accentuated his hooked nose. "In order to influence and control the future leader of the horde."

Bayor had seen the dark side of humanity but was horrified. "You are the vilest creature I ever met."

"You have seen nothing yet." The suave tone chilled the blood. "I could kill you now, but what would be the fun in that?"

"What do you mean?" Could it get any worse?

Zaal glanced down in the courtyard. Bayor followed his gaze. Anila and the

Protectors were fighting valiantly against fire from the sky, launching arrows and dodging firebolts. Then two Gripus landed next to her, and the battle heated, swords and lances against Gripus weapons. It seemed uneven.

"Yes... Anila." Zaal's voice turned even colder. "Don't get too attached to her... she is spoken for."

"You winged piece of garbage!" Bayor went for the arrow, but when Zaal raised the firebolt at him, he froze. Better stay alive. Anila needed him.

"Don't worry... we'll take good care of your precious Anila." Zaal took off into the night.

Stardust ran to her master, growling fiercely at the dark sky.

Bayor grabbed his arrow and shot. It whistled in the air, but no sound of impact. Gripus were impossible to see or hit in the sky at night.

Bayor must protect Anila. She was the Celestial Gem. Whether the Gripus knew it or not, she could not fall into their hands. He must fight at her side.

"Come on, Stardust." He hurried with the wolf down the great wall stairs toward the courtyard. Arrow ready, he ducked fire strikes from above. He couldn't let these monsters take Anila from him.

Then, as Bayor was running to her help, Zaal dropped down behind Anila and grabbed her shoulder. Sharp claws came out of his fingers and dug into her flesh.

Anila screamed in pain. Blood flowed out of her left shoulder.

Stardust leapt at Zaal, but he shot his weapon, and the she-wolf fell hard to the blue tile, fur on fire, emitting pitiful cries.

Then Zaal flew straight up with his prize and vanished into the night.

"No!" Bayor aimed his arrow but could not shoot blind, for fear of killing Anila. He scanned the night sky to no avail.

Then a loud trumpeting made the stone tremble. A signal? All the winged invaders stopped firing and flew straight up in a flapping of wings. Then they vanished into the night, darkening the moon, like a flock of migrating birds... or a black cloud with wings.

In the eerie silence that followed, Bayor realized he couldn't lose Anila.

But Stardust was badly hurt and cried weakly. He ran to the wolf and knelt. "So sorry, girl. We'll take care of you."

Someone in white robes ran across the courtyard toward him.

Bayor rose to his feet. "Master Wang!"

The master joined him quickly. "They are gone, but they will return. And now they have an army of flying soldiers with formidable weapons."

"Master Wang..." Bayor struggled to calm his mind. "They took Anila. Zaal took Anila."

The master took a slow breath. "Do they know she is the Celestial Gem?"

"How could they?" Bayor tried to think. "Zaal said she was spoken for."

Bayor's twelve warriors came down from the wall to join him in the courtyard. One limped, another held his bleeding flank, another had a burn on his arm... but they'd survived.

Bayor was glad to see them. "We must rescue Anila from these monsters."

Master Wang nodded slowly. "I agree. We cannot let the Celestial Gem fall into the wrong hands... or the prophecy could take a very dark turn for the natives of this planet."

"Do you know where they are going?" Bayor felt at a loss. "How can we find her?"

"There may be a way. They need her, so they will not kill her." Master Wang's blue eyes stared at Bayor. "Right now, we must see to the wounded."

"Right." Bayor glanced at Stardust.

Several Acolytes and a few Protectors had fallen to the deadly firebolt weapons. Curiously, none of the fallen Gripus remained on the ground. The bodies had vanished, leaving only pools of golden blood. Half-burnt feathers and ashes skipped over the blue tile, spreading a nauseating smell. Their brethren must have lifted them away.

Bayor picked up Stardust in his arms. "Where do we take them?"

"Bring the wounded to the Temple. We have medicinal ointments and potions."

Bayor carried Stardust to the Temple and left her in the capable hands of a healer. "How bad is it?"

The healer smiled. "She will be fine."

"Thank you." A weight lifted from Bayor's shoulders, but his tight chest made it difficult to breathe.

Then, by the light of torches and the many fires ignited by the Gripus firebolts, he and his uninjured warriors helped gather the wounded, and unfortunately the dead.

Returning to the courtyard, Bayor spotted Master Wang. "We tended to the living and prepared the dead for cremation."

"Thank you. Bayor, but the funeral ceremonies will have to wait." Master Wang motioned to a Protector. "We must prepare for another attack. The Gripus will return soon. They will try to reopen the gate."

A Protector standing guard atop the wall whistled. When Bayor turned around, the Protector motioned for Bayor to join him.

Bayor rushed up the step to the top. "What is it?"

"Look!" The Protector pointed to the dark horizon, where a black wave unfurled over the moonlit sand dunes.

Bayor recognized the great army approaching at a full gallop. "The horde!"

Bayor rejoiced. Whatever Zaal told his lieutenants to gain control of the horde would never hold against the trust that bound them to their Khan. He knew from comments his lieutenants made over the years that they never liked the Gripus.

Bayor should have listened to them. Now, he must face the horde and reveal the truth... and hope they wouldn't blame his misplaced trust and turn against him.

* * *

Anila came to with a start. As she gasped for air, her shoulder screamed in pain. She looked down and cried out, but no sound came out. She was flying, high in the dark sky, over forests and steep mountains, cold, unable to speak, restrained by tight golden chains. She couldn't see who held her, only feel the firm grip on her shackles.

Many Gripus flew all around her like a black cloud... a cloud with wings... the vision from her nightmare.

The flying Gripus holding her slowed the flapping of his wings as they flew above a large crater, like a well in the rock, deep and wide, surrounded by a cylindrical cliff... from which surged a waterfall, white and misty. The crater was completely invisible from the ground, only seen if one flew over the top of the high plateau. Then the Gripus holding her glided in a wide arc into the black hole, toward the bottom of the vast pit and dropped her.

Anila hit the steep slope rolling down and cried out at the sharp pain, moaning as she reached the very bottom, among broken twigs and pebbles. The faint moonlight didn't reach the depths of the deep crater.

In the darkness, she could barely make out the shadows of large nests and of tall predatory birds tending to them. Not people, not Gripus, but enormous birds the size of a man, with black feathers and the curved beak of predators. She'd never seen the likes of them... not even in the Temple archives.

Where was she? Why did the Gripus take her?

Remembering what Bayor told her about them, she realized she must be in their lair. Bayor... She would never forget the expression on his face when the Gripus snatched her. He deeply cared about her... but he'd rejected her. Although she understood his reasons, she couldn't help but resent him.

The dry stench of dirty feathers nauseated her. As she looked up to the sky, there was no sky, only the sound and the wind of flapping wings filling the upper part of the crater. She remembered her dream, but the winged cloud dissipated as the many Gripus gathered against the inner wall of the crater, hanging upside-down from the cliff like bats.

If she could figure out their next move, maybe she could warn Master Wang. She'd never communicated with him with her mind, but the Protectors did it all the time. She should try.

A large bird approached her, and Anila could only stare at its shadow. The predatory fowl pecked at her chains. They fell off, and Anila could move again, except that the pain in her left shoulder was excruciating, and she couldn't move her left arm. With her right hand, she patted her belt and boots for a weapon, a knife, a sword, an arrow... anything... but she came up empty.

The large bird held the end of her chain in its beak and flew up, then secured the chain to a ring affixed to the rock wall. A sinister metallic click indicated the lock was engaged. Then, Anila realized the other end of the chain was cuffed to her ankle.

There was no way for her to escape... unless she could cut thick metal.

She needed help. Could she send a mental message to Master Wang? To Bayor? Maybe, but she'd been unconscious during the flight, and she had no idea where she was. There were many mountain ranges, north and south of the monastery.

Anila also realized she was light-headed. From battle fatigue? Hunger? Loss of blood? Or maybe it was the rarefied air at this altitude.

Exhausted, cold, stiff, and in great pain, she focused her mind to gather the Chi, but her concentration weakened. Then her strength melted, and her consciousness slipped away.

Bayor hurried his climb down the stiff slope of Temple Rock in the pre-dawn, all the time watching the approach of his great army. The vibration of so many galloping hooves resonated through him. They drove the mounts hard, eliciting a cloud of sand and dust... like a giant wave breaking and unfurling over the land. Falcons and eagles flew above them, and he could hear their strident calls. No wonder their enemies feared the horde.

Soon, Bayor would reach the village below. The despicable traitor had just fled with the Gripus... taking Anila with him... after wounding her. The murderous swine must pay for that outrage, and for his despicable lies and sins.

But if or when he returned, Zaal wouldn't be alone.

Bayor must retake control of the horde before the Gripus attacked again. He only hoped his lieutenants weren't brainwashed or under some kind of mind control. There was much he didn't know about Gripus technology. Anything was possible.

Down in the village, Bayor went to the stables and saddled his stallion. Then he waited on the road, facing the desert. Soon, the vast horde slowed and halted, then they spread over the wide road, partway up the dunes, and dismounted. Bayor rode toward them calmly.

Only four of his lieutenants rode to meet him. The woman in charge of morale wasn't among them.

The oldest lieutenant saluted from the saddle. "My Khan! It is so good to see you alive and unharmed. Are you all right?"

Strange statement. "Why should I be harmed?"

"Zaal told us you were in mortal danger, my Khan, prisoner of Master Wang in the Temple." Even in the predawn, the lieutenant's face looked shocked. "He sent us here to rescue you."

"Zaal lied to all of you. He lied to me as well." Bayor lifted his chin. "Where is my other lieutenant?"

The old man lowered his gaze. "Zaal decapitated her for questioning his word, my Khan."

"Zaal will pay for his treachery." Bayor wanted to shout his anger, but slowed his breathing instead. "Many things have changed. We were attacked by an entire force of winged men with extraordinary weapons. They will return soon. We need to coordinate our efforts with the Protectors."

"Yes, my Khan." The lieutenant cleared his throat. "According to Zaal, General Torino, leading Prince Altan's army, is also on his way here. He left a day's march behind us, but we took shortcuts and pushed our mounts, so we made great time."

"Prince Altan's army?" Bayor shook with anger inside. Why didn't he see this coming?

Of course, Altan would betray his race in exchange for the imperial crown… he craved absolute power.

The lieutenant cleared his throat. "What are your orders, my Khan?"

Time to lead. "The horde will defend the Temple rock against Altan's army. The archers will join the Protectors atop the walls to fight the winged invaders."

The four lieutenants saluted.

The old lieutenant spoke. "My Khan, our loyalty is and will always be to you."

"Thank you for your support, my friends. Together we shall overcome the obstacles." Bayor sincerely hoped it would be the case.

In the predawn, while the horde set up their defensive positions, Bayor led a large contingent of his archers up the rocky slope to the Temple grounds. As they entered the courtyard, they could see the devastation—crumbled walls, blackened from the fires.

All the fires were now extinguished, but the smell of smoke and Gripus feathers persisted. Acolytes swept away debris, black feathers, and broken tiles. Drops of golden blood marred the blue floor in places. The Acolytes also collected arrows, abandoned spears, swords, and bows… as well as Gripus firebolts.

After directing his archers to organize the defense with a group of Protectors, Bayor stepped resolutely across the blue-tiled courtyard, toward the Temple. Time to plan Anila's rescue.

Inside the Temple, in the soft light and soothing silence, the wounded were resting peacefully on thin cotton mats, with clean bandages. Bayor went straight to Stardust. The she-wolf slept comfortably and didn't seem in any pain.

He caressed her head gently. "Good girl. Thank you for trying to protect Anila."

Master Wang emerged from a back door in the Temple and motioned for Bayor to join him.

Bayor followed him into an adjacent room, where a dozen Protectors sat in a circle on a large mat, in deep meditation. The early morning light filtered through small openings near the roof. Fragrant incense filled the air.

Bayor recognized the familiar faces of the Protectors who had travelled with Anila. Although in the beginning they all looked alike, with their wide black pants, white tunics, weapons belt, shaved heads and large Yin-Yang tattoos, he had learned to distinguish these twelve from the others.

Master Wang stepped to the center of the meditating circle and motioned for Bayor to come and sit with him. "Do you know we can use your special emotional bond with Anila to locate her?"

"You can?" Bayor felt heat on his face, glad the Protectors' eyes were closed. They wouldn't notice his embarrassment. How bold of Master Wang to mention his special attraction to Anila! But he suspected they all could read his emotions, although not his mind. Being an Immortal had its privileges.

"Wherever Anila is held, it must be the Gripus stronghold." Master Wang spread his wide robes and sat facing him. "Focus on the Chi as you visualize her, and we will find her together."

Bayor closed his eyes and focused on Anila's lovely face. At the sight of her, he could barely breathe, so much love and regret filled his chest.

Master Wang's soft voice penetrated his meditative trance. "I can feel her. She is alive... wounded, tied up, cold, and powerless, in a hidden pit, an artificial crater in the mountains. Not accessible due to high cliffs. Around her I see large nests, with giant predatory birds... and above her, blocking the light, is the Gripus army."

Bayor could now see the images Master Wang was projecting in his mind. Anila lay unconscious and bleeding from the left shoulder. His heart went out to her. He could also feel the twelve Protectors witnessing the vision with him and strengthening his Chi.

As Master Wang's vision widened to give an aerial view to encompass more of the scenery, a live map of the region revealed itself. Bayor could see the stone crater, and so did the Protectors. The crater definitely looked artificial in its perfect regularity... as if drilled.

The plateau had a steep cliff all around, with a waterfall surging from it and flowing into a small lake... surrounded by a forest. Even the cliff shone like glass. Beyond the green forest at its base, a wide strip of desert spread all the way to the monastery.

When the vision faded, Bayor opened his eyes.

Master Wang nodded. "Now, we know where she is detained. These Protectors, who traveled with Anila before, will accompany you and a small group of your warriors to rescue her."

"We shall need fast mounts." Bayor felt excited at the thought of rescuing her. "We can hide our advance under the forest canopy."

"You will also take the few firebolt weapons we gathered after the battle..." Master Wang stretched and reached toward a bundle, brought it to the middle of the mat and loosened it. Several firebolt weapons spilled in front of him, slick and shiny, the size of a dagger, with a thick gripping handle, and many luminous dials.

The Protectors stared at them.

Bayor took one and turned it around. It felt surprisingly light. "What are all these luminous markings?"

Master Wang raised his brow. "I believe these firebolts also double as tools and can be used in many different ways... like to dig a tunnel through hard rock quietly." Master

Wang smiled. "Of course, we'll have to experiment first."

"That could come handy." Bayor's chest filled with hope. The mission to save Anila seemed less impossible. "We will find her and bring her to safety. I promise."

"I know you will. You all will." Master Wang rose in one fluid motion. "Anila is the Celestial Gem. We cannot leave her in enemy hands."

"We won't." Bayor would never give up, nor would the Protectors. He also realized he would gladly die to protect her life.

Chapter 15

Stretching his wings in the morning sun, Zaal breathed in the strong scent of his brethren... the smell of black feathers. Hundreds of Gripus hanging upside down from the wall of the crater stirred, and the flapping of their wings as they righted themselves created swirling air currents.

Last night, they succeeded in opening the Celestial Gate. Unfortunately, their victory was short, as Master Wang somehow managed to close it... in a record time, too. But there would be more battles. With larger numbers and superior weapons, the Gripus would prevail.

Zaal's spirit soared. He felt so liberated after telling his arrogant former charge the truth about his parents and his true place in the world. How he'd enjoyed the shock and horror in Bayor's green eyes. Immortals were so arrogant to think they were the best at everything... and destined to rule. But compared to the Gripus, they were naïve, inexperienced, and oh so gullible.

A burst of trumpets echoed in the crater, calling the Gripus to attention. All conversations ceased, and the flapping of wings softened. Then, in front of the griffin banner, a very imposing and very stern Great Gripus rose and hovered. Zaal had never seen him before. His impressive amount of gold coverings glittered in the morning sun, blinding whoever might stare at him.

Zaal's heart faltered. Was this the leader of the newcomers? Where was the familiar patriarch of Zaal's clutch? His searching gaze found him in the background, wearing much less gold than before, as he hovered in the new leader's shadow, outranked and cast aside. Zaal could barely hold his anger at such unjust treatment of his beloved patriarch.

The newly arrived Great Gripus rose higher, staring at the entire flock. "Last night's botched operation was a total disaster." The thundering voice matched the imposing physique. "Thousands of our soldiers remained stuck on our home world and never crossed the gate. You let a puny Immortal seal the gate shut. How can you call yourselves Gripus?"

The consternation among the winged warriors was tangible. Zaal could sense their shame and humiliation. They had superior weapons, the advantage of flight, and still had to flee...

But why did they give up so easily? Who gave the order to withdraw, and why? During the battle, when the trumpets sounded the retreat, no one questioned the order, or who had given it. Something didn't add up.

Did the new leader order the retreat so he could blame the local Gripus for the failure and take charge of the native clutch? His entire race was known to have superior political skills and a great mastery of schemes and intrigues. Zaal's anger mounted as he realized this likely scenario had duped his brethren.

He returned his attention to the newly arrived Great Gripus.

"In light of this new development, we must regroup and rethink our strategy. We must control the gate at any cost. It is vital to our reconquest of this planet." The Great Gripus took a deep, sonorous breath. "Local Envoys, make your reports!"

Envoy Zilon hovered to the fore and bowed. "Prince Altan is with General Torino and his army, ready to attack the Temple, in exchange for the imperial crown and his chosen bride. He is our ally, and his army is on our side."

Zilon bowed and hovered back to his place in the circle.

Zaal came forth next. "I secured the girl Anila for Prince Altan, as it is part of the deal Zilon made. She is right here, out of reach of any native or Immortal. I sincerely apologize for my failure to rally Bayor Khan himself to our cause. The promise of the crown didn't win him over."

"You had Bayor Khan in weapon's range during the battle. I saw you. Why didn't you kill him?" The cold statement sounded ominous.

Zaal faltered, taken aback. At the time, hurting Bayor by stealing his woman seemed more important. "Great Gripus, my mission was not to kill him, but to abduct the Immortal woman, and I did."

"Don't you ever think like a strategist?" The Great Gripus shook his head. "Since Bayor Khan refused our generous offer of the crown, he is of no use to us and can only cause problems. He constitutes a threat to our plans and must be eliminated."

"He will be, Great Gripus." Zaal forced a smile. "The barbarian horde should be arriving at Temple Rock tomorrow. They believe their Khan is a prisoner of Master Wang, and Wang must die for him to get free. As their commander, I shall lead them to battle against the Temple."

"Are you certain of that?" The Great Gripus sneered. "My spies just reported that while you slept, the barbarian horde already reached Temple Rock. But instead of attacking the Temple, they turned their attention outward, and are ready to pounce on Prince Altan's army."

"How could they travel that fast?" A sudden chill coursed along Zaal's spine. In his hurry to humiliate Bayor and take away his woman, he'd failed to account for the zeal of the barbarians and the speed of their mounted horde. "I apologize, Great Gripus. I didn't expect them to get there this early."

"Shame on you, Envoy Zaal. Because of your negligence, Bayor Khan has retaken control of the horde, and you are to blame. You failed to convince the barbarian Khan to join our cause. You neglected to kill him when you had a chance, and you underestimated Master Wang's ability to close the gate. Now, you have lost control of the entire horde." Each word from the Great Gripus sounded like a condemnation.

Mortified, Zaal bowed. "I humbly apologize, Great Gripus. I swear I will correct this oversight."

"You had ample time to carry out your mission as Bayor's mentor and military commander for over two decades, and still, you failed!" the voice thundered. Then the Great Gripus raised his gaze to the entire assembly. "This is the kind of incompetence that will not be tolerated under my command."

The newly arrived Gripus soldiers whistled and banged their gold wrist bands against their breastplates, to communicate their disapproval of Zaal.

Shame burned Zaal's ears. He'd never felt so humiliated. He lowered his gaze. The former Great Gripus had been kind and fatherly to him, because they were from the same clutch. But all these new soldiers bowed to a different kind of authority.

The Great Gripus raised one hand, and the flock quieted. "Envoy Zaal, you are hereby stripped of your gold, your title, and demoted to the lowest soldier rank. You will fight on the front line, and sacrifice your life in battles to come, to facilitate Gripus victory."

Zaal could barely contain his rage. He was an Envoy, a Mentor, Commander of the horde... not a lowly soldier. But he was helpless against the Great Gripus. If the Great One pointed his golden finger at Zaal, it would be instant death.

Still, Zaal would have his revenge. He would make Bayor pay for this ignominy with a slow, excruciating death.

* * *

When Anila came to, she pushed herself from the ground to sit up, but fell back and cried in pain. Her left shoulder, stiff and raw, encrusted with dried blood, refused to move, paralyzed like her arm. At least, it wasn't her sword arm. The pale light of day didn't reach the depths of her monumental dungeon. She lay at the very bottom of the crater, among gravel, dead feathers, and giant bird nests.

She shivered. From the cold? A fever? Or from blood loss?

Overhead, the Gripus flew in and out of the crater, busy with preparations she did not understand. Anila sensed the strong excitement among them and realized they were up to something... something wicked, no doubt.

With great effort, grinding her teeth against the pain, she slowly pushed herself up in a sitting position. She shuddered as the specter of fear threatened to swallow her, but she remembered her training. No fear. As long as she still lived, she would keep fighting and would never accept enslavement.

Although light-headed, Anila must focus on the Chi, figure out where she was. She was still chained to the crater wall above her head... with shiny yellow metal, but not gold... something much harder.

Could she break the chain? With a rock? with the Chi? Even if she did succeed, there was no way for her to escape, especially in her condition. The slick, vertical walls prevented climbing, the bottom was solid rock under the gravel, and she could not fly.

She feigned dejection, keeping her head down between her knees, observing the Gripus guarding her. Three of them. They carried firebolt weapons and didn't seem friendly with the large predatory birds tending to the nests. One even kicked a bird who didn't get out of his way fast enough. So, the birds were lowly servants.

"Hey!" She called to the closest Gripus. "I'm hungry... and my shoulder needs a healer."

The Gripus guard took a few steps closer and squinted at her. "Why should I care?"

"You abducted me for a reason." She forced a semi-friendly smile. "If I die, you will have failed your mission... and I'm sure your superiors do not like failure."

The Gripus straightened his frame and adjusted his gold belt... on which hung a firebolt and small sophisticated devices... or were they also weapons? "The Great Gripus doesn't care about you at all, Immortal slime."

How did he know she was Immortal? Anila only learned it a few days ago. "So, why did you abduct me?"

"You are the future emperor's prize." The Gripus sneered.

"What future emperor?" Anila should keep him talking. Maybe she would learn something useful.

"Prince Altan... another Immortal slime." The Gripus spat just a step away from her foot."

"Altan?" So, the cowardly prince was in league with the Gripus... no big surprise.

"You see... we don't care about you at all." The guard scoffed.

"Not even to feed me?" She managed to sound weak and miserable, although she doubted the Gripus had any empathy.

The guard shook his head, visibly annoyed by her insistence. "The birds may have some slop to spare."

"Thank you." Good. She watched the Gripus walk toward a large bird.

Apparently, the Gripus did not know Anila was the Celestial Gem. How could they? But if they ever found out, or if Altan figured it out, the dark side of the prophecy could yet come to pass, condemning the planet to millennia of tyranny and suffering without hope.

The Gripus tended to think long term, over generations... like Zaal raising Bayor over two decades. Fortunately, Bayor found out what he was and secretly nurtured his Immortal virtues and his connection with the Chi.

But if the Gripus forced Anila to become Altan's mate and carry his heir, they could kill her and Altan, then raise the Immortal emperor themselves with Gripus mentors... That would give them total control of the empire, and they could oppress the planet unchallenged... for millennia to come.

Anila took a deep breath. Enough self-pity. Even seriously wounded, she was a strong warrior. She had the Chi on her side. She would never let that happen. She would kill Altan rather than carry his seed. Surrounded by hundreds of powerful enemies, she would fight to her last breath rather than surrender to an evil fate.

Her stomach protested at the thought of food, but in order to fight, she must remain alive and regain her strength.

A black bird the size of a man, half-walking and flapping his wings, carried a small bowl with its beak and dropped it in front of Anila. Some pale green slop spilled onto the gravel.

"Thank you." Anila nodded her thanks to the bird, who shrugged and clip-clopped away toward a bulky nest.

She inspected the green sludge. Her stomach protested. Not appetizing but there were seeds floating in it. Seeds were good. She dipped one finger and tasted it. Fermented milk with greens and tubers. Better than she expected. She picked up the bowl and drank the entire contents. Then she took a few slow breaths to make sure the food would stay down.

At least, she wouldn't have to fight on an empty stomach.

Feeling a little stronger, she glanced at the guards, hovering above, paying her little attention. She looked around for signs of vegetation in hopes of finding medicinal plants for her shoulder. No such luck. Nothing grew on rock. Then something caught the breeze, hanging from the side of a bulky nest. A large spiderweb. Could she reach it?

Estimating her chain was long enough, she slowly inched toward the nest, hoping not to attract attention. Spiderwebs could be used to prevent infection and heal wounds. Maybe it would work for her. She couldn't reach it with her fingers, but she picked up a stick fallen from a nest and used it to snatch the spiderweb.

She glanced up to make sure the guards didn't notice, then returned to her previous spot. Lifting her torn shirt, wincing as the fabric stuck to the raw flesh, she managed to place the spiderweb between the shirt and the messy wound. Good.

Now, she must rely on the Chi to find out where she was held, then make contact with the monastery... like the Protectors did. They would be looking for her, and she wanted to help. So, she sat, her back against the vertical cliff for much-needed support. Then she crossed her legs and closed her eyes, sinking into a deep meditative trance. All things and people were connected in the Chi.

But her head was spinning. She felt herself falling into a black hole and lost consciousness.

* * *

Even by scant moonlight, Bayor recognized the high cliff and its waterfall from Master Wang's shared vision. He kicked his stallion's flanks, hoping Anila would still be alive when he reached her. His rescue team of twelve Protectors and twelve horde warriors had made good time at night across the strip of desert.

The dense forest now hid their approach as they advanced swiftly among cool vegetation and all kinds of snakes, birds, and predators welcoming the predawn. By first light, they reached the base of the dark cliff

268

hiding the Gripus lair. From the forest floor, it looked slick and shiny, like glass. Definitely artificial.

The white waterfall surging from the cliff thundered into a small lake in a cloud of mist. A brook sprang from the lake to run down through the forest.

At the water's edge, under the canopy of trees, Bayor dismounted and led his black stallion to drink. Then he contemplated the slick wall, smooth and impossible to climb. Looking up through the foliage, he could see Gripus flying in and out above the cliff, but no one guarded the base. Why would they? They believed it was impenetrable.

Around him, warriors and Protectors dismounted. Thirsty from the ride, the animals snorted in anticipation as they approached the water's edge and drank, scaring a flock of geese that took flight. The steeds shared happy whinnies and shook their manes. A few pounded the earth with their hooves.

Fortunately, these sounds blended with the roaring torrent of the waterfall, the bristling of the leaves in the wind, the loud bird songs, the cries of prey falling to predators, and the trumpeting of big animals warning other males of their presence. Bayor counted on these natural sounds to also mask the subtle whine of the digging tools.

Master Wang was right. The firebolt weapons had many settings and many uses. Tunneling through stone was one of them...

and they could do it fast, without dust or gravel residue. When they tried it at the monastery, it pierced a perfect round hole the size of a man through a giant boulder in a matter of seconds... with almost no sound. Amazing technology.

The challenge would be to find a starting point out of sight from the flying Gripus.

As he stared at the waterfall, the fresh smell of the turbulent water reminded him of the northern mountains of his youth. Bayor realized there might be a recess or even a cave behind the water curtain... it was a common feature of waterfalls at home.

He signaled the head Protector. "Let's slip behind the waterfall. Maybe we can start the tunnel there."

The head Protector nodded. In a single line, they circled the pond, crouching among the vegetation, until they stood against the cliff wall, inching their way toward the roaring water. So close to the fall, the sound of the cataract drowned all others, and thick mist filled the air and dampened their clothes.

Bayor watched his steps as he felt his way around the base of the cliff. Focusing on the Chi, he secured each step, rooting his feet to the energy of the stone. As they followed the slippery ridge, he squeezed between the water curtain and the slick wall. His heart beat faster.

"Yes!" He stepped inside the large recess in the stone, not quite a cave, but a grotto deep enough to hide the entire team. "This hollow space will provide the perfect place to remain unseen as we start drilling," he yelled over the cataract.

The head Protector pulled a firebolt from his belt and checked the settings. As he angled it up in the general direction of the crater, he touched his Temple. An image of the rock and beyond appeared in the air in front of them. Bayor could see the bottom of the crater through the stone, and the large nests, and the giant birds, and Gripus guards hovering... three of them.

Collapsed at the bottom, half-propped against the crater wall, Anila lay still, her ankle cuff attached to a chain anchored to a metal loop high above her. With her head down, she looked asleep... or unconscious. Was she breathing? Bayor couldn't tell.

His heart went out to her. The Gripus would pay for making her suffer. But remembering the Chi, he took a slow breath to calm himself. "How far do we have to drill?"

The head Protector tapped the weapon, and a dial appeared above it. "Not too far for these firebolts. The bottom of the crater is almost above us, less than a hundred steps in that direction."

Hope bubbled in Bayor's chest. "We have to be careful not to hurt Anila. We should emerge a safe distance away from her."

"Wise." The head Protector nodded. "Wounded and chained, she can't get out of the way."

"How dare these beasts chain her like an animal?" Bayor imagined how painful and humiliating it must be for her.

"The chain shouldn't be a problem." The head Protector offered a rare smile. "A weapon that can disintegrate stone should be able to break or melt metal."

"Let's hope so." Bayor couldn't afford to fail. He would break the chain with his bare hands if need be. The Protectors valued Anila as the Celestial Gem, but to him, she was so much more.

He focused on her image but could not sense her Chi. She was too weak. Instead, he sent her reassuring thoughts. *"Anila, hang on. I'm coming for you."*

* * *

A slight vibration emanating from the stone beneath her jolted Anila awake. She must have lost consciousness... again. She glanced around and straightened her back against the crater wall, stifling a cry as pain pierced her shoulder. She couldn't move her arm.

The strange vibration brought her wide awake. The gravel at her feet trembled slightly. She focused her mind on the source of the tremor. It came from below, under the bottom of the crater. Volcanic activity?

Unlikely. She suspected this crater was artificial.

Focusing her mind, she detected a void below. Were there caves underneath?

She heard Bayor's voice calling in her mind. *"Anila, I'm coming for you."*

Was she delirious? Then she sensed his presence, as if he stood next to her. She felt his body heat, recognized his familiar scent of sage, leather, and steel. She turned and was disappointed to be alone, but she could feel him nearby, close to her.

He had come for her. Her chest overflowed with gratitude. He did care for her deeply, and so did she.

When Anila focused on the activity below her and visualized it, Bayor stood in the blue glow of a firebolt weapon, surrounded by his twelve-warrior escort. The faces of the twelve Protectors from her previous expedition also flashed on her mind. Would it be enough warriors to fight their way out? There were so many Gripus high above... fortunately, only three guards watched the bottom.

What was the plan? Anila wanted to help, but what could she do in her wounded condition, too weak to use the Chi, chained to the wall, with a very short range of movement? She might as well be dead weight.

She glanced up at the three Gripus guards who hovered above her, busy comparing their gold coverings. Since they had no physical contact with the ground, they probably couldn't feel the subtle trembling of the rock below. Good.

One of the big predatory birds jumped down from its nest, cocked its head to stare at the ground with one eye, then pecked at the shaky gravel. No! The large bird deployed its wings and flapped them frantically, emitting a loud cackle. An alarm call?

The three Gripus guards above her straightened, all senses in alert. Hands went to their firebolt weapons as they stared at the screaming, dancing bird... but birds could not speak. The three guards stared at the bottom of the crater then looked at each-other and shrugged. Since they could neither see nor feel any threat, they dismissed the stupid bird and returned to comparing their gold coverings.

Anila's gaze went upward. The hundreds of Gripus who had crowded the place earlier seemed to have flown the lair, probably to prepare their next attack on the monastery. Few remained, and they seemed oblivious to the imminent incursion.

Remembering her training, Anila prompted herself to breathe deeply, slowly, from the diaphragm. No fear. She must stand ready.

Then the crater floor opened several steps away from her, with a big swoosh of air. Horde warriors sprang out of it, brandishing swords and firebolts, followed by the Protectors.

Several Gripus flew down the crater, shooting firebolts at the invaders. Others sounded the trumpets, calling reinforcements.

Anila stared at the gaping hole in the ground, looking for Bayor. Her heart beat so fast, she thought it might jump out of her chest.

Chapter 16

Firebolt weapon in one hand and scimitar in the other, Bayor ran out of the tunnel and emerged into the crater. Spotting Anila, he ran in her direction. She needed him. He must get her out of here quickly... before the entire Gripus force arrived.

Two Gripus guards, hovering above, glanced down at the air disturbance and yelled the alarm. Then they dropped in front of Bayor, blocking his way. He switched into combat mode, focused, determined.

Dodging the flash of a firebolt, he fired his own, then plunged his scimitar into enemy flesh. The two Gripus collapsed in a puddle of golden blood, but more Gripus fell from above upon his small group of warriors. He aimed, fired, and slashed his way toward Anila.

Large birds cawed, batting black wings, and flew talons-first at the rescuers' faces, then pecked at their eyes. Fending them off and protecting his face with one arm, Bayor severed a Gripus arm and then sliced a wing with his scimitar. No time for hesitation. Lightning flared, feathers flew, and gravel exploded around him. The stench of gold blood and brimstone spread with the smoke of burning nests and feathers.

Choking on dust, Bayor couldn't see Anila through the haze. He must follow his instinct and march in the direction of the rock where she was chained. But where was it? Where was she?

The clamor of battle, the clash of steel, the sizzle of burning flesh, the cries of the wounded, the guttural yells of the victors now surrounded him. Bayor kept an eye out for Zaal... but he must not yield to his desire for revenge. He'd come to save Anila. Focusing on the Chi, he slowed his breathing, all senses on alert.

As if in slow motion, he fired bolts of lightning, pierced chests, severed limbs, struck gold plates, and charged anyone in his way. His foot connected with low obstacles, and his scimitar dripped with golden blood. The metallic smell reminded him of other battles.

Bayor had always hated killing, but these abominations couldn't be left alive. They threatened everyone on this planet. They must be destroyed. And Anila must live.

A bright explosion flared overhead. A Gripus weapon? His ears rang, and sharp pain made him lose his balance. What was that? He struggled to get up but failed. All around, his warriors were falling under the sonic assault.

But the persisting light from the sonic weapon also pierced through the haze, showing him Anila, collapsed and leaning against the cliff. She had picked up a Gripus weapon and was aiming it at her captors, head against her shoulder to cover her ear.

Bayor shook his head to clear the loud ringing in his skull and ran awkwardly toward Anila. He tripped and fell onto the gravel. His firebolt escaped his grip and fell.

A Gripus dropped in front of him and aimed. Before Bayor could retrieve his weapon, the Gripus buckled and fell backward with a big hole in his chest... from Anila's weapon. How he loved this woman.

As the infernal sound still hurt his ears, Bayor struggled toward Anila.

She aimed at her chain with her firebolt. The golden metal melted, and the softened links broke. When Bayor reached her, she looked up at him with wide amber eyes, then grimaced through the sonic pain. Grime and dust covered her hair and face. "Let's go."

She rose to unsteady feet but her leg gave out, and she collapsed against him.

Bayor grabbed her waist to steady her. "Let me help."

He slid his arm under her good shoulder and lifted her with great care, ignoring his precarious balance. Then he carried her in front of him, still firing his firebolt as he hurried toward the open tunnel, struggling to keep his feet under him.

A Protector emitted a shrill whistle... the signal to disengage.

The rescuers returned to the tunnel, some in a disoriented haze, others on their hands and knees, and many Gripus followed them. Once inside the tunnel, the infernal sound of the new weapon diminished.

The warriors lit their torches as they ran, but Bayor carried Anila and didn't dare disturb her. She looked pale, her eyes unfocused, and her skin felt clammy.

He turned his head to glance back... So many Gripus behind him... Good. As soon as his team crossed the black markings he'd made on the side of the tunnel earlier, he yelled, "Now!"

His warriors lit the wicks with the torches and threw their clay pots full of black powder behind them. Then they ran ahead as fast as they could. So did Bayor, careful not to shake his precious load.

The entire mountain shook and grumbled as many explosions collapsed the tunnel upon the Gripus who had followed them inside. It sounded as if the lower part of the crater had collapsed as well. Good.

Ceiling dust fell on Bayor and the rescuers as they forged ahead. An avalanche of gravel and stones rolled after them like a flow spreading a thick cloud, then stopped. Everything went quiet. He could hear everyone breathe. The infernal sound that assaulted their ears had completely ceased. What a relief.

Still holding Anila, Bayor stopped, leaned his back against the wall, and took a deep, measured breath to slow his heartbeat. "Everyone accounted for?"

The warriors and the Protectors looked at each other in the torchlight, counting their friends.

"Everyone is here." The head Protector nodded. "What was that sound that hurt our ears and made us fall?"

"I think it was a sonic weapon... a vibration meant to confuse and weaken the enemy." Bayor glanced around at his warriors. "How many Gripus weapons did you collect?"

A few of them had several firebolts tucked into their belts. Their leader smiled. "Maybe thirty, my Khan."

"Good." Bayor eased Anila gently onto the tunnel floor and knelt beside her. "We should rest a while."

Anila smiled her approval.

A warrior glanced up at the rock ceiling above their heads. "What if they dig after us?"

"They won't." Bayor didn't mind explaining. "The explosion destabilized the rock. The entire crater will collapse upon them if they try to drill. Besides, drilling would kill their own men trapped in the collapse."

"But they can fly." Another warrior exclaimed. "They will search for us from the sky."

"Most likely, but the waterfall hides the tunnel entrance, and they have no way of knowing in which direction we went underground. There are many caves and natural tunnels all through these mountains." Bayor hoped they would be safe. "Send sentries to the waterfall to check on Gripus activity."

"Yes, my Khan." The warrior fisted his chest and left.

Bayor took a slow breath and gazed upon Anila. She was trembling and pale, dark short hair sticking to her clammy forehead. She needed a respite. "We should stay here until the Gripus abandon their search."

The head Protector pinched his lips. "Are you certain they'll give up so easily?"

"Yes," Anila answered weakly. "They don't care about me. I'm only Altan's prize. They have bigger plans to worry about. They are planning an attack... very soon."

"Yes. They want to reopen the Celestial Gate." Bayor moved Anila's medallion to the side, sensing its energy tingling through his fingers. Carefully, he lifted the torn fabric of her bloodstained tunic and freed her shoulder from the garment.

Anila flinched but quickly smiled. Her caramel skin was soft and smooth. The wound was deep and encrusted with blood.

Bayor chuckled as he saw the spiderweb filaments. "You did a good job to prevent infection."

"That's all I could find near me in the crater." She gasped under his probing touch.

"Sorry." Bayor signaled to one of the Protectors.

The Protector nodded and turned around.

Bayor smiled at Anila. "Master Wang procured some medicine from the monastery. It should help you."

"Thanks." Her shoulders relaxed. Blood oozed from the wound.

The Protector brought a pouch, set it on the tunnel floor and spread it open.

Bayor inspected a variety of clay jars, marked with the names of the ointments they contained, as well as vials of various potions. He selected some rolled bandages, a healing balm, and a potion against infection from a familiar plant.

Then he nodded to the head Protector, who took the pouch to others in the group who also needed care.

Bayor handed the vial to Anila. "Drink this. It's bitter, but it will prevent that wound from poisoning your blood."

"I know." She adjusted her position and glanced up at him. "But how do you know so much about potions? Are you also a healer?"

"Healing is part of being a warrior." He helped her raise her head so she could drink. "Everyone needs care after a battle."

"I never thought of it that way." She took a sip, grimaced, then tossed the entire dose down her throat and shook her head in a quick shudder. "That's potent."

"Yes, it is." Bayor chuckled. He opened the jar and applied the medicinal balm directly to the wound, covering it and massaging it deep into the tissue. "Does it hurt?"

"Not that much." All the time, Anila stared at him as if she were seeing him for the first time.

He met her amber gaze. "What is it?"

"Thank you for saving me, for taking such good care of me." A tear rolled down her cheek. "No one ever did anything like this for me before."

Taken aback, Bayor felt a catch in his throat. "Maybe it's because you are so strong and independent, there was never a need."

"Maybe." She closed her eyes, relaxing under his massaging fingers.

Around them, the others remained quiet, taking care of their own injuries, mostly burns, cuts, bruises, and a torn knee being set into a brace.

Bayor secured the bandages around Anila's shoulder, then pulled her torn tunic over it. "And thank you for saving my life, by the way. That last Gripus might have killed me when I was down."

"That's the least I could do for my savior." Her hand reached for his and rested there.

He relished the warm contact. He could feel her energy returning... her Chi merging with his, effervescing throughout his body. What a wonderful feeling.

"My Khan." A warrior approached with a hatchet and a wooden block. "Maybe now I can remove that ankle cuff?"

"Yes." Bayor reluctantly freed his hand from hers and rose to his feet. "This is not the kind of jewelry we want on our precious Anila."

The tender way she gazed up at him made him melt inside.

* * *

After rest and food inside the tunnel, Anila felt a lot better as some of her strength returned. She had never thought of herself as valuable. It felt strange to be cared for by the people she admired. Especially Bayor.

Once in a while, a warrior would venture out and return to appraise Bayor on the Gripus search.

When everyone was patched up, the entire group moved closer to the exit behind the waterfall, where the sound of the cataract drowned all conversations.

Finally, one scout returned, out of breath, shouting over the water noise, "The search is over! The Gripus have left the crater!"

"All of them?" To Bayor, it sounded unlikely.

"Looks like it." The man nodded for good measure.

Anila wondered where they went. It couldn't be good. "They plan to attack tonight. I can feel it."

Bayor nodded. "Me, too."

He signaled to his warriors, and the head Protector did the same. All stood up and slowly inched their way out from behind the waterfall. In single file, they navigated the narrow ledge along the bottom of the cliff just above the lake... leading down to the forest floor and the wooded banks.

When they reached the mounts waiting at the water's edge, Anila realized something. She remembered her abduction, and the she-wolf leaping at the Gripus holding her.

She looked around. "Where is Stardust?"

"Not here. But she is safe." Bayor smiled as if to reassure her. "She suffered burns from the Gripus weapon, but she is in good hands with the Temple healers. She will be fine."

"I'm glad." Anila wouldn't want an innocent animal to be maimed or die for trying to save her.

When Bayor offered a boosting hand to help her get on a young bay mare, she accepted gracefully. She noticed the different animal and the barbarian saddle with high metal stirrups. "What happened to the white mare?"

"She was too old for this mission. Our mounts are young, strong, and bred for speed and endurance." He checked that her foot was secure in the stirrups.

"I see..." Anila realized the trip home would be difficult in her condition.

"We'll have to ride hard." He flashed a sad smile. "Sorry."

Anila glanced up. "Won't the flying Gripus returning to the lair spot us on the ground?"

"Have no fear." Bayor patted the mare. "The forest canopy will hide us. We can blend with the many animals who inhabit this jungle."

"Then what about the desert?" There would be no forest there.

"We'll have to cross the strip of desert in the open at a full gallop... and hope the Gripus are too busy elsewhere in the shadows to notice us. They hate the bright sunlight anyway." Bayor vaulted onto his black stallion. "On these fast mounts, it will take most of the day to get back to the monastery."

Anila wasn't sure she could stand a hard gallop in her condition. But they must reach the monastery before nightfall, before the attack. The fate of the Celestial Gate and the fate of the planet depended on it.

* * *

Later that day, just before sunset, Master Wang walked into the Temple, the floor of which had become an infirmary. The smell of camphor blended with that of aromatic plants and fish ointments. On the thin cotton mats lined up against the walls, Protectors, Acolytes, and a few villagers lay at rest, bandaged and sedated, some meditating to accelerate their recovery.

Healers went from one patient to another, changing bandages, checking a pulse, and touching a forehead for signs of fever. Others used acupuncture needles at the corresponding points of the body to fix a specific problem.

As Wang approached Anila's mat, he was glad to see her breathing regularly, relaxed, eyes closed, although her aura seemed diminished. Her energy was low. But this could be remedied.

At her side, curled up in a ball, a white cat purred. Good old Cottonball. The cat knew she was hurt and contributed his good vibrations to speed up her healing process.

The head healer came toward Wang and saluted. Then he knelt at Anila's side to remove her shoulder bandages. Her red jasper medallion seemed to glow, for some reason. What could it mean?

Wang cringed as the healer bared the ghastly wound. It looked worse than he imagined. "How is she doing?"

"I sedated her, Master. She feels no pain. But she lost a lot of blood, and the hard ride home took all her energy. She has none left to fight her way back to health." The healer glanced up at Wang. "The Gripus claws did great damage to her shoulder, ravaging muscles, tendons, and bone.”

“I can see that.” Wang needed Anila whole.

“The damage could be permanent. She could be crippled for life, unable to ever shoot a bow or wield a long pole.” The healer lowered his gaze as if in apology.

Wang needed Anila to be in perfect health and physical condition for the destiny she was dealt. He handed a small vial to the healer. “Give her this elixir. It should heal her quickly, without crippling effect, or even a scar.”

“Elixir?” The healer took the vial with reverence and bowed. “Thank you, Master Wang, for this rare and amazing gift.”

Anila opened unfocused amber eyes and gazed upon Wang. “What elixir?”

Wang was glad to see her awake. “It is formulated to heal an Immortal from any injury in no time at all.”

“Thank you, Master Wang.” Anila’s heavy eyelids closed again.

Wang touched the healer’s shoulder. “Take good care of her. She is our most precious hope.”

“I will, Master.” The healer bowed. “Should we get ready to receive more casualties? When do you expect another attack?”

“Anila mentioned the Gripus might attack tonight. She was right. I can feel it.” Wang sighed. “We should all be prepared.”

"We shall be, Master Wang." The healer saluted, right fist in left palm, from his kneeling position on the floor.

Wang walked away and glanced back to see the healer helping Anila drink the elixir. As he strode out of the Temple, he hoped the next battle could be won, but he faced a strong and ruthless enemy. He and his Protectors would be tested to their limits... and the stakes had never been higher.

If they failed to protect the Celestial Gate, or the Celestial Gem, the entire planet was doomed.

* * *

In the reddish glow of the setting sun, Bayor straightened in the saddle and gazed upon Prince Altan's army, spreading over the desert beyond the horde. He could feel a sense of unease snaking through his warriors. Fear was the enemy.

He turned his stallion to face his lieutenants. "Altan and Torino probably learned that you no longer follow Zaal's orders. They must know you will defend the monastery."

A lieutenant pointed. "My Khan, look, Torino is deploying his archers to the front line, hoping to rain death on the horde."

Bayor brandished his scimitar to the sky, a familiar signal for his warriors. "Raise the shields!"

The lieutenants yelled orders. In the fading light, rectangular sections of walls made of palm fronds and clay rose from the ground at an oblique angle, facing the enemy. The warriors must have dismantled all the huts in the village, while the villagers found refuge in the caves. The makeshift shields would catch Altan's arrows... but they would not protect the horde from Gripus' weapons raining death from the sky.

Bayor had a bad feeling about tonight. Night battles were always tricky. And this time, he didn't have the advantage of surprise. Also, he wanted to avenge his parents, and Anila... He wanted payback for all the lies, betrayals, and manipulations he'd suffered from Zaal over the years... without knowing it.

The need for revenge was poisoning his Chi. Anila would not approve... nor would Master Wang. Bayor closed his eyes and took a slow breath to clear his mind. He must let go of his selfish desires, let the anger slide off him, and become one with the Chi.

As the sky darkened, Bayor dismounted and gathered his lieutenants in the command tent.

When he had their attention, he took a deep breath. "I'm counting on you to stop Altan's army from reaching the monastery. Use all your resources... even the golden eagles, if they will fly at night."

The master ornithologist bowed. "They are well trained, my Khan. They will fly."

"Good." Bayor took a deep breath. "I will take the rest of our archers to the top of the wall. From there, they can fire on Altan's soldiers and on the enemy attacking from the sky."

"Yes, my Khan!" The four lieutenants said in unison.

"Remember, no fear. Remind the horde that we are not fighting for ourselves but to save the entire planet, including their families back home. There is no future for any tribe without victory." Bayor gazed at his trusted lieutenants, fixing their faces in his mind, hoping to see them all alive after the battle. "Good luck to you all. Remember to be one with the Chi. Let it show you the way to victory. May the Chi protect us all."

"May the Chi protect our Khan!" The four lieutenants took a knee, fisting their chests in the most respectful salute.

Bayor turned around to hide his emotions and walked out of the tent. Time to prepare for his battle.

Chapter 17

Anila screamed in her nightmare, then sat up, wide awake on the sleeping mat. Not her mat... she glanced around. The Temple... transformed into a healing hall. She remembered. She was back at the monastery... wounded. But she felt fine.

Other patients lay on other mats along the walls. Some mumbled in their sleep. A cool breeze carried the smell of camphor and medicinal herbs. From the faint moonlight seeping through the openings near the ceiling, it was way past sunset.

Cottonball purred, curled into a ball against her thigh, and Stardust was lolling her tongue over sharp fangs, staring at her with big yellow eyes. The she-wolf sported a bandage around her shaved belly, but she seemed eager to get out.

Anila scratched the canine's head. "Where is Bayor?"

She must hurry. In her dream, he was dying. He needed her. He was in great danger... or would be, very soon. Right now, everything seemed quiet. The attack hadn't started yet, but it would happen tonight.

She patted Stardust's shoulder. "When the time comes, we must watch over Bayor. He will need our help."

Stardust barked and wagged her tail. She was ready for some action.

Cottonball rose to his paws, stretched and yawned.

Anila sprang to her feet with no effort, surprising herself. She wore clean practice clothes. She examined her shoulder. No bandages, no scars, as if the wound was never there. She rotated her left shoulder and felt no residual pain. Her energy had returned. Master Wang's elixir had performed miracles.

"Cottonball, Stardust, let's go." Ignoring the healers, busy with the wounded of the last battle, Anila ran out of the Temple, bare feet silent on the smooth stone, with the great wolf and the white cat in tow.

The courtyard was dark and quiet, but heavy with tension. She could see the shadows of many archers atop the great wall. The attack must be imminent. She could feel the tension in her bones. Where was Bayor? He needed protection.

But first, she should find her weapons... and get some shoes to protect her feet. Battles were messy.

Quietly, she tiptoed toward the practice hall, where the oil lamps burned and the Acolytes had gathered. As she entered with Stardust and Cottonball, she sensed the young ones' panic. They all spoke in a frenzy, unfocused, out of breath, running around without direction. Where were the other teachers? Probably defending the walls.

Anila seized a long pole and pounded the end on the floor three times. Silence ensued.

"Sifu Anila? What's happening?" The girl's big, round eyes pleaded with her.

"We must prepare for an attack." Anila realized the students were scared. "But first, let's breathe and focus on the Chi. Remember, no fear. Still your mind."

She raised her arms and took a deep breath, filling the bottom of her lungs, held it, then released it slowly through the nose. The students imitated her, and she could sense a measure of calm returning to the group.

After a few calming breaths, she addressed them. "The Protectors are preparing for battle, and so should we."

"What should we do, Sifu?" Another student, a boy.

Anila realized she was their only leader in this instance. The responsibility of command was enormous, but teaching had taught her to lead. She let her training take over. "You are Chi warriors in training. Get ready for battle as well."

"The Protectors told us to cover our ears." The girl covered her ears with her hands.

"Your ears?" Anila remembered the paralyzing pain in her ears during her rescue.

"Yes, Sifu. They say the Gripus have a weapon that hurts the ears." The boy was adamant.

"It's true." Anila owed them the truth. "We should all put cotton in our ears and cover them with headbands." She made eye contact with one student after another. "You know how to use weapons. Choose your favorite, the one that fits your skills. Real weapons, not practice sticks."

The students' faces sobered. They nodded and scattered toward the lethal weapons racks.

Anila spotted a pair of boots and her bow, arrows, and sword, just where she used to keep them. She silently thanked the good soul who bothered to return them there. She also grabbed a belt to hook her sword... and a few explosive jars. When she looked up, all eyes were on her.

Anila straightened. "Do not yield to fear. Our enemy doesn't believe in the Chi. They think we are helpless and weak, but we are strong when we use the Chi."

A first-year student planted herself in front of her. "Sifu? What if we are not very good at weapons, yet?"

"Fair question." Anila projected her voice. "First-year students go to the drums! As soon as the enemy is spotted, you bang these drums as hard as you can, and keep the rhythm going strong."

"But Sifu, with our ears covered, who will hear the drums?" A boy asked.

"The vibration of the drum is more than just sound. It penetrates the rock underfoot, the stone buildings. We can feel it in our chest. All of us fighting will draw energy from that vibration."

"Yes, Sifu." The girl saluted and walked away, lowering her muffling headband.

Several other first-year students did the same.

Those who had chosen the bow now faced Anila.

She gazed at their young faces, hoping they would be safe. "The archers should take their post along the roof lines, so you can shoot up in the sky and down on the ground."

The archers saluted, lowered their earmuffs, and left.

"Those of you carrying a sword or spear, make sure the blade is sharp. You will fight on the ground with me." The main courtyard would be the most dangerous spot. "And remember that we must protect the Celestial Gate at any cost."

"Yes, Sifu." They all saluted, right fist in left palm, acknowledging the order.

"Only the oldest Acolytes will handle the explosives." Anila pointed to the chest containing the jars of black powder. "And remember to always shield yourself behind a wall or a building before lighting and throwing those."

"Yes, Sifu." The advanced Acolytes stood with resolute faces, several clay pots hanging from their belts.

Anila considered this army of young souls ready to do battle. They were innocent, pure, and so brave. She felt guilty, taking them on such a dangerous assignment, but if the Gripus won tonight and opened the gate, the fate of these young Acolytes would be worse than death.

"Lower your earmuffs." Anila did the same, then raised her spear, giving the signal to follow her. "Let's go!"

* * *

Wang stood between the two pillars of the mighty gate, hoping he was up to the task. With the few ancient instruments he had access to in the monastery, he had programmed the gate to remain closed. But that may not be enough. If the Gripus gained physical access, they had the technology to override his program and open it anyway... like they did last time.

But this time, the Protectors were prepared, forming a circle at the base... arrows and firebolt weapons aimed at the dark sky... the Gripus had such an advantage, dropping from above, unseen.

Wang's best hope resided in the Chi, creating a protective shield to fend off any assault on the gate from the sky. He hoped the Protectors would hold their ground.

How he wished for the airships and spaceships available to his siblings. But none

of these remained on this humble planet...
and his people would not return for decades.

From a distance, he saw Anila, leading a group of Acolytes to battle. The elixir had done its job. Wang was glad she recovered and stood ready to fight. He also noticed the new archers lining the rooflines of the many buildings. Acolytes. Well played, Anila.

A bright flash and a detonation high in the sky made Wang cover his ears with his makeshift muffs. Bayor was right. A sonic weapon producing a debilitating vibration... But the sudden boom of the big drums shook the ground underfoot, producing a counter-vibration, weakening the effect of the harmful sound. Who directed the drummers? It could only be Anila.

The sonic weapon ceased as the enemy realized it wouldn't work. Now, deadly fire rained from above, like it did before. But this time, Wang had a way of lighting the sky. He signaled to a Protector on the wall, who nodded understanding.

Hundreds of fireworks went up, exploding in bright colors, causing chaos as they detonated among the flying Gripus. They illuminated the skies above, making the Gripus easy targets for the archers... and the firebolt weapons Bayor and his team had brought back from the crater.

But Wang's first concern was to protect the gate.

Bayor glanced up as the fireworks flew and exploded, revealing a sky full of flying Gripus. He aimed and fired arrows as fast as he could. He was glad he'd identified the sonic weapon in the crater. The Temple defenders were prepared and would not be weakened by it.

Beyond the great wall, the horde was fighting Prince Altan's army. Some Gripus bolts ignited the raised panels protecting the horde from enemy arrows. General Torino now directed his archers to use flaming arrows to burn these makeshift shields. Soon, the entire barbarian camp would be set ablaze. But Bayor trusted his lieutenants to handle that battle.

For now, he must protect the Celestial Gate... but he also wanted to find Zaal and resolve his personal issues with him.

A flight of Gripus flew over Altan's army, picking up soldiers and taking them to the air, then dropping them into the courtyard.

Bayor saw Anila with a group of Acolytes, running to meet Altan's seasoned soldiers in battle. May the Chi protect her.

* * *

The fireworks lighting up the sky at regular intervals showed Anila not only her targets, but the entire courtyard, which had become a battlefield.

Now, many Gripus were diving, dropping soldiers in red armor in the middle of the yard, then flying back up to avoid weapons fire.

Anila directed her young troops toward the new threat, dodging lightning strikes and throwing black powder jars at any obstacle.

When she glanced at the Celestial Gate, several Protectors knelt around Master Wang, lending him their Chi to spread an energy shield over the tall pillars. It seemed to work at repelling the Gripus who came too close... for now.

A Gripus with an arrow in his chest fell from the sky at Anila's feet, dripping golden blood. She motioned to a group of Acolytes. "This one is yours. Practice your skills, but be careful, even wounded, he is armed, and extremely dangerous!"

"Sifu? You mean we should kill?" The young voice trembled.

"Yes. Pure evil cannot be saved. It must perish before it destroys us all."

The young warriors rose to the challenge, determination on their faces, and rushed to finish off the fallen Gripus. Anila could feel their excitement, the battle madness and pride at overcoming a superior enemy. Right now, they had no fear... but how long would it last?

More soldiers in red armor dropped into the courtyard, quickly met by determined Acolytes... and by Stardust. Even the Temple cats joined the fight, attacking the fallen enemies, scratching their eyes and biting their faces, so they could not use their weapons against the Acolytes. Good kitties.

Then Anila spotted a tall foe in silvery armor. Prince Altan? Instead of fighting, he was sneaking along the Temple walls in the shadows. For cover? In hopes of stealing the Celestial Gem?

Anila thought of the wounded recovering inside the Temple and rushed to meet him up the Temple steps, barring his way.

When Altan saw her, he halted and faced her, raising his firebolt. "What are you hoping to prove, Anila? You cannot win. You cannot overpower me with a sword against a firebolt. Make no mistake. You will be my slave bride and carry my heirs."

Anila's anger built up in her chest. She wouldn't let this treasonous snake steal the imperial throne, betray his entire race, or take her to his bed. "Even if we lose, I will sooner kill you or die rather than bend to your will."

"Then, I'm afraid I will have to kill you." He grinned and waved his firebolt, aiming at various parts of her body. "A shame to extinguish such a strong Immortal. Our children would have been superior in every way. Not that I would ever let them reign, as I would likely outlive them... but they would have made strong underlings to help me control the empire."

Anila couldn't let this vile prince win. The sword in her hand seemed to move of its own volition. She lunged, and the firebolt flew off Altan's hand.

Startled, he drew his sword and adopted a fighting stance. From his impeccable form, she could tell he had trained for many years... possibly a lifetime or more, since he had Immortal blood. He might be a coward, but he was skilled.

Her first moves confirmed it. He repelled all her attacks, agile as a cat, quick to react, offering no opening for a strike. Would he kill her right here and now? Maybe she could distract him. "I think we should talk about this."

"Too late." Altan snorted. He had a strong will and a strong body behind his steel. He didn't falter, he didn't retreat, he advanced with great strength.

Anila started to doubt herself. Although not a Protector, she was a Chi warrior. Then she realized what she'd forgotten... her superiority over Altan. She relaxed her stance and focused on the Chi. Let the energy of the universe guide and strengthen her.

As soon as she felt the Chi flowing through her, she made progress, forcing Altan to step back, pinning him against a wall. He quickly escaped, but she trapped him again. Then he lunged close to the ground and retrieved his firebolt.

As he aimed the weapon at her head and pulled the trigger, Anila ducked, turned and sliced his flank, right below the breastplates. The weapon's fire struck the side of a Temple column, in a shower of small stone fragments.

Altan fell backwards as if in slow motion. His weapons clattered on the stone. The expression on his face was one of pure disbelief as he rolled backwards down the Temple stairs. Jets of red blood poured and sprinkled all around as his head hit each stone step.

Anila descended the steps slowly. One look at his bloody face, broken body, and still eyes told her Altan was dead.

She felt a great emptiness in her chest... a great sadness. She had no problem killing Gripus, and Altan deserved his fate for betraying his race. Still...

* * *

Bayor rejoiced when he saw Anila down in the courtyard, standing over Altan's body. If only he could find Zaal.

As if he'd heard Bayor's vengeful thoughts, Zaal dropped before him and hovered, sneering. For some reason, he wore less gold than before... a smaller breastplate, and bangles instead of wide cuffs at his wrists, and none on his wide belt.

Wishing he were holding his firebolt, Bayor pointed his scimitar. "I was hoping to find you."

"My Khan!" Zaal's tone dripped with venom. "I owe you the displeasure of my fall from grace. You thwarted my plans, halted my promising rise among the Gripus. You cost me my exalted position as an Envoy. Because of you, I was shamed in front of my peers, stripped of my gold, and demoted to the rank of simple soldier."

"It's a small comfort to know you suffered because of me." Bayor struggled to contain his anger.

"I'll make you suffer before killing you." Zaal hovered in a slow circle around Bayor. "You will ask for death as a mercy."

Forced to constantly turn to face him, Bayor held his scimitar high but couldn't control his rage. "You killed my parents, gained my trust through lies, conspired with our mortal enemy, killed my favorite lieutenant, and betrayed me and the entire horde. For that, you deserve to die!"

"We'll see..." Zaal raised his firebolt, slowly, deliberately.

With his free hand, Bayor drew and aimed his own firebolt at Zaal's face, enjoying the irritation he saw there. He wanted to trust the Chi, but the need for revenge was too strong.

Zaal's trigger finger moved.

Bayor vaulted and landed behind Zaal as the shot hit empty space. With his firebolt, Bayor struck one wing. Liquid gold surged from the wound, and fire ignited the feathers.

Zaal screamed, turned in midair and landed on his feet. Then he shot Bayor's hand.

Bayor cried in pain and dropped his firebolt. Zaal patted down the burning feathers and retracted his damaged wings. Then he drew a blade and faced Bayor with pure hatred on his dark face.

Zaal's other hand grew sharp claws… the same claws that damaged Anila's shoulder. Angry heat crept up Bayor's neck and face.

But while Zaal succumbed to pure rage, Bayor realized he must not. Focusing on the Chi, he grounded himself and focused on his purpose. Wielding the scimitar in wide arcs, he jumped and rolled and attacked. But Zaal knew his former master's fighting technique too well and counteracted each time.

Remembering one of Anila's moves, Bayor bent his knees low, lunged and struck from below, surprising Zaal with a stab to the heart.

Golden blood spurted from the wound, matching the gold torc. Zaal grimaced, and understanding twisted his face. "My clutch brethren will avenge me!"

Zaal slowly collapsed, atop the great wall, his golden blood spreading on the stone.

* * *

Anila stopped fighting when Stardust howled... not at the moon, but at fighters on the wall.

Bayor! Anila's heart beat faster. Several Gripus dropped from the sky and fired firebolts at Bayor!

"No!" Anila watched in horror as Bayor lost his footing and fell down the narrow stairs along the wall.

Stardust at her side, she ran toward him, as he rolled down, all the way to the blue tile of the courtyard, halfway to the mighty pillars of the Celestial Gate. Was he still alive?

As she reached him, he lay on his back, not moving. All around them, the battle raged, but she only had eyes for him. He was still breathing, but barely.

A strange vibration made her look up. She realized Master Wang's shield had collapsed and no longer protected the gate.

Instinctively, she bent over Bayor, to protect him from the fire raining from the sky. When she did, her medallion fell from her tunic. His medallion was also exposed, and as if attracted by each other, the two halves touched and immediately locked together.

Before Anila could understand what was happening, a great light surged and formed a protective dome around them and over the Celestial Gate. Stung by the blinding light, the flying Gripus froze and dropped from the sky, disintegrating on their way down.

The Acolytes ran to finish them off, but didn't have to, as they turned to ashes before hitting the ground. "Sifu, they are gone. All of them... gone."

The few soldiers in red armor from Altan's army, confused and stunned, dropped their weapons in surrender.

"You did it!" Master Wang ran to Anila and Bayor. "The medallions were the key. Now we know how to defeat these horrible creatures. I only hope we got them all."

The dome-shaped luminescence softened then vanished. The medallions unlocked, but Bayor's life-signs were failing. He was unconscious, bleeding from many wounds, and with severe burns. "Master Wang, he needs your help."

Master Wang dug into a deep pocket and produced a small vial. "I have just what he needs."

Anila rejoiced, recognizing the elixir that had saved her earlier. Bayor was an Immortal, but he teetered at the brink of death.

She held his head as Master Wang made him drink the elixir.

A horde messenger ran toward the group. "My Khan! We have overcome the prince's army and killed General Torino. Prince Altan is nowhere to be found."

"Prince Altan is dead." Anila couldn't help the satisfaction in her voice.

At the sight of his unconscious Khan lying on the blue tile, the warrior turned to Master Khan with worry on his face.

"Do not fear." The master smiled. "Your beloved Khan will be back on his feet within a day or two."

"Days?" Anila had healed faster than that.

Master Wang gazed at her. "His many wounds are more severe than yours."

Anila realized he should be dead, and how lucky they were for Master Wang's elixir.

The horde warrior bowed to Master Wang. "I'll report the good news to the lieutenants."

"Please, do so." Master Wang motioned with his hand.

The warrior turned around and hurried out of the courtyard through the gate.

When Anila gazed down upon Bayor's bloody face, he opened his deep green eyes.

"How are you?"

No response came, but she could feel a glint of awareness in the green depths of his gaze. She gently stroked his bloody hand. "Don't worry, you will recover."

She was so happy to see him aware she didn't care about having an audience. She let tears of joy fall onto his face and gently kissed his full lips. When she came up and met his gaze again, she felt herself blush at the strong emotions he'd awakened inside her.

Epilogue

Two days later, Anila hurried across the compound in the direction of the Temple. She had seen Bayor in a dream, fully recovered. She hoped it was true.

The ashes of the dead Gripus had been swept and buried deep in the caves, below Temple Rock. So were the ashes of the dead Protectors and Acolytes, cremated on a pyre the next day. All living things returned to the Chi upon death.

A rare winter shower had cleared the air of the stench of battle. The monastery was once again pure and clean. Anila had felt its renewed energy when she practiced her Tai-Chi form on the wall, the past few mornings.

The classes had resumed. Soldiers and warriors helped the villagers rebuild their homes, replant, and water their fields. Normal life slowly returned.

She quietly entered the Temple, where all the wounded from the battle were recovering, most of them still asleep. As she walked toward Bayor's mat, her heart beat faster. He was sitting up, awake and conscious.

"How do you feel?" She knelt beside him, unable to erase a silly smile.

He smiled back. "Still a little weak, but otherwise, better than ever."

"It's so good to see you whole." Anila choked on the words. "For a while, I wasn't sure Master Wang's elixir would work. You were in such bad shape."

"It's over now." He took her hand and kissed it.

Anila enjoyed his contact, the tingle of his energy mingling with hers.

"Master Wang told me what happened." His voice sounded like soft music. "Thank you for saving my life."

"You saved mine first. I couldn't let you die." She shrugged. "Besides, the elixir saved you, not me."

His deep green eyes gazed into hers. "So, what do we do now?"

"I want you at my side." She blurted the answer, automatic and strong. No hesitation.

"Good. I can't imagine my life without you in it." His brow rose. "But who's the boss?"

"No one." She had thought about it and hoped he would accept the deal. "We get joined as lifetime soulmates and crowned together, we reign together, we decide together."

He stroked his chin. "What if we don't see eye to eye on certain issues?"

"We'll find a compromise. We already agree on everything important." She squeezed his hand "Why fight it?"

Bayor chuckled. "Why indeed?"

"Glad to see you resolved your differences." Master Wang's teasing tone as he walked toward them said he always knew they would. "After all, you were destined for each other long before you were born."

Anila no longer cared that she didn't have a choice. "Then let's formalize it, right here, at the Temple."

Master Wang smiled. "I will see to the preparations. Should we do this on the next double full moons?"

"Sounds perfect." Anila didn't know what the future held, but she had the most important thing in the world, a loving and capable soulmate. She had no doubt that together they would accomplish great things.

* * *

On the next double full moons

The crowd cheered and the drums banged happily, as Anila and Bayor stepped out of the Temple onto the terrace, both of them dressed in shimmering Immortal robes. Anila's heart pounded as she gazed upon the assembled crowd of special guests, as well as lieutenants, soldiers, horde warriors, Acolytes, villagers, and hundreds of Protectors.

Even the wounded who could sit attended in a special section, bandages and all. The crowd gazed back at her and Bayor with love, and she could feel their strong positive energy. In the few empty spaces between the groups, the blue tile of the courtyard gleamed under the winter sun.

A cool breeze revived the trees and flowers, and the birds trilled their peaceful song. The aroma from the kitchen carried notes of unfamiliar spices and exotic foods. The joining and coronation feast, from the food supplies of both armies, would represent all the different tribes of the new empire.

A sweet flute melody signaled the entrance of Master Wang, also in shimmering robes, freshly shaved, and wearing a black pill hat. He stepped up to face Anila and Bayor, then bowed his head. "Do you swear to love and respect each other in the Chi, and protect each other for as long as you live?"

Anila nodded. "I swear it."

"I swear it," answered Bayor in his baritone voice.

Then Master Wang faced the crowd. "Immortals from beyond the stars have been waiting for this day for centuries. This is a happy occasion, bringing hope for this entire planet."

Master Wang now turned to face Anila and Bayor again. "Will you be the fair rulers who will bring peace, harmony, and prosperity to this world? Do you swear to protect and defend its people, to govern them in peace with great kindness?"

"I swear it," Anila said with a strong voice.

"So, do I swear," Bayor added in a lower register.

"Do you swear to place the well-being of the empire above your own?"

"I swear it," they both said in unison.

Anila melted into Bayor's bear hug. Their medallions merged, and a warm bubble of radiant happiness shone brighter than the sun.

A happy roar rose from the crowd at the glowing manifestation of their union.

Then the medallions separated and the new Empress and Emperor turned to face the crowd.

Master Wang raised his hands, asking for silence. "Will the military and political leaders now come forward and pledge allegiance to their new rulers?" He stepped aside for the important guests to approach the terrace.

A slow procession of horde lieutenants, officers in Altan's defeated army, as well as lesser nobles and tribal leaders from all around, climbed the Temple steps and then filed in front of the imperial couple, bowing or taking a knee and pledging allegiance to both.

Anila was glad for Bayor's political knowledge and experience. He seemed to have a kind, personal remark for each of them, while she barely knew who they were. After the last pledge, the Acolytes brought tables and benches to the courtyard for the important guests.

Master Wang sat at the imperial table with the officers, tribal chiefs, noble leaders, and a few Protectors. Meanwhile, the local residents, soldiers, and warriors sat on rushes in the courtyards, practice halls, and all available buildings.

Everyone seemed to be having a great time. The food was superb, and the loud music and singing would continue late into the night... especially with the barbarians sharing their tika with everyone willing to try it and daring them into acrobatic feats.

But it would be improper for an empress to drink and dance like a barbarian. Besides, it was her wedding, and all Anila could think of was being alone with Bayor, and telling him how much she loved him, and how much she appreciated his support, his kindness, and his quiet strength.

As they sat side by side, watching the festivities, she took Bayor's hand. "It seems our lives will never be the same..."

Bayor smiled. "True, but tomorrow we'll ride, and for a while we shall travel all over the land to meet our new people."

"I know... that should be fun." She smiled back. "But what about tonight?"

"Tonight, I'm all yours... and you are mine." His green eyes sparkled with mischief.

"Then let's get out of here." She winked at him. "Master Wang arranged a room with a bed for our wedding night."

"A bed in a monastery?" He tsked. "Isn't that against the rules?"

"For a Protector or an Acolyte, yes... but not for the imperial couple."

"This is a slippery slope toward a life of luxury and privileges..." He winked at her. "But I'm willing to make an exception."

"In that case, let's go." Anila rose from her seat, and so did Bayor.

He took her in his arms and kissed her lips, slowly, like someone who enjoyed all the good things in life. She responded with a passion she didn't know she had and came up all flushed and warm.

The dancers applauded and the musicians stopped, but Anila motioned for them to continue playing. "Have fun without us. The night is young."

Bayor chuckled at a joke one of his lieutenants made, petted Stardust, then he waved good night and took Anila by the waist. "So where is this special room with a bed?"

Although she was nervous about what would come next, Anila felt his kind energy, the warmth of his hand, his strong arm around her waist, his breath on her neck, and she knew everything would be fine... tonight, and for centuries to come.

The End

Award-winning author Vijaya Schartz never conformed to anything and could never refuse a challenge. She likes action and exotic settings, in life and on the page. She traveled the world and claims she comes from the future. Her books have collected many five-star reviews and literary awards. She makes you believe you lived these extraordinary adventures among her characters. So, go ahead, dare to experience the magic, and she will keep you entranced, turning the pages until the last line. Find more about Vijaya at

https://www.facebook.com/profile.php?id=100046373155653#

Vijaya Schartz' books also published by BWL Publishing

BLUE PHANTOM SERIES:
Book 1 - Angel Ship
Book 2 - Angel Guardian
Book 3 – Angel Revenge

BYZANTIUM SPACE STATION SERIES:
Book 1 - Black Dragon
Book 2 – Akira's Choice
Book 3 – Malaika's Secret

AZURA CHRONICLES SERIES:
Book 1 - Angel Mine
Book 2 - Angel Fierce
Book 3 - Angel Brave

CHRONICLES OF KASSOUK SERIES:
Prequel: Noah's Ark
Book One: White Tiger
Book Two: Red Leopard
Book Three: Black Jaguar
Book Four: Blue Lioness
Book Five: Snow Cheetah

ANCIENT ENEMY SERIES:
Book 1 - Anaz-Voohri
Book 2 - Relics
Book 3 - Kicking Bots

SINGLE TITLE SCI-FI ROMANCE:
Alien Lockdown
Snatched

ARCHANGEL TWIN BOOKS:
Archangel Book 1 – Crusader
Archangel Book 2 – Checkmate

Medieval fantasy based on Celtic legends:
CURSE OF THE LOST ISLE SERIES

Book One – Princess of Bretagne
Book Two – Pagan Queen
Book Three – Seducing Sigefroi
Book Four – Lady of Luxembourg
Book Five – Chatelaine of Forez
Book Six – Beloved Crusader
Book Seven – Damsel of the Hawk
Book Eight – Angel of Lusignan

CONTEMPORARY ROMANCE:
Ashes for the Elephant God
Asleep in Scottsdale

BWL Publishing
bwlpublishing.ca

www.ingramcontent.com/pod-product-compliance
Lightning Source LLC
Chambersburg PA
CBHW070103120726
47909CB00002B/479